EVERYONE DIES
IN THE
GARDEN
OF
SYN

MICHAEL SEIDELMAN

Book Two In THE GARDEN OF SYN Trilogy

Chewed
Pencil
Press©

Printed in the United States of America. Seidelman, Michael. Everyone Dies in the Garden of Syn / Michael Seidelman p. cm. ISBN 978-0-9949695-3-8. Young Adult—Fiction. 2. Fantasy — fiction. 3. Cystic fibrosis —medical 4. Young Adult—Fantasy. Alternate Worlds —fiction. First Edition

Cover Design by extenededimagery.com, Copyright © 2018 Chewed Pencil Press

978-0-9949695-3-8 (tr. pbk)

Dedicated to my sisters, Sara and Jodi

Prologue

A Tale of Two Faces

FUELED BY ADRENALINE AND RAGE, Bryce Stevens chased Darren Silva through the cornfield.

"I'll kill you!" Bryce shouted, shoving cobs out of his way. Bryce, eleven years old, had bleached-blonde hair, now tousled and scattered with bits of broken leaves and threads of corn silk.

Not far ahead, Darren was out of breath. Sweat was dripping down his olive-complexioned face. He was terrified. Bryce was three years older and much stronger. He'd beaten up kids a lot bigger for a lot less.

As Darren blasted through the last of the stalks and left the cornfield, a startled crow shot into the sky. Darren tripped on a crack in the asphalt and fell, scraping his knee, and didn't notice the crow light up as though a bulb inside it had been turned on. The bird faded from sight as if it had never been there. Mere seconds later, Bryce made a hasty exit from the cornfield and grabbed Darren by the collar.

"You ratted me out," Bryce growled.

"I'm s-sorry," Darren whimpered.

"I could be expelled! You know that? My parents will kill me!"

As Bryce's fist smashed into Darren's face—once, twice, again and again—people, animals, and insects in the boys' vicinity lit up like fireflies. By the time Bryce had finished pummeling Darren, every one of those creatures had vanished.

Darren's nose was bleeding. One eye was swollen shut. Bryce would have continued hitting him if it weren't for a man out walking his dog.

"Hey! Leave the kid alone!" His dog started barking and tugging at the leash.

The boys faced the man just as he and his dog froze, one of the dog's paws hovering above the road in mid-air. They lit up like the others, except that the flesh of the glowing man flowed to the dog like mercury from a broken thermometer. The dog's fur-covered body stretched over to the man. In slow motion, the man could be seen screaming, but no sound escaped his warped lips.

Where the man and his dog had stood seconds before, fur, slime, flesh, and bone melded, while body parts fell to the street. Now, there was no man. No dog. Just a mess of bloody remains and a newly created Frankenstein-like monster. Parts of the two beings merged into one. But only for a second. Before this creature had time to take even one breath, it brightly lit up and was gone.

"What the—?!" Bryce jumped backwards.

He and Darren froze in mid-air. Light streamed through their skin, encompassing them. Each boy felt unimaginable pain as flesh, bones, and organs splattered outward, zigzagging into each other's bodies.

The excruciating merge seemed like an eternity to Darren Silva and Bryce Stevens, but in reality, it took less than fifteen seconds for the two boys to be torn apart and formed into a brand-new child. That child lit up and vanished into thin air, never to be seen again on this earth. All that remained was a pile of leftover skin, bones, and guts on the asphalt.

During the next ten minutes, over one hundred beings disappeared from the Southlands community of Redfern, Washington—humans, animals and insects. Only discarded body parts were left behind.

The town of Redfern would never be the same.

* * *

When the boy opened his eyes, he was lying in an enormous garden. He had no memory of this place or of any events in his life. Even his name had been forgotten.

He rubbed his eyes, trying to make sense of his surroundings. Not the pond, the trees, or the beautifully manicured garden, mind you, but the oddities. First, the Garden was surrounded by thick fog. Second, a totally out-of-place spiral staircase ascended into a cloud that was nowhere near the height of the sky. And then there was the old house, inside of which a screaming match between a man and a woman raged.

As the boy wandered, he found others living in this Garden. Some people, some monstrosities—different combinations of animals and humans. The hybrid-beings creeped the boy out for reasons he couldn't explain. Everyone seemed to get along though, so the boy made his best effort to do so too.

A man named Adam and a woman named Root took the boy in. They called him Coleus, after a colorful plant in the Garden, because the combinations of the different hues were like the boy's face. Coleus didn't understand, until he saw his reflection in the pond.

He did not like what he saw. Like some of the monstrosities in the Garden, Coleus looked like two beings formed into one. One side of his face had pale skin and blonde hair, the other side olive skin and dark hair.

"Why do I look like this? Am I a monster?"

Adam reassured him that he was not a monster. However, he wasn't human either. Coleus was like the monstrosities—the Creepers. "This is okay," Adam told him.

It was not okay to Coleus—he was not a monster. "I am a boy," he insisted. Not a blend of shapes and colors like that hideous plant.

From that moment on, the young boy felt nothing but contempt for Adam and Root. However, he was just a boy who needed care, and decided not to make a big deal about it. At least not yet. He did insist on never being called Coleus. "Just call me Cole."

Shortly after, the sky suddenly darkened. The weather changed, dead birds fell from the sky and airplanes crashed into the woods that existed inside the mysterious fog. Cole knew this Garden was unusual. No one ever fell ill, and any wounds, scrapes, and even broken bones rapidly healed.

While the people and the Creepers built homes, farmed the land and built a community, Cole explored every corner of the Garden. Even though he was a young boy, if someone had a question about something in the Garden, they knew Cole was the best person to ask.

He befriended some of the kids living in the Garden. Secretly, he hated them all. Especially the Creepers, the monsters who were nothing like him. Not in any way. Still, Cole always wore a smile. He tried hard to be a part of the community, not wanting to seem like an outsider, like the mysterious couple in the big house.

Terrible arguments often erupted in that house, screams echoing throughout the Garden. Sometimes there were different screams—screams even more horrific than just from arguments. Genuine screams of terror. Children's screams. Even the human-reptilian

Creepers didn't dare knock on the door to see if everything was okay. Everyone knew there was something sinister going on in that house, something that chilled them to the bone.

One day, Cole spied on the house. After the couple left, he snuck inside. His exploration revealed some odd things—a gurney, papers strewn about, countless computers and the strangest of all—a machine inside a glowing dome. He didn't know what to make of it.

The man and woman were often gone for long periods of time, but about three years after Cole found himself in the Garden, the couple moved in permanently. And, they had a baby.

A few years later, he met their daughter. She was playing with a doll at the foot of the wooden staircase behind the house.

"What's wrong with your face?" she asked.

She was only a little girl, a girl who knew no better, but Cole wanted to grab her by the throat and watch her turn purple as the life drained from her body. It took every bit of willpower to do nothing but smile. That's what a normal boy would do, right?

Her mother called over the railing. "Bethany, come inside. You shouldn't be out there alone."

As the girl reluctantly went inside, Cole thought about how seldom he saw her. Perhaps she was imprisoned by overprotective parents the same way he was imprisoned in a body he didn't belong in. Shortly after that, the killings started. A man was found at the top of the mysterious staircase, his head bashed in. Another was found on the stairway platform with his throat sliced open. A young woman was thrown over the rails of the stairway platform.

Cole didn't care about the people who died. Fewer wretched souls to deal with. As only humans had been killed, the people in the Garden concluded that the Creepers were responsible. The thought of those monstrosities taking precedence over a superior species enraged Cole.

The night the young woman was found dead, Cole was eating dinner when Adam brought up the subject of the murders. At first, Cole was encouraged that Adam and Root blamed the Creepers for the deaths. But then Adam said something Cole would never forget.

"Don't you worry, Cole. We'll protect you."

"From the killer?"

"No, not the killer. There is talk about humans revolting against Creepers."

"We won't let them touch you," Root said. "You're not like the others."

To be fair, Cole's guardians had alluded to this from the day they gave him his name, that he was different. But this time they were close to speaking the words—the lie.

"What do you mean?" Cole asked.

"You know," Adam said. "You're not like the other Creepers."

Finally. They spoke their minds. Their true feelings rose to the surface. His own guardians.

Cole shoved his chair from the table and stood up. "I am not a Creeper!" he screamed, storming out of the cabin.

When Cole returned hours later, Adam and Root were asleep. He stood at the end of their bed, clutching a wooden baseball bat, and used it to nudge each of them awake.

"What's going on?" Adam asked the dark figure standing over him. "Is that you, Coleus?

"My name isn't Coleus! I am *not* a Creeper!"

Cole slammed the bat down hard again and again, with more strength than one would imagine for a boy his age. His guardians' screams dwindled. The only sound was the crushing of bone and the mushing of flesh as the bat continued to pummel. All his bottled-up urges of violence were released at once. He felt a rush like never before. Cole felt more than just satisfaction. He felt freedom.

He grabbed the red canister of gasoline he had left by the door and splashed it over his guardians' remains, on the floor, and against the walls. When the canister was empty, still holding his weapon, he he left the cabin. The coast was clear. He tossed the bat inside, lit a match, and threw it through the doorway. As the flames engulfed Cole's home like a bright, vicious beast, he ran from cabin to cabin banging on doors, begging for help.

Nothing remained of the cabin but ash. Everyone, human and Creeper, was horrified by Cole's loss. He told them he had been awakened by a shadowy creature who said, "Die humans!" and that he was barely able to run out of the house before the flames spread. When he shed some fake tears, everyone did their best to comfort him.

Cole was proud of how he had fooled everyone.

The Garden's human residents held a private meeting and a decision was made. The Creepers must leave the Garden, by will or by force, before there were more killings. Some considered that the couple living in the big house should be included in making such an important decision. Memories of children screaming haunted them and they were frightened. No one wanted to do anything that might make those people angry.

Cole leaped from his chair. "Since it was my guardians who were killed, I want to make a case for the Creepers' banishment!"

There was hesitation to allow a kid to take on this task. However, Cole pressed on until the adults conceded. Cole was not forthcoming about the true reason he wanted to talk to the family. It wasn't only to get their permission. If they were against the idea, only he would know.

Something strange occurred when he knocked on the front door of the house. A girl's raspy voice answered, "It's open."

Cole went inside cautiously, leaving the door ajar. The house was dark, only a scant amount of light streaming through the curtains, the open door and from the glowing blue dome. The girl was standing in the shadows of the doorway that led to the basement.

"Who are you?" she asked.

"Who are *you*? Where is the family who lives here?"

"Who *are* you?" she asked again.

"My name is Cole."

"I'm Syn. It's just me here. The family...they are gone."

"Step into the light," Cole said. "So I can see you."

There was a long silence. Just as Cole was about to ask again, the girl took two steps forward. She wasn't older than ten or eleven, fully clothed in a black robe. All that was visible was her face, and that left a lasting impression. It was not only burnt and scarred, the skin was bubbling like soup boiling in a pot.

Syn waited for horror to darken Cole's face. He wasn't horrified though. For some reason, Cole felt a connection with this girl, this girl he had just met. A connection he had never felt with anyone else. And, she felt a connection with Cole, the first since being taken from her family as a young child.

Cole and Syn talked for hours, sharing each other's tragic stories. Syn revealed how she had trapped her torturers in the very place they had imprisoned her for years. Cole told her about things he had never shared with anyone. His hatred of Creepers. The urges for violence he had as far back as he could remember. He even confessed about murdering his guardians. Syn didn't pass judgement.

What Cole didn't know was that while Syn truly did sympathize, she had decided to use him to further an agenda of her own. She feigned friendship. Told him she would handle the banishment of the Creepers and how in return, he would spread fear of her to the residents of the Garden to keep them away. He would tell them that she was a woman, not a girl, and that her name was Synister. That she was the queen of the Garden and heard every word they spoke. That if they left her alone and stayed away from the house, she would allow them to live in her kingdom. She needed this so she could work on her plan. And maybe this boy could help with that too.

Syn kept her word. The Creepers were banished to the sewers beneath the Garden. Cole kept his part of the deal. He made certain that the others in the Garden would know her only as Synister and that she was to be feared. She liked that. Only he would dare come knocking at her door.

Cole put on a cheery face and continued to befriend everyone in the Garden, giving Synister any information she might find useful. When Cole visited Synister, he dropped the charade and became his true self. In time, something unexpected occurred.

Perhaps it was loneliness. Perhaps it was more than that. As Cole and Synister spent more time together, she began to enjoy Cole's company. Aside from her prisoners, Cole was the only person she had direct contact with. She looked forward to his visits. Yes, he was a murderer. And, he was a monster. Maybe that was another reason why she related to him. They shared the same rage at their unfortunate circumstances.

As Cole and Synister matured, their friendship evolved. Cole fell in love with her. She had feelings for him too. But love? She wasn't sure. Her feelings might have been what they were because she had no one else. He was familiar. He loved her more than she would ever love him. That was okay. She would have someone to hold her, someone who was loyal.

Synister needed Cole as much as he needed her. For more than just companionship. She had a plan. A plan that would allow her to live a more normal life in a real world. To have skin that didn't bubble. To not feel unbearable pain during every living moment. To have someone to take care of her. She needed Cole to help her kick off her plan. Cole didn't like the plan, but he would do anything Synister asked, so he helped her build a machine.

Then, he crossed over to the other world and brought a new girl to the Garden—the other Syn. He befriended her, kept her from getting into too much trouble. Meanwhile, Synister perfected her machine.

When it was time, Cole revealed his true self to the girl he had brought to the Garden and Synister made her their prisoner.

But like so many great plans, everything went horribly wrong. The prisoner escaped. She destroyed the machines that made the Garden special and unique. And worst of all, she killed Synister, Cole's true love.

After the life faded from his lover's eyes, Cole stood at the top of the wooden steps behind the house, drenched from the rainstorm. Every time lightning flashed, he had a glimpse of the Garden—the new Garden. Thick rope was wrapped around his forearm, the other end tied tightly around his new prisoner. The girl Cole long ago fantasized about strangling. The murderer's young sister, Bethany.

"She's going to come back for me," the brave ten-year-old told her captor.

Cole stared down into eyes very much like those of his recently departed love, his face inches from the girl's. "I'm counting on it."

As if on cue, Cole heard in the distance what he had been waiting for in the cold downpour. Sounds of terror. Screams of the damned. Roars of the new hierarchy.

Once more, Cole bent down to his kneeling prisoner. "Everything is different now. Your sister made certain of that. You can hear it. You can feel it. This is a new Garden. When the sun rises, it will be a new day. Soon your sister will come for you. And I assure you, blood will spill."

Through tragedy, the demons inside were released and the two-faced teenager tore himself from a cocoon of denial. Cole finally accepted who he was. What he was. He was not human. He was a Creeper.

As he carried the gasping, defiant young girl inside the house, one hand around her scrawny throat, he knew he would never hide behind the boy-next-door persona again. He knew what he was and it was about damn time he acted accordingly.

Chapter 1

Conversations
with Dead People

DEAD IS DEAD.

That is always what I have believed. Now, while gazing at the headstone with Janna's name and date of death meticulously carved into it, and standing upon the raised mound of seeded soil covering the coffin in which her body lies, it all hits me again. She is really gone. It makes me hope that maybe, just maybe, I was wrong. That her spirit is still here with us or lingering on another plane.

The possibility of an afterlife doesn't sound as out there after all. Not more than a month ago, I saw unimaginable things. So maybe....

This is only wishful thinking, of course. Deep down, I don't actually believe Janna's journey continues. However, my friend Ebby told me that if there is even the slightest chance Janna can hear me, I should talk to her. The worst-case scenario is that I'll feel silly.

I drop to my knees, tears falling from my cheeks onto the first few blades of grass that have sprouted through the soil. There is comfort in believing that my tears are watering the grass that will grow over my friend's body. After a good cry, I wipe my nose with a tissue and cough up the usual phlegm that comes after tears. Finally composed, I talk to Janna, who I know doesn't hear me. Surprisingly, I don't feel silly at all.

I talk about my adventure in the Garden two months ago, starting with being pushed into the pond behind my house and waking up in a new world. How there was no illness or death in this strange world, and about all the bizarre things, from human-animal-insect hybrids called Creepers to the staircase that reached high into the sky. And then about the guy I met and fell for. Cole's betrayal of me. His girlfriend Synister, another version of me, kidnapped from an alternate world. Her frightening appearance, how she was tortured by my parents using other versions of me in their hopes of finding a cure for my cystic fibrosis. More than anything, I was trying to make sense of everything that happened.

I also revealed how my parents, who went missing when I was five, had been trapped in the Garden by their partner Masie Winters. That it was Masie's technology that allowed my parents to create a new world where no one got sick. How Cole and Synister trapped my parents in a hollow, white prison called the bubble. I shared about smashing the blue globe in the house and unknowingly changing the DNA of the Garden. And how after that, the healing properties that protected everyone in the Garden from illness were no more. I recalled that my rash moment of anger resulted in two lives being lost—a kind and quirky old man named Wolf, and Synister herself, who died in front of my eyes.

And then the most personal revelation from my journey: my parents had another child while living in the Garden. My perfect sister Beth. How Cole has kept her prisoner and dared me to return to the Garden and rescue her. Something that will likely result in my death.

I have always considered my life to be precious, never having thought I'd even consider risking it. But then I never had a reason to do so before. Beth is worth that risk. My sister is everything to me. Well, almost everything.

It is time to tell Janna about my other friends Ebby and Jon, who are waiting for me under an oak tree at the edge of the cemetery. Janna wouldn't be jealous. She'd want me to have other friends in my life now that she is gone. I'm apprehensive all the same.

"Janna...those are my friends, Ebby and Jon. I wish you could have met them when you were—"

I gaze at her headstone through teary eyes and whisper, "I love you, Janna." Then, forcing myself to turn away and not look back, I return to my friends.

Ebby's older brother Luke pats my shoulder when we reach the car. "You okay, kid?"

I sniffle a couple times. "Yeah."

I've known Luke since I became friends with Ebby. He's been in the military fighting overseas and hasn't been around much. He returned shortly after I came home from the Garden, honorably discharged. Luke won't talk about his time overseas or why he was sent home. But he's been a good friend since I've been home. He even visited me in the hospital the same day he returned from the Middle East.

"Syn," Ebby says, "why don't you sit in front this time? Jon and I will close our eyes and plug our ears if you two kids want to do…anything."

Ebby is far from subtle in her attempts to get Luke and me to hook up. Yes, Luke would certainly seem like a perfect catch for many girls. Tall, well-built, with the messy blonde hair of an 80's surferdude and handsome in an unconventional way. A soldier in every sense, but those sensitive eyes give away his every emotion. I know very well that he's not interested in me. Grinning, I leap into the back seat with Jon before Ebby gets around to the passenger side.

"Seriously?" Ebby says as she ducks into the front seat. "You puzzle me sometimes, Synthia Wade."

"Syn and I can close our eyes and plug our ears if you two want to do anything crazy," Jon says, stifling a laugh.

"Ew, ew, ew!" Ebby screams. "What is *wrong* with you?!"

"You want to get out right here and walk home, young man?" Luke jokes.

"No, Sir," Jon replies, still smirking. "I'll be good."

I laugh at the silliness, glad to have these guys in my life. Not only are they fun, they are incredibly supportive. They visited me in the hospital and listened to my countless stories about my adventures in the Garden. They did a good job pretending to believe me. After being released from the hospital, I took them down to the pond to show them the lightway portal that transported me to the Garden. It wasn't there. They were skeptical but didn't act like I was crazy like many people would have.

Two more weeks went by and I still hadn't found the lightway to return to the Garden. It had to be somewhere because Cole challenged me to return. Then one day I noticed a garden gnome that had decorated my backyard garden oasis for as long as I could remember. Part of his face was shaded brown. Like Cole's face, a combination of two people, one with light skin and one with dark skin. I lifted the gnome and a stream of light bolted from the ground.

When I showed my friends, they were speechless. They never imagined what I was telling them could actually be true. And now that they knew it was, they promised to help me rescue my sister. We've been planning for a week now, and Luke's military expertise might even give me an edge in bringing my sister home.

As for my parents, I fear that Cole might have killed them. They did unspeakable things to his girlfriend and there is no way he would let them live now that they aren't needed by my doppelgänger. However, I hold a faint ray of hope that they are still alive.

And so, here we are on the highway, twenty minutes into our trip home from the cemetery. Ebby and Jon are playing their favorite new game.

"I let go of Haley's hand during Red Rover in sixth grade," Jon starts, "and Addison Peters tumbles to the ground and breaks his collarbone instead of dislocating my shoulder."

"Addison doesn't make the football team in high school," Ebby continues.

"Haley doesn't end up dating him—"

"And gets knocked up by a quarterback from another school."

"Her son grows up to be president—"

"And declares war with Sweden—"

"Leading to the annihilation of the entire planet."

"That's dark," I tell them.

"And who would declare war on Sweden? "Luke asks. "Sweden!"

"The altered game of Red Rover changes the direction of world events," Ebby says. "One change in a simple game of Red Rover could trigger other changes that result in Sweden becoming a dictatorship. Anything can change the course of history. Clap two times instead of once and the entire world could change. Right, Syn?"

"It's possible," I reply, lacking enthusiasm for the game and the conversation that follows.

Their game is based on what I learned while living in the Garden. That the world we live in is just one of an infinite number of similar worlds in the multiverse. That each time a new world spawns out of an existing one, there is one change, big or small, that spirals everything in a new direction, making that world different and unique from the one it originated from. So, while one night in my world I turn off the bathroom light before going to bed, the new world would be exactly the same except that I might forget to turn the light off.

That one tiny deviation from my regular routine could potentially result in significant or minimal alterations. Still, everything and everyone would in some way be affected by that different action. Even something as seemingly insignificant as a mosquito in Zimbabwe being swatted in one world and not in another could potentially change history. I've heard this described in school as the 'butterfly effect'.

Honestly, I don't understand any of this. All I know is what I learned from Synister and Cole, and from reading theories about the multiverse. If I ever get a chance to see my parents again, they could explain it, I'm sure. I do know that other worlds exist because I have traveled to a few of them.

One of the worlds had no life aside from me. Apparently, it was the end of the world. So the multiverse isn't something that's an especially fun topic, and I certainly wouldn't want to create a game around it. But who am I to ruin my friends' fun?

"Want to create a scenario, Syn?" Jon asks.

"I'd rather discuss the plan to get my sister back. Luke?"

"Why don't we talk about it when we stop for dinner?" he suggests.

"Sure." I frown.

"Syn," Luke says, "I promise to do everything possible to get Beth back. There's nothing more important to me right now. Okay?"

"I know. I appreciate your help. When do you think we'll be ready to go? Every day that goes by is another day my sister is held prisoner by that monster."

"I know. Don't hold me to this, but I'm thinking two weeks."

That's two weeks longer than I would like, but when Luke agreed to help me he made it clear we wouldn't head to the Garden until our plan was solid, and until he could obtain weapons. If it were up to me, I'd already have gone alone. The reality is that I couldn't confront Cole by myself. Not only would I most likely die, he'd kill Beth too.

Luke exits the highway and drives past some well-known food chains. We settle on Denny's. After ordering, Ebby and I slide off the cracked vinyl seat of our booth and head to the washroom. Phlegm is building up in my chest. As someone who suffers from CF, I often have a phlegm buildup. I also know when I'm at the beginning stage of something worse. I cough a few times as Ebby opens the door to the ladies' room.

"You okay?" she asks once we're inside.

"Yeah."

I cough again while I'm washing my hands and avoid Ebby's concerned reflection in the mirror. By the time our meals arrive, I'm seriously hacking. Customers at neighboring tables are clearly concerned.

Luke waves our server over. "There has been a change of plans. We'll need our meals to go."

"We're driving straight home," I sputter. "Trust me."

He's reluctant and it isn't until we're buckled in that he finally agrees not to stop at a clinic or hospital. I force some food past my lips. If I don't eat, no one else will. Except for the coughing and awkward support from my well-meaning friends, it's a long and quiet trip home. Luke eventually turns on some classic rock to help pass the time.

Though I know better, I hope this isn't going to be too serious. This isn't about me. This is about Beth. My sister awaits rescue from the clutches of a maniac. Two weeks. What seemed far away now seems so close. So close to rescuing her, and this has to happen.

Could a basic drainage of my lungs be enough to do the trick? A couple of days' hospital stay and a quick recovery? I pine for that, though I've been through this before. And like I said, I know better.

Chapter 2

Murder at Redfern Memorial

I DID KNOW BETTER.

Four months have passed and I'm still recovering in the hospital. Just like I thought, it was a lung infection, and it caused a slew of other problems. That all said, I'm finally feeling better. Dr. Freeman, whom I've been seeing since I was a kid, will release me after a couple more days' observation. Along with tests, the usual twenty plus pills daily, nebulizer treatments, and regular daily therapies, I've been on antibiotics.

"Now, Synthia," says Dr. Freeman sternly. "You're patched up, but the symptoms are only going to get worse if you don't take extra care of yourself, eat right, and exercise."

I hate these lectures.

"We've talked before about you also having an oxygen tank with you at all times."

I furrow my brow.

"It will help you to breathe when your lungs are clogged up."

This subject has come up before and I've dismissed it each time. "I'll have to roll it around with me wherever I go."

"Yes."

I can't even think about that until I've brought Beth home from the Garden. It's going to be tough enough to face Cole without having to lug around extra baggage.

"We're optimistic about getting you on a waiting list for a lung transplant," says Dr. Freeman. "The oxygen tank is not a permanent solution."

The idea of a lung transplant terrifies me. I smile weakly at Dr. Freeman as he leaves my room. A lung transplant is the only thing that would allow me to live a long and full life. For that to happen though, someone else has to die.

I've had regular visitors at the hospital. Aunt Ruth is almost always by my bedside. She even snuck in my hairless Sphynx cat Fluffy a couple times to cheer me up. Ebby and Jon visit after school. They fill me in on the gossip (which I couldn't care less about) and bring my assignments. A hospital stay doesn't get you a pass on homework. Luke pops by at least twice a week. He deliberately schedules visits when my aunt is away so we can discuss "business."

It is a warm September afternoon, so a nurse wheels me outside. I'm sitting in a wheelchair in the courtyard with some homework on my lap, not getting any work done. All my thoughts are about

Beth and how I've failed her. How she's suffered in Cole's clutches all summer. Luke offered to enter the Garden himself, but I couldn't let him do that. If something happened to him or Beth because I wasn't there, I'd never forgive myself. I need to be there for the mission.

An old man wearing a hospital robe ambles past at a snail's pace, rolling an IV pole alongside him. He raises a cigarette to his lips. I open my mouth to speak, but someone beats me to it.

"Hey! Get that filthy thing away from my friend. She has a respiratory disease."

Startled and confused, the man turns to face Ebby.

"You want to kill yourself, go ahead. But keep that thing away from my friend!"

The confused man stumbles back in the direction he came. I cough from the smoke that has seeped into my weak lungs and admire Ebby for standing up for me. It wasn't too long ago when she couldn't stand up to a bully in school and I had to intervene.

Ebby sits down on the bench beside me and hands me more assignments. "I can't believe they let people smoke here. It's a hospital for crying out loud."

"I know, right? Thanks for that. I think that guy has dementia though."

"That won't be all he has to worry about if he circles this way again."

Oh, Ebby. "Hey, got any more gossip?" I giggle, honestly not caring to gossip. It makes Ebby happy all the same.

If I had been admitted to the children's hospital, I wouldn't have to endure smokers because smoking is banned there. It's too far away though. Aunt Ruth would have to lodge nearby and my friends couldn't visit as often. The only reason I ever went to that hospital was because Janna was there sometimes.

After Ebby leaves me in my room, the nurse checks my IV and then brings me to physical therapy to work out on the treadmill. Exercise is imperative for people with CF, though I can't overdo it. The nurse, Stephanie, is one of many nurses and orderlies here and they are all so kind. They're compassionate without showing pity.

I am escorted to my room after physical therapy and an orderly brings in a tray of food for dinner. Chicken breasts, mashed potatoes, veggies, a roll, and some unidentifiable orange soup. Stephanie returns with the enzymes I take with my meals.

I flip the channels on the TV at the foot of my bed. Home renos, talk shows with jilted lovers and mystery fathers, an episode of *Friends* I've seen a million times. Then there is the news. Only bad news, of course. A bus flipped over on the highway, a former governor convicted of fraud. A body was found.

The story about the body the police found catches my attention. It was discovered on a neighboring farm. The body is one of two suspects in a computer store robbery that made the news shortly after I returned from the Garden. It was an odd story. Two employees with no criminal record robbed the Digital Town store, stealing merchandise worth thousands of dollars. They escaped in a stolen truck and haven't been seen since. I remember this clearly because the empty truck was also found not far from my place. And now a body!

Aunt Ruth arrives as the newscaster begins the next story. "Here are some clean clothes for you to wear when you're released. And, I brought that book you want to read."

I smile, making every effort to conceal the fact that I will be leaving her again. Since I returned from the Garden, we have been closer than ever. It pains me that I might not make it back this time. She's dedicated the last eleven years of her life to me and I'm all she has. This time, I will leave her a note. Tell her about Beth and ask her to look after her if she comes home without me. I'm not sure how I will explain the Garden though. But right now, I'm just glad to have my aunt here with me. We talk for a long time.

At eleven o'clock, Lita, one of the night nurses, arrives to give me my final dose of pills—three full miniature paper cups. Aunt Ruth offers to sleep on the chair next to me. I insist that she goes home to sleep in a comfortable bed. Once she has left, I text with Ebby for a while and then pick up the book my aunt brought. I start to fade on page six but make myself stay awake to finish the first chapter.

There is only a paragraph left to read when the fluorescent lights in my room begin to buzz and flicker. My bed lamp clicks off. The familiar beeping and whispers in the hallway are non-existent. The door to my room creaks open and clicks shut. When I see him I am instantly paralyzed with fear.

Cole is wearing a white lab coat and a stethoscope is hanging around his neck. "Well hello, Miss Wade. The doctor is in the house."

The lab coat rustles as he strolls over. Those menacing eyes and that twisted grin—I'm unable to speak. He wheels a metal tray next to my bed, presenting neatly arranged surgical tools—a scalpel, a small electric saw, a razor-edged clamp.

"Dear Synthia, now it's your turn. All the other Synthias have been cut up and pried open by your mommy and daddy. Well, it's time for Dr. Cole to see what treasures are inside *your* precious body."

He removes a pair of latex gloves from his pocket and slides them on, snapping the tip of each finger with satisfaction. Dread prickling every cell of my body now, I watch his hand hover over the metal tray, fingers wriggling as if he expects one of the tools will call out to him. With a flourish, he grabs the scalpel and holds it up, pausing for effect. "Ah. This is the one."

The scalpel is pressed against my throat, his face pushed up against mine. The cold metal blade grazes my skin. "Let's see how much blood spills from your arteries after I slice your skinny little neck open."

Cole waves the scalpel high above his head and swoops it down to my throat. My eyes abruptly open. Lights are still dimmed. The book is splayed across my chest. I was dreaming! Except...my eyes come into focus. Cole is hovering by my bedside, glaring at me. For real.

"Seems you had a bad dream. I assure you, it's only going to get worse." His warm breath brushes across my cheek.

Could I still be dreaming? *Please, let me still be dreaming.*

I poke my hand out from under the bedsheet and press the red nurse call button. Three times, to declare the urgency.

The sadistic grin fades from his face, while the menacing look still blazes in his eyes. "Synthia, was I not fair? Did I not give you a chance to return to the Garden and trade your life for your sister's?"

My finger presses the red button, clicking it again and again. *C'mon!*

"Yet, here you are, months later, pathetically lying in a hospital bed. It seems that family doesn't mean as much to you as I thought it did."

"Cole," I desperately whisper. "Please."

"Please?" He grins. "Politeness doesn't get you anywhere, Synthia. Let me be blunt. One way or another, and very soon, one of Ian and Debra Wade's children will die. Which one? That is up to you."

Click! Click! Click!

"If I don't see you in the Garden soon, you'll find your little sister's body lying at the end of your hospital bed." He backs away. "Hope you feel better soon…so you can come visit me again." Then he is gone.

No nurse will answer my panicked button clicking. I try to scream for help but can barely make a sound. Off with the oxygen tubes and IV needle. I sweep my bare feet across the bed to the floor and carefully walk alongside the bed in the shadowy room. All the while, my eyes are glued to the door. Halfway across the room, I slip on something and drop to the hard floor. Wincing from the pain, I try to stand up. My hands are wet, as is my hospital gown. Not only wet. Smeared red.

Then I see her. Lita, the night nurse. Motionless, lying in a pool of blood.

Chapter 3

Return to the Garden

THE POLICE INTERVIEWED ME FOR nearly an hour. And for nearly an hour, I lied left and right.

No, I didn't see the culprit. No, I don't remember seeing or hearing anything strange. No, I have absolutely no idea who could have done this.

I told them I woke up and pressed the red button to call the nurse. When no one replied, I got out of bed to get some water and slipped on the blood.

I also lied to Aunt Ruth. Lying to her has become a regular habit since returning from the Garden. If I come back safe and sound with my sister, I'll come clean with her. She deserves to know the truth. But for now, I lie.

No, I'm sure I have no idea who did this.

But I *do* know who killed Lita. And I *did* see the culprit.

It was a monster. A monster that murdered an innocent stranger who did nothing to him. A woman who sent half of her earnings home to the Philippines so her niece could go to college. This monster has destroyed a family. This monster has my sister and will kill her if I don't hurry up and do what needs to be done.

I am lying in my new hospital room, having been whisked away from the crime scene. Aunt Ruth is sitting on one side of my bed and Luke on the other. She leaves to get a coffee.

"Can you get me my clothes?" I ask Luke. "We need to go!"

Luke shakes his head. "You should wait another day or two until you're released."

"No, I—"

"Since Cole has waited this long already, he is unlikely to harm Beth. Especially after he gave you a warning so loud and clear. He knows you will come. You need to get healthy and be in decent enough shape to face him."

I reluctantly admit that Luke is right but getting out of here as soon as possible is of utmost importance. The nurses and orderlies seem even more shaken up than I am.

Every few hours, the police come in to ask me the same questions. They certainly don't suspect me, but know I'm holding something back. The officers won't reveal information, but Aunt Ruth overheard some details of their investigation. Apparently, the culprit was caught on hospital security cams, but his hood concealed his face. They have prints of his shoes, know the size and brand name, and are following up at local shoe stores. Yeah, good luck with that.

My health is as good as can be expected, which is important considering what I will be doing as soon as they discharge me. I think of Beth, scared and at Cole's mercy.

Soon, little Sis. I'm coming.

* * *

The doctors release me from the hospital the following morning. I spend most of the afternoon lying by the pond in the garden behind my house, trying to focus on homework. The keyword is *trying*.

Aunt Ruth serves gooey homemade mac and cheese with an overload of breadcrumbs for dinner. Ebby and Jon join us and wolf down the caloricious meal. We all eat more than we should. After dinner, we have ice cream sundaes. Nothing but comfort food, not only to welcome me home but to help me forget about the murder two nights earlier. The conversation around the table is sparse. Of course Ebby, Jon, and I want to talk about our rescue mission, but Aunt Ruth can't know about that.

Eventually, I say goodbye to my friends after too many awkward silences threaten to give us away. We'll see each other soon. Aunt Ruth asks what she can do for me and continually inquires about how I'm feeling. I wish I didn't have to leave again and make her worry even more.

At 1:30 A.M., I slide out of bed and get dressed, grab a backpack full of supplies from my closet and tiptoe from my room. All the lights are out except for a plug-in night light in the hallway and another over the kitchen sink.

I place an envelope with "Aunt Ruth" neatly printed on the front between the salt and pepper shakers on the table. For Aunt Ruth's sake, even more than my own, I hope to return in one piece—with Beth. Surely my aunt will extend the same love and support to Beth that she has given me all these years.

I unlock the back door. Clutching the handle, I take one more look at the familiar before heading into the unknown. It's a nice night. A tad chilly but the sky is clear. Thousands of stars glimmer and gaze down at me. I arrive at the two-faced gnome. Ebby and Jon are already there.

"Oh my God," Ebby says excitedly. "I can't believe we're doing this."

I hold up my finger and shush her. Jon looks nervous. He says he's okay, but I know Jon. Traveling to an alternate universe? He freaks out over trying a new vegetable. And, Jon's not even going to the Garden yet. The plan is for me and Luke to enter the Garden first. Luke will return for Ebby and Jon later.

"Where's your brother?" I ask Ebby.

"Buying you a bouquet of roses," she jokes.

"We're early," Jon says, glancing at the time on his phone. "He still has ten minutes."

Ten minutes pass. Still no Luke. Another ten. And another. It's forty minutes past our meet time. We've all sent him texts and there have been no replies.

"I'm worried," Ebby says. "This isn't like him."

"Yeah, I'm worried too."

Every minute that passes is another minute Beth is held prisoner by that monster. That murderer. Each minute that passes brings us closer to the moment when Cole's patience wears thin. When he sharpens the blade of his knife and—.

I can't bear to think about it. During the ten minutes that follow, I make a decision. Probably a terrible one. Yet this can't be put off any longer.

"I'm going," I tell my friends. "Tell Luke when he gets here."

I lift the two-faced gnome and the lightway beams upwards in all its glory.

Ebby grabs my arm. "Let me go with you! I'll be your backup."

"I appreciate the offer but can't let you do that, Ebby."

"This is a terrible idea," Jon pleads.

"You're not wrong, but Beth is my sister and I'm doing this."

"You're such good friends," I say, refusing to cry. "If I don't make it back, tell my aunt I love her."

Without giving Ebby and Jon time to convince me otherwise, I step into the light. Time seems to slow down, then stop. When time returns to normal, I step out of the lightway. It remains behind me like a cylinder tower beaming light into the sky. Enough light emits that I don't need my flashlight.

The grass I'm standing on is taller and wetter than the grass I was standing on a moment ago. Light raindrops are falling. My cold-like symptoms remain. The properties of the Garden that made me healthy the last time are gone. That is on me.

Cole surely has someone waiting for me—or is even here himself. Sensing someone behind me, I spin around. Someone is here and not at all the person I expected.

"Oh. My. God." I glare at her. She is too astounded by our surroundings to notice.

"I've a feeling we're not in Kansas anymore." She giggles.

Damn it, Ebby.

Chapter 4

Jeepers Creepers

"WHAT ARE YOU DOING here?" I whisper fiercely.

"Um, well I—"

"Shhh!" I check to make sure we're alone. "Okay, what the hell?"

"You needed backup. Well, I got your back. We're besties. That's what besties do, right?"

"Seriously, Ebby?"

"This is so cool. I can't believe we're in a whole other world! But, um, why don't we go back and wait for—"

I'm about to shush her again, but realize it's too late. We both freeze as something creeps from the shadows. The glow from the lightway reveals a young woman, maybe ten years older than me, wearing a tank top and cut-off jean shorts.

Covered in brown fur, with a bald tail sprouting from behind, she is unlike any woman I've ever seen. And then there's her face. That little pink nose, constantly wiggling in every direction, very rat-like.

Before we have time to react, another figure floats down from above. At first, I see a thing of beauty. Two enormous orange and black butterfly wings that glow when they flutter. And then…between those two wings is a rugged-looking man, probably in his early sixties, built like an ox. Butterfly-Man's feet touch the grass without a sound.

Ebby's jaw is gaping and she is motionless, either from wonderment, fear, or both.

"Coleus has been waiting a long time for you," Rat-Girl says.

Butterfly-Man looks back and forth between Ebby and me. "Which one is she?"

"The skinny one," Rat-Girl says, moving closer.

I whip the tranquilizer dart gun from my pocket and shoot two darts into her chest. Her eyes roll back and her body falls to the ground.

"What the hell?" Butterfly-Man leaps at me.

I take aim. He hovers above the ground, wings flapping. The dart streaks under his arm and behind him, giving him enough time to slap my face and knock the dart gun from my hand. He grabs me by the waist and we lift off.

"Syn!" screams Ebby.

Damn it. This is not the plan.

We're about several feet off the ground when I hear two 'thwips'. We pause in mid-air. Butterfly-Man's grip loosens and we tumble to the wet turf below. It's a hard fall, and it doesn't help that zonked-out Butterfly-Man's huge wings are blanketing me. It takes all my remaining strength to move them out of the way and stand up. The sight that greets me? Ebby, proudly waving her dart gun.

"Did I do good?"

I smile. "Yeah. I knew there was a reason I let you tag along."

My body is ringing with pain from the fall, but my chest isn't any more clogged than when I got here, and that's my main concern.

"So, let's go home and wait for Luke."

"No. As soon as someone stumbles across these Creepers, I'll have lost the window I need. You should go home and get Luke."

Ebby crosses her arms determinedly. "You stay, I stay."

I sigh. "Follow me and don't say anything until we get to where we're going. Okay?"

She nods.

I guide Ebby over to the wall of fog. As we head away from the lightway, the moon's glow allows us to see where we're going without using flashlights. But it's more than the steady moonlight glow that lights our way. Other sources of light pulse, grow brighter, then darken. Just like—

As if to address my theory, a lightway pops up about twenty feet away and then vanishes. Another flashes a few feet from that. It blinks out and the original lightway flashes again before fading. Then one final lightway appears, holding steady.

I glance over my shoulder at the Garden behind us. There are more circular tubes of light, beaming from the ground, towering into the sky.

When I was last here, lightways opened in the far reaches of the fog. Anyone who stepped into a steady beam was transported to an alternate world. This time, the lightways are opening in the Garden. As soon as we enter the fog, I stop Ebby.

She is astonished. "We're in…"

"Yeah."

We are standing in a humid forest of trees, ferns and moss, entrenched in a hazy mist, barely able to see one foot in front of us. All is silent. No birds chirping, no whisper of wind.

"This foggy forest surrounds the entire Garden. Even though we're just a few feet from the fog's wall, no one in the Garden can hear anything spoken in here. The wall of fog is soundproof, for whatever reason."

As Ebby turns in wonderment, I peer into the thick of the fog. There is one major difference from the last time I was here. No lightways are flashing in the distance. I wonder why the lightways only show up in the Garden now, instead of in the outskirts of the fog. Is that something I'm responsible for? When I smashed the glowing blue dome that powered the

Garden's healing properties, did I cause this to happen?

"What now?" Ebby asks.

"We're going farther into the fog and then to find my friends. They might know where Cole is holding Beth. Maybe she's not in the big house with him. Creepers could be guarding her elsewhere, like in the sewers."

Ebby excitedly awaits more details.

"The plan I worked out with Luke is to check Rose's cabin first. Rose and Flint might not be there anymore, but if they are, we'll go in. If not, we leave."

"Right."

"Listen Ebby, I appreciate that you have my back. But as you've seen, this isn't an ordinary place. Cole is a psychopath. So are the Creepers. The lightways never used to flash in the Garden, so there might be other changes I don't know about. What I'm saying is—"

"Be careful. Got it."

I'm sort of glad Ebby is here. I load her dart gun and hand it to her, then remove a metal bar from my backpack and slide it through a loop in my jacket pocket. With our hands clasped, we exit the fog.

We're alone, at least for now. Moving in the direction of Rose's cabin, we stay close to the wall of fog in case we need to escape. Clouds have drifted over the moon, but lightways flashing nearby still light our path.

We stop for a minute to rest by the well at the far end of the Square. The fresh air must be helping because I feel good. Good for me, anyway.

After a brief rest, a couple of minutes later we arrive at Rose's cabin. I approach the window, motioning for Ebby to stay put. It's pitch-black inside, so I get my flashlight. I switch the setting to dim and shine the low beam through the glass, slowly moving it from left to right. A boy is sleeping on the couch.

Could it be...? I squint to make out his face. *Yes, Flint!*

I shut off the flashlight, joyous that Flint is okay. If he's in the house, Rose is surely in the other room. My thumbs-up calls Ebby over. We approach the door.

"Let me do the talking. We're going to startle them enough, waking them in the middle of the night."

Ebby is excited and apprehensive. "Luke is gonna be ticked at us for doing this without him."

I carefully open the door and, like I expected, there is a creaking noise. Leaving the door ajar, we slip through the crack. I shine the flashlight so Flint can see my face. As I gently shake my friend's shoulder, his eyes flutter open. He squints.

"Syn!" Flint scrambles to sit up.

The floor in the other room creaks. My excitement to see Rose again is busted by the unexpected.

"Help," Flint says quietly, his voice resetting from sleep.

Help?

Then louder. "Help!"

The sound of heavy footsteps come from the other room. Rose?

There is fear in Flint's eyes as he screams at the top of his lungs. "Humans! Humans!"

What the hell?!

The flashlight slips from my hand. Something sits up in the bed behind the couch. I squint to see a boy covered with green scales. Hurried footsteps approach. A light is flicked on. Ebby gasps.

Totally not Rose.

A gigantic Creeper, crocodile-human hybrid, possibly one of the guys who chased me through the sewers a few months ago. And a second one behind him.

They creep closer.

Chapter 5

Creepers Creepers Everywhere

"RUN!"

Dazed, Ebby doesn't hear me. I whack her shoulder to snap her out of it.

"Run!"

We bolt for the door. Sudden pain pierces my shoulder as claws tear through my skin. I yank Ebby by the hood of her jacket and she follows me towards the Square.

A deafening scream roars. "Humans!"

Footsteps are in hot pursuit. My eyes are fixed on the lightway in the center of the Square. Ebby grabs my hand as we run to the light. However, as soon as we step inside, the lightway fades.

About to exclaim a "Damn it," I cough instead. My lungs are filling with phlegm. Footsteps are closing in on us.

"Syn?"

"We have to keep going," I choke.

I motion for Ebby to follow and we scurry to the back of the Garden, racing through the wall of fog. My legs come to an abrupt stop. Ebby stops too. I squint beyond Ebby's hazy silhouette to see through the mist.

"We have to lose whoever is following us." I find Ebby's hand and fold it into mine. "Put your other hand out, so you don't slam into a tree."

There are footsteps behind us.

"Spread out," someone with a deep voice orders.

I draw Ebby closer and put a finger to my lips. Quietly, we move to the right, rather than heading deeper into the fog. The Creepers will probably go in a straight line and since they can barely see what's in front of them, maybe we can lose them. I don't feel so good and barely manage to keep myself from coughing. The less noise we make, the better our chance is to escape.

The voices and footsteps grow fainter. We creep along for another few minutes and stop. Neither of us says anything. We only listen. Silence.

"We escaped."

"For now, anyway." I let myself cough and realize how congested my chest is. Not surprising. I did just get released from the hospital. But, I also planned for this. "Hang on a minute."

I let go of Ebby's hand and rummage through my backpack, eventually finding three inhalers. I rub my thumb over each one to feel the scratches I made to tell them apart in the dark. Or in this case, a very thick fog.

I puff from the bronchodilator, which is meant to open my airways. Back into my backpack, puff the second, a hypertonic saline to clear the mucus from my lungs and open my airways. Then I inhale the Pulmozyme inhaler, which helps thin the mucus. A few deep breaths....

"Better?"

"A bit."

I drink some water and hand the bottle to Ebby, glancing around for any sign of life around us. "We need to keep moving."

She gulps some water. "Syn, you have a plan, right?"

"Not to let them catch us."

"Well, duh. I mean beyond that. You thought you would find out where Beth might be from that boy and sneak into the house or wherever she is being held, without Luke's help. But your little friend betrayed you, and now we're on the run. There's no more sneaking in anywhere or surprising anyone."

"I know."

"And you know I'm with you all the way," Ebby adds. "If you're in this, I'm in this. But I don't want to die, and I know you don't either."

She's right. Whatever I thought could be accomplished here without the trained Marine by my side is kaput. How do I save Beth if Cole knows I'm here and we're being hunted by Creepers? I royally messed this up.

"The longer we stay in the Garden," Ebby says, "the better the chance that Luke will rescue us. But how will he find us? This place is massive, and in this foggy forest you can't see your shadow."

"You're right, Ebby. I should have waited for Luke. When Cole finds out we're here and took down Butterfly-Man and Rat-Girl…"

Ebby giggles at the names I use.

"…he might take his anger out on Beth."

"Don't beat yourself up. The question is, what do we do now?"

I know what Ebby is hoping my answer will be. Even though it's the last thing I want, it's the only reasonable option.

"Okay, new plan," I tell her. "We'll leave the fog, hope we don't get caught by a two-legged crocodile and head to the lightway. We allow some Creepers to see us go through the lightway. If a pissed-off Cole comes to our world to get me, we blindside him and go rescue Beth. If Cole doesn't follow us home, we find Luke and return to the Garden with him."

Ebby pats me on the back. "I like that plan. Keep your dart gun ready."

"Hopefully I don't have to use it this time." Before I have a chance to reach for my backpack, someone grabs my shoulder.

"I got one!" a woman's voice shrieks.

Whack!

The woman cries out and her grip on my shoulder releases.

"Let's go," Ebby yells. "Hurry!"

We race through the fog again, hurried footsteps following closely.

"They're getting away!"

Ebby squeals and narrowly misses a tree, stumbling, her dart gun flying from her hand.

I scoop up her gun and help her to her feet. "Come on!"

Now I hear footsteps and voices in front of us too.

"They're surrounding us!" I guide Ebby to the right, in the direction of the Garden. The cover of the fog isn't going to protect us anymore. My coughing continues as soon as we return to the Garden. There is movement in the shadows ahead.

"There!" a raspy voice yells.

We U-turn and tear in the opposite direction. *How much longer can I keep this up?*

"Where to now?" Ebby gasps.

"You'll see. Stay close."

My legs are weak by the time we arrive at the bog. Maybe we can make it to the other side and lose them in the fog. As I set foot on the peat trail, something dives for us from above. It swoops closer, green scales barely visible in the faint light.

"Creeper!"

Ebby shrieks as its talons hook onto her shoulders. She is swept over me and into the sky, dangling precariously. They disappear into the darkness, Ebby's screams fading rapidly.

"Ebby!" I scream, and then have to kneel and hack my lungs out. I'm coughing up phlegm as another shadowy form approaches. A Creeper bird like the one that took Ebby. They resemble pterodactyls from the Jurassic period. Truly frightening. My thoughts dart from panic to regret over the friend and sister I've failed.

As the Creeper bird lunges, something slaps against my back. I'm yanked towards Ebby's terrifying screams and fall to the ground again! Before I can comprehend what is happening, I bounce upwards like I'm on a bungee cord and then drop again. Feeling sick to my stomach now, my feet are dangling above the trail as I'm flown through the bog by some unseen force. Everything is a blur. Ferns and brush whack against me. I'm lowered, my feet skimming the surface of the bog water and I am lifted again. The bog is soon behind me and my feet are hovering above the grass in the Garden. Suddenly, I am yanked upwards and land on the fourth stair of the spiral staircase.

Last time, I climbed this staircase to the platform high in the sky and found out that the healing properties of the Garden had no effect up there. Since there are no healing properties in the Garden anymore, and I'm already feeling awful, I'm more concerned about who, or what, awaits me at the top, and who has hold of me.

I'm dragged up the stairs and tugged through the hollow center into the cloud floating at the top. Once through the cloud, I tumble onto the platform, landing in complete darkness.

I hack my lungs out, wincing as pain from the scratches on my shoulder, and scrapes and bruises from the flight through the bog rip through me. Surprisingly, after a few seconds, the coughing stops. The pain dissipates. The fluid in my lungs clears.

Someone strikes a match. The flame lights a tall candle in the center of the platform. A familiar creature crawls over to me on eight legs.

"Child," Maya says. "You should not have returned."

Chapter 6

Kiss of the Spider-Woman

Maya!

Should I be afraid or relieved? The last time I saw Maya, she helped me escape the Creeper-infested sewers, but only after her kids convinced her not to eat me.

"Thank you. I think."

Her mischievous grin suggests I may wish to rescind my gratitude. "This is for your own good," Maya says. "Don't scream."

With that, Maya blows out the candle, yanks the strand of web attached to my back and flings me over the railing. *You better believe I scream!* I bounce way up, but this time I am fastened to a giant web. It's pitch-dark.

The good news is that aside from the very real fear of falling to my death, I feel triumphantly healthy. As I learned during my last visit, this place is more than two flights of stairs high. I'm in the sky, possibly above the clouds, and this sky belongs to another world. How this is even possible is beyond me. The only people who could explain it are my parents. If they are alive, that is.

Someone whispers in my ear and I shriek.

"Didn't I tell you not to scream? Child, you must be silent until I say otherwise."

"But—"

"Not a word," Maya whispers. "Not. One. Word."

I do as she says. Hanging above the clouds from a thin strand of web, my fate is in her hands. I manage to calm down and clear my mind, but nothing can make me forget about Ebby. Or my guilt. She's here because of me. Because I was too impatient to wait for her brother. And now who knows if she's even alive?

Strangely, I hope the Creeper took her to Cole. What a giant reptilian bird would want with her is too horrifying to consider. At least Cole might hold her as more leverage to make me turn myself over to him.

Suddenly, there are thumps on the platform above. Then a beam from a flashlight, and a woman's voice.

"Nothing."

"Look closely," a deep male voice urges. "Any webs?"

"Not a one."

"Hand me the light," orders the man.

Maya covers my mouth and forces me backwards as the flashlight beam shines where we were hanging mere seconds ago. It hovers around the outside of the platform. Then the light falls back.

"Alright," the man says. "Let's go."

I patiently wait for Maya to tell me when it's safe. Without warning, she flings me up and over the railing, slamming me onto the hard platform.

"Ow!"

"Listen," Maya says as she lights the candle again. "I only helped you because you did as I asked before. You freed us all from our confinement underground. You kept your word when I didn't believe you would."

Technically, we should be even. I did that in exchange for her not devouring me. However, I feel no need to remind her of that.

"But you did more than that," she reminds me. "You removed the Garden's protection from illness. And, you killed a girl."

"No." I lower my head in shame. "I mean, it was an accident. I would never kill anyone on purpose."

"I figured. But you have angered the two-faced snake. He has convinced most of the Garden's residents that you killed his love. That you destroyed what would prevent us all from our eventual demise. He claims that you've made our utopia no better than the places one can escape to in the light."

"I was angry and did a terrible thing. I didn't know what would happen. It is my fault. But don't they realize who freed them from the confinement of the sewers? Didn't you tell them that?"

"I did. But your old friend Coleus says otherwise, and he can be very convincing. When he keeps his temper in check he can be quite charming."

"Yeah," I confess. "I'm aware."

"Know that he does not fool me. Some do believe me. They are grateful to you for their freedom. We are outnumbered though and keep to ourselves. We're not welcome. As lethal as I can be, I cannot take on all the Creepers in the Garden. Nor would I want to. They are simply misguided."

"But Flint...."

"Who is Flint?"

"A friend. A boy who is living with, um, the Creepers. He's the one who ratted me out for being here."

"A loyal friend, indeed. I know of whom you speak. He is one of us, you realize."

"I do. Flint was raised by his mom, Rose."

"He was a kind boy. Taken away from his mother when it was discovered he was one of us. He lives with us now."

"Why would he betray me? It's only been a few months since I saw him. Where is his mom? Where are all the people who lived here?"

"Where do you think they are?"

"Are they...? Did he kill them?" How could that be possible?

"No, nothing that drastic, though some humans are no longer with us. Coleus had them all rounded up, and they now live where we did. Below."

The sewers. My friends, Lily, Rose, Nell…. I think of poor Wolf, who died because of me. Who else might have died under Cole's charge?

"Now, young one," Maya says. "They will check up here again for you. You must go home."

"I can't go home. Not yet."

"You are being hunted by dangerous creatures. Some would bite your head off in one snap. Why would you want to stay?"

"I don't want to stay. I *need* to stay. Cole has my sister."

"The young girl. Of course. There is a resemblance."

"Have you seen her?"

"I have seen her from time to time. Coleus ties her up when he takes her out."

Hearing of Beth being tied up doesn't comfort me, but knowing she is still alive does.

"And now, a Creeper has flown off with my friend Ebby."

"I have saved your life, Synthia Wade. We are square." Maya scurries around me. "I will get you home if you wish but will not join you on a suicide mission. Your friend is most likely dead. Your sister is probably still alive. Accept that and go back where you belong."

"No! I won't believe Ebby is dead. She came here to help me. We were about to head home for help when she was captured. I can't leave her. I won't."

"You're a stubborn child." Maya crawls to the cloud and the exit. "And a stupid one, I'm now starting to realize."

I stand up, easily and without effort. "Thank you for saving me. Now it's my turn to do the saving."

"Enjoy your short stay in the lion's den. I expect that the next time I see you, your pretty face will be torn off at the neck and planted on the ground next to the feet you're standing on."

She leaps over the railing, leaving me vulnerable and alone. I watch the flickering candle, hoping her gruesome prediction won't become a reality.

Chapter 7

Shellshock

I HAVE A PLAN. Not a great plan, but it's a plan.

Assuming there is still a hunt on for me in the Garden, there is no telling how many Creepers have joined in the search. It's vitally important to get to fog cover and find the big house as soon as possible. If I waste time, it could be at Ebby's expense. Plus, Cole could climb up here and find me.

It's time to move on. I remind myself that there are three things in my backpack that will come in handy after I go below the cloud: an inhaler, a dart gun loaded to capacity, and a long metal bar that fits nicely in my palm.

Fastening the dart gun onto my belt, I step through the cloud. It's still dark on the other side and I can't see anything. There are no lightways nearby. As expected, my chest clogs up rapidly. There is still pain from being flown through the bog and from being banged around on this stairwell while attached to Maya's web. That I can live with. But my CF symptoms need attending to or they will get worse. I smack my chest repeatedly to help release the mucus in my lungs, and then take a puff from the inhaler. Finally, some relief.

The sequence of flashing lightways conveniently guides my way down the staircase. I slip the inhaler into my jacket pocket and zip it shut. Taking the long metal bar in one hand and holding the railing with the other in case the light is lost, my descent begins, one step at a time. Loud voices reach my ears as I approach the bottom.

"You check the platform."

"Yeah. Meet you in the bog."

Damn it. I have no choice but to run down the rest of the stairs and hopefully get there before the Creeper that is headed my way. My feet slip off the third step to the bottom, launching me forward to fall hard on the grass, the dart gun flying off my belt on impact.

Ouch.

I stand up in the Garden, face to face with another strange Creeper who is staring into my eyes. He looks like a mustached, middle-aged Joe Schmoe, except that he has two massive lobster claws instead of hands. Claws that could easily snap my head right off. I grip the metal bar firmly.

"Well, look what we have here." He turns to yell at his friend. "Hey, Gary!"

During that brief second, I whack him between his legs with the metal bar. Lobster-Man leaps back in pain and instinctively moves his massive claws to protect his injury. His arms are thick and have enormous heft, so he is thrown off balance and falls over. He struggles to get up with his bulky claws. Those claws are a great weapon, but they seem to be more of a hindrance. Lucky me!

Keeping an eye on Lobster-Man, I slide the metal bar into my backpack and pat my hands around on the wet grass, frantically searching for the dart gun. Lobster-Man is still flailing around, trying to get up, screaming for his friend. *Where is that gun?* Someone is moving closer.

"Gary! It's the kid. I found her!" Lobster-Man grunts.

Got to find the gun!

"Yeah, yeah…I'm comin. I'm comin!"

Gary is in sight now, coming closer. *Found the gun!* In the nick of time. I brush past the downed Lobster-Man and dash across the farm. After a hard-left turn, I slow to avoid exerting myself any further. There is still movement around me though, and voices in the distance. *Gotta keep going.*

I peer over my shoulder after reaching the fog. No one around. *Phew.* Carefully dodging trees, I travel far enough north through the fog to be sure to have passed the end of the Garden, and then turn right and head to the border of the fog. When I reach the fog's exit, I take a moment to rest, before poking my head out for a peek.

I'm surprised and pleased to see that I'm exactly where I want to be—in front of the big house—the two-and-a-half-story duplicate of my house. The front door is wide open, muffled voices drifting through. The front lights shine brightly, illuminating the yard. In what was once a beautiful garden with perfectly manicured flowers and plants, weeds are rampant and dead leaves, fallen petals, and pine cones have decomposed into mush.

A Creeper is standing at the bottom of the stairway, guarding the house. He's a well-built, balding man with a humongous turtle shell on his back. Clearly fast asleep, he's doing a lousy job guarding his post. As I'm wondering how he can even stand upright, he falls forward like a domino.

I duck my head back into the safe fog cover. If Turtle-Man was sleeping before, he is certainly awake now. A few minutes later, I poke my head out again. Turtle-Man is lying on the lawn and would be looking straight at me if his eyes were open. I duck back into the fog.

The threat of harm to Ebby increases every minute, but getting caught won't do her—or Beth—any good. I will remain hidden in the fog until I'm sure that anyone capable of stopping me is no longer around. Could one of those voices from the house belong to Cole? Or maybe Ebby, or Beth?

I sneak another peek. Turtle-Man is still out like a light. If Cole knew he was sleeping on the job, all hell would break loose (not that it hasn't already). It's hard to tell if anyone is still in the house because the door is now shut. Could I sneak around the sleeping turtle dude? Even if he wakes up, I can tranquilize him before he has a chance to scream. Or, if he stands up, a quick shove would cause him to lose balance again.

Sliding the dart gun from my belt, I step through the fog. The worst lookout guy ever is still snoozing directly in the path leading to the stairs. I tiptoe past him, hoping to avoid another coughing fit. While I'm passing the sleeping Creeper, his eyes fly open and he grins.

I've been played!

I raise the dart gun. Turtle-Man spins in a circle and the dart bounces off his shell. He jumps to his feet faster than I would have thought possible and whirls around like a madman, whacking me off balance. The dart gun is knocked from my hand. The metal bar flies out of my backpack and rolls a short distance.

Now, with Turtle-Man looming over me, I try to reach the metal bar. It's too far away. If I get up quickly enough and surprise him, I might be able to knock him over, though that won't keep him down long. When I'm about to make my move, the front door opens.

"Ebby!"

Her cheeks are tear-stained. She can't speak. A thick rope is tied tightly around her throat. Both hands are tied behind her back. Standing behind her, holding the rope, is the big bad in the flesh.

Cole.

Crouched on either side of him are the reptilian dog Creepers I faced last time, drool hanging from their jaws.

Cole stomps down the stairs, tugging poor Ebby behind him, Creeper dogs in tow. "Well, well, well." He lowers his face over mine, mockingly. "Look who finally showed up. It's about damn time!"

Chapter 8

Firestarter

THIS IS NOT THE COLE I remember. His hair has grown out and he is disheveled. Several days of stubble protrude from his cheeks and chin. The friendly demeanor he used to deceive me has vanished. The angry, vindictive Cole that captured Beth and shoved me into the pond is wearing a wide grin with a hint of malice.

He kicks the metal bar out of the way to make sure I can't reach it. "You found the present I left by your hospital bed?" he mocks.

"You're a murderer," I growl through clenched teeth.

"Am I?" He gloats. "If you had come sooner, I wouldn't have had to resort to such drastic actions. If it's anyone's fault that poor woman is dead, it's yours. At the very least, you're an accomplice."

I do my best to convince myself there isn't any truth to that.

"Honestly though," Cole continues, "you have made it worth the wait. Do you know why?" He yanks Ebby closer, choking her in the process. She begins to cough.

"Because you've brought me a new toy to play with." He grins, a sadistic spark dancing in his eyes.

"Let her go!" I angrily rise to my feet. "Beth too. Take me instead."

"I thought you were a smart girl, Synthia. I have the upper hand. You have absolutely nothing to offer."

He's right. That's why I need to rescue Beth rather than turn myself over in exchange for her freedom. Cole's word was meaningless. Now, I might have thrown Ebby into the fire as well. Even though I hold no chips, there must be some way to bargain with him.

"You said—"

"Screw what I said!" Cole's outburst sends spit flying against my cheek, violent temper breaking through his playful taunts. "You killed the only person I ever loved. Now it's my turn to take everything from you!" He slaps my face so fast I barely see it coming.

"Bring her inside," Cole orders Turtle-Man, "while I prepare for a public execution."

As Ebby is dragged away, squealing, I see what at first looks like a piece of string dangling in the air. Then I realize that it's a web attached to the metal bar, which is now swinging towards me. I catch it in mid-air and promptly jab the two prongs at the end into Turtle-Man's chest, just as he grabs at me.

A dazzling blue rod of electric current jolts my foe. His eyes roll back in his head and he lands with a thud. Still breathing, as Luke promised, but convulsing from shock.

Maya squeals. Her five children, considerably larger than the last time I saw them, leap off the roof of the house and surround Cole, Ebby, and the Creepers. If Maya's kids were standing on two legs they would be about my height. A familiar shadow looms across the front yard as Maya stares down at us from the roof, like a prophet watching over her disciples. "Let the girls go, Coleus!"

"You're waging a war, Maya!" Cole shouts, restraining a now furious Ebby. "You have a handful of warriors while I have an army."

Two figures cross the carport and pause to watch the standoff. One looks human, a woman about ten years older than me. She is stark naked! Standing next to her is a man who looks like a beetle standing on his hind legs.

"Maya, let Coleus go," Beetle-Man says in a very human voice. "You don't want to make an enemy of him over these pesky humans."

"We *should* do as you suggest, Markus," Maya shouts. "But we will *not*. I was going to let the humans fend for themselves, but my children insisted otherwise."

"That's right," the spider-Boy named Jeremy says. "That girl is our friend."

"Well then," the naked girl says, "it seems there is no convincing you." With that, she blends in with her surroundings and virtually vanishes into thin air, like a chameleon. Markus darts for the circle of spider children, but is flung off the ground by one of Maya's silken threads. He bounces down, then bungees upwards and hangs from the roof. Chameleon-Gal reappears without warning and punches Jeremy in the face, then flashes out of sight again.

Cole sics the Creepers at the spider children. Before they connect with their targets, Maya flings them up to hang on either side of Beetle-Man, barking and drooling.

With the spider kids distracted, Cole uses the moment to plow into two of Maya's children, knocking them over like bowling pins. Poor Ebby is dragged along with him, squealing angrily. He lunges at me, hands poised to strangle, but I'm prepared. In a flash, the tip of the metal bar zaps him in the chest. His body convulses and he falls at my feet.

The metal bar was designed for more than just whacking turtle-men.

Ebby is coughing from the rope around her neck. I bend over to remove it. Chameleon-Gal pops up again, her hand balled into a fist. Before she can hit me, she is flung into the air and hangs from the roof on another thread of Maya's web.

Maya leaps from the roof to the grass. She and her children assist me in untying Ebby by nibbling on the rope. She is free in no time.

"It's over, Ebby," I reassure her, and hug her tightly.

More Creepers, unimaginable human-animal and human-insect combinations, rush forward. While Maya wraps Cole up in her web, another enormous shadow falls across the yard. The gang of Creepers halt in their tracks as a silhouette of another human spider, even larger than Maya, calls down from the roof.

"If anyone lays a finger, claw, paw, or whatever on my mate, my children, or their friends...let's just say that my family will enjoy a very hearty meal."

"That's my Thomas," Maya says, smiling for the first time that I've ever seen. She faces me and Ebby, her smile fading. "Syn, we'll get you and your friend home safely now, and then you must never, *never* come back."

"I'm not leaving without my sister."

"Why, you ungrateful—"

"Mom," Jeremy interjects. "It's her sister. I'd never leave Tasha behind."

Maya glances from Jeremy to Tasha. "Go into the house then. Find the sister. Hurry!" She nods at her mate. "There are some here that don't fear Thomas."

Ebby insists on coming with us. As we race up the stairs and into the house, Cole screams, "I'll kill you all!"

"Nice guy, Syn. You sure know how to pick 'em," Ebby jokes.

Amazed at how well she has recovered from her ordeal, I ignore the jab at my one-time worst ever crush. I'm tired, not feeling well, and need to find Beth and get us home.

"I'll check upstairs, you search down?"

"Yeah. Look everywhere."

"Got it." Ebby heads for the stairs.

"Ebby?"

She stops and turns around.

"I'm so glad you're okay."

"You better be." She grins. "You think Luke would go out with you if you got his sister killed?" She turns and dashes up the stairs.

I laugh as I race to the room that would be my kitchen at home. Last time it was littered with old computers and a broken dome. The shards of the blue dome I smashed are gone. Only the machine I destroyed is still sitting there. The one that created the Garden's healing properties, and that caused my other self to die when I smashed it to smithereens. I cast that memory aside and scan the rest of the room, surprised. All the broken computers and screens are gone, replaced with brand-new state-of-the art equipment. Where did Cole get these? What is he using them for?

I shake off questions that threaten to distract me from our mission and begin to search the first floor— everywhere. Nothing. I open the creaky basement door, flick the light switch on the wall, and fly down the stairs. There is more brand-new computer equipment stored here. No sign of Beth.

Ebby is waiting for me at the top of the stairs. "She's not upstairs. I'm sorry."

"Let me go up," I say between coughs, hacking up more mucus.

Ebby gently rests a hand on my shoulder. "I checked everywhere. Under beds. In closets. In drawers, even. She's not there."

I'm filled with dread. Could Cole have killed her? Am I too late? Then something else strikes me. "The bubble!"

"Huh?"

"The blank reality where Synister kept my parents trapped for years. Maybe they are still alive and in there with Beth. We can save them all!"

I dash over to the one computer that has a mouse sitting next to it. The screen wakes from sleep mode with one click of the mouse. Excitedly, I click from icon to icon, while Ebby looks over my shoulder.

Suddenly, there is a loud thump on the roof. Then another. Too loud to be Maya, Thomas, or their children. The kitchen door is flung open and a Creeper bursts in—a man with human arms and legs, covered in fur, bat wings protruding from his back.

Before Bat-Dude can move any closer, a silken thread attaches to his back and he is yanked away. He tumbles down the wooden staircase at the back of the house.

Maya's daughter Tasha scurries inside. "You need to leave. Now!"

"I need another minute!"

There are several more thumps on the roof. Something is moving towards the front of the house.

"You don't even have thirty seconds."

Ebby looks at me with desperation. "Syn…?"

"Yeah, I know."

We spring away from the computer and race outside, down the steps, slipping and tumbling down the last few. Sprawled on the grass, I start coughing again. Thumping sounds on the roof are moving closer, making me forget how bad I feel. Ebby helps me up and as we run from the house, I glance at the roof. The Creeper that flew off with Ebby looks poised for another flight mission and standing beside it is another of the same. Ebby is shaking, no doubt recalling her recent ordeal.

The Creepers begin to screech, their gigantic wings spreading. We run! Afraid to look back, suddenly grateful for the sight of Maya and her family hanging on webs from nearby trees.

Thomas' voice booms down. "The girls come with us!"

Another voice projects from behind us. "I don't think so."

We spin on our heels and find ourselves facing

Cole, who is now wearing a metal backpack and holding a colossal gun of some sort. I suddenly realize what it is!

"You and your family should have stayed on the sidelines, Thomas," he sneers. "Your fate was sealed when you partnered with a murderer, the enemy of every Creeper who lives in the Garden."

I gasp as Cole lifts the flame-thrower. An instant inferno explodes from its barrel, setting Thomas on fire.

"Thomas, no!" shrieks Maya.

Ebby and I cover our ears as bone-chilling squeals pierce through the Garden. Thomas hurls himself from the roof in agony, writhing and twitching violently. I am unable to look away from the horrific scene, unable to look at Maya or her children, my heart breaking.

As quickly as it all began, Thomas' flaming body is still. His children wail at the horror they have just witnessed. Cole brandishes the flame-thrower again, igniting Tasha and three more of Maya's offspring. They make no sound, hardly knowing what hit them. Their tiny bodies scatter next to their motionless father, spiraling trails of smoke in their wake. The crackling flames still simmering Thomas' crisp corpse break the brief, paralyzed silence.

Maya is hit next with the same flame before it fizzles out. She collapses and manages to roll over and put out the flames that are roasting half her body. She spins a strand of webbing up to her horrified, surviving child on the roof.

"Retreat!" she orders.

"But D-Dad," Jeremy stutters. "And T-Tasha, Ba—"

"Gone," Maya says. "They are gone."

Ebby and I are cowering on the ground, covering our heads. We watch with great sadness as Maya and her only remaining family member depart.

Rustling sounds bring our attention back to our precarious situation. More Creepers prowl into view. I recognize only Turtle-Man, nicely recovered from his earlier electric jolt.

Cole grins and nods at the two Creeper birds on the roof. "Bon appétit!"

They spread their wings and hover over us, tauntingly, as our hair streams every which way. Ebby squeals and grabs for me, but they casually lift off and land in front of the charred corpses, which they immediately begin to devour. Ebby throws up.

"Not looking so good, ladies," Cole says mockingly. He motions to someone behind us.

Bat-Dude grabs a screeching Ebby by the waist, lifts her a few feet, then drops her next to me.

"I promise you will feel better real soon." Cole snickers, and cocks the flame-thrower at a terrified Ebby. She staggers to her feet. "There are consequences for aligning with a murderer." His forefinger clasps the flame-thrower's trigger.

Chapter 9

Suspect

I'M FEELING SICK AND CAN'T seem to move. My friend is about to die! Instinct takes over. I hurl myself at Ebby, knocking her out of the line of fire.

A gunshot echoes throughout the Garden as the flame comes to life. It misses us and whizzes for Turtle-Man. Another gunshot. A flame shoots into the sky and peters out.

Confused by screams of agony coming from Cole, I turn around and my jaw drops. There is a hole in the palm of his bloodied left hand. Light shines right through it! His shoulder is bleeding profusely. His legs give out and he sinks to his knees, gripping his shoulder.

Someone glides from the shadows, clutching a handgun. Luke!

The Creeper birds have interrupted their charred smorgasbord and are slinking towards Luke, ready to tear him apart. Luke cracks the gun on Cole's head, knocking him down. He slides the gun into his holster and yanks the flame-thrower off the ground.

"Don't make me," he warns, aiming it at the two Creepers.

They study him intently, then spread their giant wings and take flight.

"Phew," Ebby says in a quiet, relieved voice.

"You okay?" Luke asks, jogging over.

Ebby nods.

I cough. And cough. And cough.

Ebby gets to her feet and looks down at me. "Syn?"

I force myself to stand.

"Gimme a sec." Luke returns to a barely conscious Cole. He grabs a fistful of Cole's hair and lifts his head up to face his own. "Where is the girl? Where is Beth?"

Cole cackles. "You think I'll tell you? That I wouldn't take that handy bit of info to my grave?"

Luke drops Cole's head and my bloody nemesis fades away into dreamland. Luke glances at the group of Creepers surrounding us. We're outnumbered.

As they approach, Luke unfastens the straps to the machine on Cole's back and slips into them. He picks up the gun and holds it with both hands, brandishing it at our enemies. "Anyone follows us and you're toast. Figuratively and literally."

He clicks the flame-thrower gun into a clasp on the side of the machine and picks me up as if I weighed nothing. "Ebby, follow us."

"But…Beth," I sputter between coughs, staring at Turtle-Man's blackened shell, simmering and smoking on the grass.

Luke doesn't respond. He carries me through the orchard, then into the fog. We move briskly, Ebby keeping pace with Luke despite the danger of colliding with a tree.

"How do you know where you're going?" she asks.

He offers no answer. I grin in spite of myself. I had drawn Luke a map of the Garden and he obviously memorized it.

We travel in silence for what seems like an eternity, finally stopping at a small plane that must have been downed when the Garden was created. Thoughts about whether or not it is empty are immediately abandoned at the sight of Jon standing there.

"Hey, guys," he says, nonchalantly. "Something tells me we're not in Kansas anymore."

"That was my line." Ebby punches him in the shoulder. "And your timing sucks!"

It finally registers with Jon that Luke is carrying me. "Geez! Syn, what happened? Are you okay?"

"She will be," Luke replies, setting me down on a dusty seat in the plane. "Jon, grab the bags."

Jon looks around, flustered. "Right." He disappears briefly into the mist, returning with a hefty red sports bag and smaller blue one. I know the contents of each.

Luke unzips the blue bag, lifts out a battery-powered generator and sets it near the plane's door. He opens the red bag and takes out a therapy vest like the ones they use to treat patients at the hospital. Luke helps me remove my backpack and then slips the vest over my head and around my abdomen.

"Beth," I say again between coughs. "Need to—"

"Syn, Syn, Syn. You can't help Beth until you help yourself." Luke switches on the generator and plugs the vest cord into it.

"I know we don't have much choice," Ebby shouts above the rumbling of the generator, "but this is not exactly going to help us with discretion."

"The two-faced terror is out cold and his minions will wait for his orders. That said, Jon, it couldn't hurt for you and Ebby to keep an eye out for unwelcome visitors. Have the dart guns ready. Jon knows where they are."

Jon hovers over me. "Are you going to be okay?"

I offer the best smile I can muster and watch him go into the mist with Ebby.

Luke removes the air-pulse generator from the red bag and attaches it to my vest. I am grateful that he knows exactly what to do. I tug the vest until it's above my hips while Luke adjusts the closure clasps.

"How is that? Is it on correctly?"

"Perfectly."

"Good. I'm going to turn it on for five minutes and stand guard. You take it easy."

Luke leaves for a moment. He returns with the flame-thrower and is wearing Cole's backpack. He bends down to be heard over the vibrating noise of the vest and the rumbling of the generator. "I'll be a few feet away. Shout if you need me."

The vest rhythmically inflates and deflates. There is nothing to see but fog, nothing to hear but the busy generator and vest. My thoughts return to Beth. There's nothing I can do until I'm in a better state, but fear of what Cole might do to her is difficult to ignore. I'm hoping he'll place his own recovery ahead of his vendetta.

And Poor Maya. Witnessing her mate and four of her children burning alive. They were just kids! They died trying to help me. Including the nurse at the hospital, Cole has killed six times because of me. I promise myself that there won't be a seventh. If there must be, it will be me. My sister needs a chance to live too. Nobody else should die because I lost my temper and unintentionally killed the love of Cole's life.

I turn the machine off, endure a coughing spell and switch the machine back on. Ebby and Jon come to check on me.

"You okay?" Ebby asks.

"Yeah."

"Ebby filled me in on all the action," Jon says. "I'm so jealous that you guys got to see some real live Creepers."

We both give Jon a look.

"Okay, fine. I practically peed in my pants just seeing the two unconscious ones you two took out. Pretty badass, by the way."

"Syn?" Ebby touches my arm. "You were willing to take the brunt of the flames to protect me." A tear streams down her cheek.

I desperately want to talk, but my voice sounds all Darth Vaderish. Instead, I squeeze each of their hands affectionately. Then, cough my lungs out and turn off the vest.

"You two need to leave," I say, gradually finding my voice. "Luke can handle himself, but I can't have anything happen to either of you."

Right on cue, Luke appears. "Syn, turn the vest on. Time isn't on our side."

I do as he says. Ebby and Jon leave to stand guard again. Luke still thinks it's too early for anyone to venture out here to find us, let alone find our exact spot. He's probably right.

"Listen," Luke says. "I was going to ream you out for dragging Ebby into this without waiting for me. But Ebby told me she didn't give you much choice. That said, you still should have waited for me. Did you actually think you could do this by yourself?"

I can't meet his eyes. He's right. I was impatient and put my life and my friend's life at risk. Beth's too, because if anything happens to me, I won't be able to rescue her. Cole won't let her go without a fight.

"Where were you?" I ask, finally raising my eyes to meet his.

"So, funny thing. Guess who shares my shoe size and brand? The hooded lunatic who left bloody footprints throughout the hospital."

"No!"

"Yup. The cops had no other leads and took me to the station for questioning. Took my phone too."

"You're a suspect?"

"I am," Luke sighs. "I wasn't under arrest, so they didn't have the right to confiscate my phone. They insisted on questioning me even after my request for a lawyer. They will have a hard time holding me unless they get something concrete though, like a motive, which I don't have. I'm not too worried and you shouldn't be either."

"You arrived in the nick of time." I frowned. Poor Luke. No wonder he got Cole so good. Though Cole was also about to fry his sister.

"I'm not supposed to leave the state." Luke chuckles. "But they didn't say anything about other worlds."

I don't laugh with him. None of this is funny. I turn off the vest, cough a bit, turn the vest back on. I am starting to feel better. Hopefully this will be the last time. We can't afford to waste any more time when we need to focus on rescuing Beth.

"Now here's the thing." Luke leans closer. "Seeing you and my sister almost get killed. Knowing all the threats here—those two flying beasts are enough to deal with. Cole is a madman. I can't let you guys stay here. We have to leave."

"Take Ebby and Jon home," I say firmly. "I'm staying."

"That's crazy, and you know it."

"I get that you can't leave your sister here. Well, that is exactly how I feel about Beth, the sister I never knew I had!" I turn off the vest. "I'm not leaving without her."

Luke sits there watching me cough for what we both hope is the last time. "Damn it." He takes a Twinkie from the red bag and rips the package open with his teeth. Once my coughing subsides, Luke hands me the snack. "Twinkie? Check out the calorie count on this baby."

I chuckle while Luke helps me remove the vest. He returns it to the bag as I enjoy the delicious combination of sugar, fat, and preservatives.

"Okay, we have to pack up and move," Luke says, zipping up the bag. "And you're stubborn as hell, so new plan. I move you somewhere else. Somewhere you can rest and recuperate. I'll take Ebby and Jon home and come back. Then *together*," he eyes me sternly, "we'll get your sister back. Deal?"

"Deal," I confirm, just as Ebby and Jon return.

"Footsteps and voices!" Ebby whispers fiercely.

"We have to—" Jon is grabbed from behind, then Ebby.

Chapter 10

The Rattle and the Glow

AT FIRST, JON AND Ebby's captors appear to be a man and a woman. Although, as they come closer, it is clear that they are anything but human. The female Creeper looks like any other woman in her late thirties, except that her skin is shining, and not in a good-makeup-day sort of way. She's literally glowing like a firefly, bright enough to illuminate the other Creeper.

He looks like a middle-aged man, until you see his—tail? There is an actual snake attached to his lower back, with a rattle at the end that is shaking like a maraca. Snake-Man opens his mouth and his jaw drops almost a foot past his shoulders. A pointed tongue flicks between two large fangs. He looks primed for a feast.

"Let them go," Luke orders.

Snake-Man hisses and engulfs the top of Ebby's head with his super-sized jaw.

"Give up the sick girl," Firefly-Woman demands over and above Ebby's shrieking, "and you can have these kiddies back."

"Deal!" I move forward, eagerly.

Luke grabs my arm. I wink so only he can see and he lets me shake him off. "Luke, it's the only way!" Adopting a defeated posture, I sidle over to them, saddened by the terror in my friends' eyes.

Snake-Man releases Ebby's head. His jaw snaps shut and expands into a sinister smile. "Hands up, Syn."

I raise my arms, the dart gun tucked under the sleeve of my jacket.

"I'm not stupid," he says. "Drop the weapon."

I reluctantly let it slide to the ground.

"Come here," he says. "Very slowly."

"Let go of my friends first."

Snake-Man grins at Firefly-Woman and his tail rattles excitedly. Firefly-Woman knocks Jon to the ground and takes Ebby off Snake-Man's hands. He grabs me before I have time to react. *This is not how this was supposed to go down.*

"We'll hang on to this other one for now," says Firefly-Woman. "To make sure Hero Man doesn't try anything."

"You promised!" Luke growls, lunging forward.

Snake-Man's jaw drops again, gaping inches from me. Luke stops in his tracks. The putrid odor of the Creeper's breath is nauseating. To ward off panic, I watch Jon heave himself from the ground, darting my eyes in the direction of the gun he dropped.

Alas, he doesn't seem to take the hint and stumbles over to Luke, pleading, "Let them go. Please!"

"Katya," Snake-Man says facetiously. "The boy said puh-lease."

She groans with feigned defeat, yet her face glows increasingly bright. "I guess we have no choice but to release them then."

They laugh uncontrollably, providing me with the perfect distraction. I kick Jon's dart gun over to Luke and duck.

Luke fires. Another dart pierces Snake-Man's chest. I wrestle free of my captor as his eyes roll back. He collapses.

Luke points the dart gun at Firefly-Woman and she yanks Ebby in front of her as a shield. "You'll hit her, Hero Man," she warns, inching backwards with her hostage. "You know that."

With Katya focused on Luke, I take cover in the fog.

"Where'd she go?!" Katya shrieks. She looks at the downed Snake-Man in disgust. Then glares at Luke again, almost daring him to shoot.

I sprint over to Katya and pick up the dart gun Ebby dropped. Before Katya can turn around, I shoot her twice in the back. She keels over and her glowing face dims.

"Ebby, you okay?"

Ebby nods. She's trembling.

Luke and Jon race over.

"We gotta go," Luke says. "Now!"

Luke slings the flame-thrower onto his back and aims his gun in the direction of the approaching footsteps. Ebby, Jon, and I collect our supplies and when we're ready, Luke takes my hand. Jon grabs Ebby's hand and we move on. Voices and footsteps pursue, but as we follow Luke's lead, zigzagging between trees, the sounds fade. At one point we stop to listen. Nothing.

"I think we lost them," Luke whispers. "Follow me."

I'm pretty sure I know where Luke is taking us. After another long while, we stop again.

"Where are we going?" Jon asks. "Home?"

"Home, soon," Luke says. "First we need to make a stop."

"The sewers?" I ask.

"Yup."

"The sewers?" Jon groans. "Seriously?"

"Syn is staying. She can't be convinced otherwise, so I need to get her someplace safe. The cabins are occupied by Creepers and we can't leave her alone out here."

"We can't leave without her," Ebby says.

"It's not up for discussion, Sis."

"No, it's not," I say, not expecting Ebby to argue the point any further. She's already had her life threatened several times. "Ready?"

"Yeah, let's go," says Luke.

He leads us back to the Garden through the fog, at the ready for any surprise Creeper attack. We arrive in the bog at the spot where I sank into the mud the last time, and accidentally found the entrance.

"Why here?" I ask. "What about the other entrance I told you about?"

"It's heavily guarded," Luke says. "If we knock them out, Cole will know exactly where you are."

"Right." I doubt that even Cole knows about this hidden entrance because I only stumbled upon it by accident. If his guards don't catch us going through the known entrances, he won't even think to look for us in the sewers. Smart.

"Will you be okay holding your breath?" Luke asks, kindly omitting "in your condition?"

"I have no choice."

"Okay," Luke says. "No one speaks until we arrive at our destination. Not a word. When we are safely there, I have snacks for everyone."

"Twinkies?" Jon says excitedly.

Ebby and Luke shush him.

Besides safety—and another Twinkie—what I look forward to the most is seeing my friends again. And, making sure they are okay.

I go first, stepping off that familiar rock into the tar-like mud. Unlike last time, I don't flail about. I remain still with my arms by my side, hold my breath, and let myself sink farther into the muck. When my head drops below the surface, I reach to the right. A little farther, until the sensation of cool air is felt on my fingertips.

I slide from the mud into the shallow pool of water on the cement floor, coughing up mud and mucus that is already building up in my lungs again. Ebby's hand pokes through next. She's covered in mud and coughing profusely. Together, we pull Jon out. Luke arrives last. We splash each other with water and rub off all the mud we can, carefully cleaning our weapons too. Ebby and I wring out each other's hair and wipe off the two sports bags.

Unlike the last time I was here, the place is all lit up. I squint down the long tunnel as far as I can see. In addition to torches, circular battery-powered lights have been fastened to the walls, providing ample light for safe passage.

"Listen! I hear something," Jon whispers.

We hold our position, ears perked, eyes peeled. Sure enough, splashing footsteps are approaching.

"Okay," Jon says. "Forget what I said about wanting to see Creepers. I've seen enough for a lifetime."

"There aren't any Creepers down here," I tell him, hoping to hell I'm right. "Just friends."

Several long shadows are cast in our direction, followed by five figures. Humans. It's my good friends Rose and Lily, the usually chipper Dawn and two kids I barely recognize. They look so different from the people I left more than four months ago. They are barefoot, wearing dirty, tattered clothing, and their skin is filthy, like they haven't bathed in ages. Lily's once flawless and long golden locks of hair are matted and dirty brown. Worst of all, my friendly, happy, and outgoing friends look miserable. Dawn and the children stay back. Rose and Lily approach.

I try to smile but can't manage it. "Lily. Rose."

"Syn," Lily says in a voice I hardly recognize. "What are you doing here?"

Rose brushes past Lily. "You shouldn't be here." She smacks my face, knocking me to the concrete.

"Hey!" Luke takes a step, but I raise my hand to stop him, numb with shock.

Meanwhile, Rose and Lily are looming over me.

"You shouldn't have come back," Lily says coldly, stinging my heart.

As I try to get up, she shoves me down again. Rose's words hurt more than her physical assault. "You filthy little miscreant. I had hoped you were dead."

Chapter 11

A Frosty Reception

IT SHOCKS ME TO SEE the once sweet Lily act this way. However, it's not the first time. When I returned to school after my post-Garden hospital release, I noticed a girl smoking pot outside the gymnasium door with a group of grungy-looking friends. Her hair was dyed black, her nose, one eyebrow, and bottom lip were pierced, and she was wearing black lipstick to round out her distinct Goth attire. I had seen that girl before but never paid much attention until that day I made the connection. In my world, she was Lily's doppelgänger.

"What ya looking at, Sicko?" she had said, followed by her friends' laughter. One of her acquaintances sarcastically offered me a puff of their joint.

This girl's name wasn't Lily. It was Gwen. Gwen Dubois.

I had wondered what circumstances would have a sweetheart in one world be a goth bully in another.

But now, the teenage girl standing over me has a more similar demeanor to Gwen than the Lily I knew.

I cough a few times. Jon rushes to my side to help me up.

Ebby stands protectively between them and me. "Leave her alone! She's sick."

"Oh, poor Syn has a cold," Lily sneers.

"What the hell is the problem here?" Luke demands. "I thought these were your friends!"

"We thought so too," Lily says.

"You should leave," Rose orders. "Go back to the world where you belong."

"You blame me," I say quietly.

"Of course we blame you," Lily says. "You *did* release the Creepers. Right?"

I lower my head in shame. "It wasn't supposed to turn out like this."

Will they ever believe me? Yes, I bargained with Maya, agreeing to destroy the device that emitted a high-pitched sound that pierced the ears of Creepers. It would have killed them if they didn't take cover. They had been condemned to the sewers where the device's range couldn't affect them. I destroyed the device in return for Maya sparing my life and she promised that no humans would be hurt. Did I truly believe her or had I convinced myself that she was telling the truth?

"Isn't it your fault that the Garden no longer protects us from illness? And death?"

"Yes," I tearfully admit. "That was an accident. I didn't know that would happen."

"An accident?! People died because of that," Rose retorts. "Wolf. Hopper. Who knows how long Nell has…."

"W-what?" *Oh my God. What have I done?* "What happened to Hopper? And Nell?"

"Hopper was perfectly fine during the day," Lily says. "That night I went to his cabin to see Nell. She and Fern were crying over his body. He was alive one moment and then suddenly, dead. Just like that. Because of you."

Even though crying causes mucus to build up in my lungs, I can't stop myself. Hopper was innocent. Nell considered him her father. He must have had some condition that the healing properties kept at bay.

"And…" I can barely get the words out, "Nell?"

"She's sick," Rose says. "We don't know what's wrong."

Nell is my age, and Lily's best friend. At least she's alive. Maybe we can take her to a hospital in my world. Perhaps she still has a chance.

"All this because Cole didn't love you? For god's sake, you only knew the boy a few days!"

"Whoa, Lady," Ebby chimes in before I have a chance. "That is *so* not what happened."

Luke puts a hand on Ebby's shoulder. "Why don't you let Syn tell them what happened?"

"We know!" Lily exclaims. "Cole turned her down, she lost her temper, and destroyed everything that made the Garden special."

"No," I say quietly, "that's not true."

"Cole told us," Lily insists. "He was my friend for years and all of a sudden you show up and turn him into a psycho."

"No. Cole was pretending to be your friend. He is mean and ruthless. Always has been. He pretended to be my friend too. It was all a ruse."

"You expect us to buy this?! Cole and I were friends, ever since we woke up here as kids."

"I'm sorry, Lily. But the truth is that Cole isn't who you thought. He didn't break my heart. He was in love with—"

"With who?" Lily demands. "Nell and I were the only other girls his age in the Garden."

"No, that's not true. There was someone else our age. Synister."

"Oh, come on. Synister? She stayed in her house and didn't talk to anyone. And besides, she was a grown woman."

"No, she wasn't a woman. You only think that because of what Cole told you. Let me ask you this: Did anyone other than Cole and me ever see Synister up close? Without her mask?"

Lily and Rose exchange glances. Are my words finally getting through?

"Synister was a teenager like me," I went on. "Exactly like me. She was experimented on for years and was so sick, even the Garden's healing properties couldn't help her. She was in immense pain all the time. Her skin bubbled like lava. Despite this, Cole loved her. He would do anything for her. And then…" I pause. "She died. That's why Cole lost it."

Rose and Lily are speechless.

"Synister and Cole captured me for some weird science experiment. I escaped and tried to defend myself. Smashed everything in front of me, including the glass dome. I didn't know what it did, but now it is clear to me that it somehow preserved or controlled the Garden's healing powers. I deserve the blame for that. Still, Cole lied to us. He was Synister's spy, not our friend. Rose, you would have found Wolf's body minutes after Synister died."

Lily's eyes overflow with tears. Rose puts an arm around her shoulders.

"It's true," Ebby says. "You know it is."

"If this is true," Rose says, "it's still Syn's fault as much as it is Cole's."

"You're right," I confess. "I'm so sorry."

"Sorry?!" Rose exclaims. "Cole took Flint from me, because he's a Creeper. Did you tell Cole about that?"

"No, of course not. I promised not to tell anyone."

"Well, he knew. He warned Flint that if he didn't stay with the Creepers and show them his loyalty, they would kill me."

That explains why Flint ratted me out. He was trying to protect his mother. "I'm very sorry, Rose." I reach a hand out and she waves it away.

"Why are you here, Syn?" Rose asks. "Why did you come back?"

"For Beth. Cole has her."

"Who's Beth?" Lily asks.

"My sister."

"The girl…" Rose starts to connect the dots.

"Yes, that young girl. The one I asked you about, and you wouldn't tell me who she was."

"We didn't know her name," Rose says. "She was seen in the Garden from time to time. Cole told us that Synister didn't even want us to talk to her."

"We weren't sure," Lily says, "but we thought she might have been Deb and Ian's daughter. The man and woman who used to live in the house."

"She was."

"But you said she's your sister." Lily is confused.

"I only found out about Beth after coming to the Garden. Now she is Cole's prisoner. He threatened to kill her if I didn't return to rescue her."

"But, if Beth is your sister," says Rose, "then—"

"Ian and Deb are my parents."

"Your parents?" Lily is stunned.

"I still have faint hope that they are alive."

"Get it now?" Ebby asks. "Syn isn't the enemy. That two-faced monster is."

I gesture to Ebby, Jon, and Luke. "These are friends from home. They have come to help me."

"Things haven't gone so well," Ebby says.

"Understatement of the year," Jon mutters.

Lily looks into my eyes, expressionless. I can't tell what she is thinking. Suddenly, she wraps me in her arms.

"I'm sorry, Lily. About everything."

Luke approaches Rose. "Does Cole know about the entrance we just came through?"

"No. That is how we sneak in and out to get supplies from the lightways."

"Would you mind if Syn stays here?" Luke asks. "I'm going to take these two home and then return."

"Luke, we should stay here with Syn." Ebby protests. "For one more day. I don't want to leave her yet."

"I don't know," Luke says wearily. "There's probably a search party out for you guys."

"We could all stay down here today," Ebby offers. "And then go home tonight."

Luke looks defeated.

"There's space," Lily says. "Everyone else is still sleeping. They will be for another hour or two. We were up early to prepare meals for today. The others won't be happy to see you, Syn, but I'll tell them the real story."

"Thanks."

"What's on the menu?" Jon asks.

"Pretty much what we have every day," Rose says. "Rats and rice."

Jon gags.

Ebby punches him in the arm. "Oh, grow a pair."

Lily sets us up in an empty concrete corridor, providing sleeping bags and sheets of cardboard to put underneath them. It's cold, but we're all exhausted and despite the uncomfortable conditions, sleep beckons.

* * *

It takes me a moment to realize that I'm not in my bed at home. I sit up. Ebby is sprawled across her sleeping bag, staring at her phone. She puts it down when she sees that I'm awake.

"Morning, Sleepyhead."

"Is it morning?"

"Barely."

"What time is it?"

Ebby looks at her phone. "Just past 11. It sucks that there's no cell connection down here. Thank goodness for Candy Crush."

Poor Aunt Ruth. She must be freaking out because I've disappeared again. At least Jon's and Ebby's parents think that they are at an overnight school hiking trip. The trip is real, as are the permission forms they signed. Their attendance not so much.

Luke lives alone and took time off from his security job. So, it's just poor Aunt Ruth who is worried sick. She's like a mother to me and was left with nothing but a note. I feel horrible about that.

I try to cough up some phlegm. Ebby hands me a pitcher of water. "Thanks." I take out my pill container. As I swallow twenty-four pills, Jon and Luke join us in the corridor.

"You were supposed to bring food," Ebby says.

Luke tosses us some granola bars and Pop-Tarts.

"You don't want what they're having," Jon says.

"I won't know unless I try it."

"The rat is actually not bad," Luke says. "With seasoning, it tastes like chicken. How are you feeling, Syn?"

"Okay."

"Great. I have some good news and bad news for you. The good news is that I visited Nell and for the time being, she is okay. I think she has vertigo and gave her a Gravol. She's already feeling better."

"Couldn't vertigo be a symptom of something more serious? Like a brain tu—"

"Unlikely a brain tumor at her age. When I bring you and Beth home, I want Nell to come with us and get proper medical attention."

"What's the bad news?"

"I wanted to give her something to cheer her up, so our Twinkie count is down by three."

"I am not okay with this," Jon jokes.

After I finish my morning therapy regimen and have something to eat, Ebby, Jon, and Luke take me to see Nell. We cross through a massive compound the size of the Garden, if not larger. All the corridors have battery-powered lights attached to the walls so it's easier to see the layout this time. While we don't have to worry about any Creepers sneaking up on us, it's understandable that we share looks of antipathy with people who pass. Luke leads us to a metal door.

"Come in," Lily's voice answers Luke's knock.

He slides open the heavy door, old hinges protesting with scraping sounds like fingernails scratching a chalkboard. The room is compact. Nell is lying on a mattress that's pressed against one wall, a few personal belongings scattered at her feet. Lily is sitting cross-legged on a sleeping bag that is spread over a sheet of cardboard next to the bed.

"What is *she* doing here?" Nell asks Lily.

"She wanted to say hi."

"Um, how are you doing?" I immediately wish I could stuff the words back in my mouth.

"Not good, thanks to you!"

"Listen, I want to—"

"Save it. I might live because of your friend here," she eyes Luke, "but I am sick because of you."

"But Nell," says Lily, "you know that it was an accident."

"I don't care! Because of her, Hopper and Wolf are gone. Forever!" Nell glares at me. "I don't ever want to see you again!"

Lily stands up to comfort her. Nell waves her away.

I have no words. Luke ushers me into the corridor. On the way out, I almost turn to glance at Nell. Almost. With heavy hearts, our close-knit group sadly trudges along the corridor.

Ebby watches me wipe away some tears. "I'm sorry, Syn."

"Don't be. She's right about everything."

"Syn, tonight after it's dark," Luke begins, "I'm going to take Ebby and Jon home. I don't suppose you're join—"

"No."

"Okay. I won't be gone long."

The sound of my name echoes down the corridor and footsteps splash through the shallow water behind us. "I'm sorry about all that," Lily says, running up to us.

"It's okay."

"So, Ian and Deb are your parents."

"Yeah?"

"Well then," Lily says, "There is something you might want to see."

Chapter 12

The Voltway

LILY AND I HAVE FEW words to share. On the surface, we're getting along again, although there is still an unspoken tension between us. We're not the friends we were during the week I was first in the Garden. She's far from the stoner goth girl at my school, but the turmoil of the last few months has obviously had a profound effect on her. Although she seems to have looked past the role I played, a certain vibe tells me otherwise.

We pass some former residents of the Garden. I remember most of their faces but know few of their names. They all have one thing in common—disdain at the sight of me, even Teng and Tian, the sweet Chinese couple who could barely speak a word of English. They always wore smiles. Now Tian looks weak and is hunched over, leaning against her husband. Their brows are lowered in scorn.

We stop at a metal sliding door. As Lily slides it open, chills travel up and down my spine. I have no idea what to expect except that whatever is in here somehow relates to my parents.

The concrete room is about half the size of my bedroom. It could easily be a storage space, but it is empty, except for a chair and an older PC on a desk. The PC is plugged into a wall socket (that's *functional?*). A young Asian man about Luke's age is sitting in front of the computer.

"Syn," Lily says, "this is Lundy."

Lundy strides over and we shake hands.

"The infamous Synthia Wade. Nice to meet you."

Unlike the other residents of the Garden, Lundy doesn't show any ill will towards me. I don't recall seeing him last time I was here and yet for some reason he looks familiar. Wait a minute! The news story I watched in the hospital about the two computer store employees who robbed their employer. One of them was found dead. Lundy is the other one!

I pull my hand away. "Y-y. You're that guy!"

"Who?" Lily asks.

"He robbed a store with some guy. The police think he might have killed him."

Lundy steps back. "Whoa, whoa, whoa. That is not what happened."

"How do you know this?" Lily asks.

"It was on the news!"

"Listen to his side of the story," Lily says. "Lundy didn't kill anyone."

"I swear to you, Syn. I'm not a murderer. I'm certainly not here by choice, either. Hear me out."

I nod. I admit I'm curious.

"Yeah, so I worked at Jasper Tech Town after I finished high school. Part-time in sales when I was in school and full-time on their tech team once I graduated, refurbishing second-hand systems. My buddy Dave worked there too. We were hanging out at the beach drinking beer one night after work when a guy in a hoodie approached. He knew our names and where we worked. When the guy took off his hood, we saw that he was a freak. He literally had two faces!"

Cole!

Lundy sees the shock on my face. "Yeah, that guy. He showed us pictures of our family. My parents and little sister. Dave's girlfriend and mom too. He said he had guys outside each of their homes and if we didn't do exactly as he said, he'd have them killed."

"I believe you. But what could Cole have wanted?"

"The guy told us he needed a bunch of computer systems."

Of course. The new computers in the house. This is starting to add up. "And he wanted you and Dave to steal them?"

"Exactly. But the guy had no clue about anything tech-related. My grandmother knows more than he does. He just rambled on about lightways, weather systems, and alternate dimensions. Honestly, I thought the guy was insane."

He isn't wrong.

"Coleus was flustered that we had no clue what he was talking about. So he listed off details about the systems he was replacing. Really old tech, but we understood what he needed. The guy had Dave drive a truck to the alley behind the store. I turned off the alarms and took the stuff from the loading dock to the truck. We knew we were on the security cams, but this guy was crazy. We feared for our families' safety."

"Let me guess. He took you to a beam of light and you hauled the stuff through to the Garden."

"That's right."

"But your friend," I say as delicately as possible. "Did Cole kill him? And why are you down here?"

Lundy lowers his head. "Coleus had us set up the new systems. Setting up the hardware wasn't a problem. Transferring programs we've never seen before from old hard drives, some of them damaged, was a challenge. Dave didn't have a tech background like I did. He was self-taught and accidentally short-circuited a hard drive and the lightways, the ones that used to appear in the outskirts of the Garden. They popped up inside the Garden instead. Cole was furious. Beat him and dragged him away. I tried to stop him. Honest."

"I get it now," I say. "I'm sorry about Dave. And everything you were put through."

"Thanks. Somehow, I knew you weren't the monster people said you were."

His backhanded compliment is probably the nicest thing anyone down here has said to me so far.

"Cole sent Lundy down here," explains Lily. "Occasionally a Creeper or even Cole himself comes to fetch him when they need him to fix equipment."

The poor guy is trapped here. Some of the blame falls on me since I was the one who smashed the computers. "So, Lily told me there's something I should see that's related to my parents, Ian and Deb."

That sets a spark under Lundy. He slides into the chair in front of the computer. "Come over here." He clicks the mouse.

I'm looking at a black screen with two columns of filenames. All the files in the first column start with *MWinters* (Masie Winters, surely) with most followed by numbers.

MWinters587946
MWinters47988
MWinters556

MWinters_test_site is at the end of the list.

I'm intrigued, but my curiosity is more strongly focused on the other column of files. Each of those filenames starts with *IWade* or *DWade*, followed by numbers.

IWade5579
IWade777564

DWade6798976
DWade9997465

Each column has ten files.

"What are these?" I ask.

"I don't know. But both of you go stand against the wall over there," he motions to my left, "and watch."

Lily and I do as he says and Lundy double-clicks the first file in the second column, *DWade98975*. A confirmation message pops up. When asked if he wants to continue, Lundy clicks "Yes". My heart is pounding with anticipation. I have no idea what to expect.

Nothing happens at first. After many long seconds, a lightway beams from the concrete floor through the ceiling, about three feet from Lundy's chair.

"What is this?! Where does it go?"

"To a new world. We've only traveled to one, which took us to three others. Nothing significant to see, but we didn't stay long. It was my first time earth-hopping and I was kind of freaked out. Okay, majorly freaked out. We grabbed supplies and left. Only did that once."

"Why? It seems like the perfect way to gather supplies without worrying about Creepers. Not that I endorse theft or anything."

"Show her the freaky one," Lily says.

"Yeah. After we returned I discovered this." Lundy is extra cautious to make sure we're hugging the wall. He double-clicks the last filename in the first column.

MWinters_test_site

I'm beginning to think that whatever is supposed to occur isn't going to, when there is a buzzing sound. A black cloud fills the space where the lightway was and takes the shape of a tube. Unlike the lightway, this tube is all black—like outer space without any stars. Every couple of seconds, a bright yellow and blue bolt of electricity crackles through the black tunnel, traveling from the floor through the ceiling.

"I call this a voltway," Lundy announces proudly, like he's announcing the name of his newborn.

"Does it take you anywhere?"

"Yeah, it does." The excitement has drained from his voice. He double-clicks the filename and the electrical bolts vanish. The black cloud fades like steam after a hot shower. "Where though? Who knows?"

"It's probably best not to try and find out," Lily adds.

"Why is that?"

"Well," Lundy explains, "after we sent a rat through, two guys here volunteered to go."

"Jade and Mackie," Lily says.

"What happened to them?"

"I stayed here waiting for them to return," Lundy says. "Hours after they left, Jade's arm reached through the voltway. I grabbed it, but…. but only the arm came through. Ripped from the rest of his body, like something got him before he could escape."

"Something?" More chills run up and down my spine.

"We kept the voltway open for weeks. It eventually closed by itself. Mackie never returned."

Wow. I don't know what to think. It's safe to assume Jade is dead. Is there any chance Mackie could still be alive? And what is Masie's supposed test site?

"We were afraid that whatever did that to Jade might come through so once it closed, we didn't open it again. We felt it best not to take a chance going through the lightways the other filenames open either."

"We put a ladder in the wall of mud you guys came down through," Lily says. "When we need supplies, we leave that way and sneak through a lightway in the Garden, hoping no Creepers catch us. The folks here are more willing to risk that than share Jade's and Mackie's fate, whatever it was."

I'm speechless. The hardships these people have gone through, because of me.

"I thought you'd want to see this, Syn," Lily says. "Since your parents had something to do with it."

"Thank you."

"What brings you back to this crazy place, Syn?" Lundy asks.

"Cole has her sister out," Lily blurts. "She came to rescue her."

"Beth?" Lundy asks. "Beth is your sister?"

My heart is pounding so hard I half expect it to rip through my chest.

"How do you know Beth? Is she okay?"

"I often see her while working at the computer stations in that house. She seems okay."

"I'm so relieved. My friend Ebby and I searched the house and couldn't find her."

"I know where she is," Lundy says. "He mostly keeps her in something he calls the bubble."

"I know about the bubble! That's where I thought she might be but didn't know how to get into it. Plus, Creepers were trying to get into the house and we didn't have time to figure it out."

Lundy smiles. "I'll walk you through it. You can open it yourself. I even know that bastard's password."

A ray of optimism engulfs my spirit. *I'm going to get my sister back!*

Chapter 13

Mangled

ABSENTMINDEDLY, I WATCH JON ram the remains of a Twinkie into his mouth. Ebby and Luke are sorting supplies and choosing weapons to prepare for their trip through the Garden to the lightway.

"We're leaving the flame-thrower here," Luke says. "I don't like what it can do, and Cole won't be able to get his hands on it if it's hidden down here."

While I sit on my tattered sleeping bag with the vest vibrating against my chest, I'm not stressing over Ebby and Jon leaving. All I can think about is seeing Beth again, determined to forget about possible obstacles and only allow positive thoughts.

When the vest treatment is finished, I snack on beef jerky and Twinkies. Protein and calories. I take the vapor treatments from my backpack.

"Hey Ebby, what time is it?"

"A quarter to one."

Luke wants to leave at 2 A.M. He plans to get Ebby and Jon home safely, collect more weapons and food, plus some Gravol for Nell. When he returns we'll devise a plan to rescue Beth. Though Luke is firmly against it, I insist on escorting them to the lightway. I know Luke can handle himself, but I feel like Ebby and Jon's safety is my responsibility. They're only here because they wanted to help me.

At 1:45 A.M. we leave our gritty guest quarters. I say goodbye to Lily while she's asleep. Not that it's necessary since I'll have returned before she is awake. It just feels like the right thing to do.

Climbing up through the mud wall is a lot easier now because of the ladder. I hoist myself onto a large rock and Luke pulls me out. We splash ourselves with bog water to get as much of the muck off as possible. If we do bump into Cole or any Creepers, we don't want to give them any clues about the sewer's secret entrance.

After we're all suitably armed, Luke leads us into the fog where there is no chance of us being seen. Other than the sounds of our breathing and footsteps, there is complete silence.

The lightway home is close to the bog, but we go as far as we can through the fog so they can't track us back to where we came from. Luke clutches his gun with both hands, ready for anything. He promised me he wouldn't shoot to kill and would only use it as a last resort. I'm holding the metal bar—actually, an electric prod—and the rest of the group is carrying dart guns.

We leave the safety of fog cover. Two familiar Creepers are guarding the lightway, standing with their backs to us—Rat-Girl and Butterfly-Man.

"Why would Cole trust the same two imbeciles we took down so easily before?" Ebby whispers.

I shrug. Ebby is right. Plus, now that he knows we're here and might try to escape, wouldn't he have more than two Creepers on guard? Something isn't right.

There is something lying on the ground ahead— actually, not something. Someone! My breath catches at the sight of a mangled body. The woman's neck is twisted so unnaturally it looks as if it is detached from her body. Someone who fell from the sky. I put a finger to my lips, but am too late. Ebby squeals and Jon slaps his palm over her mouth.

The Creepers whirl around but Luke already has one gun in each hand aimed at them—a dart gun in one and a handgun in the other. He shoots two darts into each of their chests and they collapse. Perhaps I was wrong to worry. Maybe this is all going to be okay.

Luke holds the dart gun to his lips, motioning for us to stay quiet. Ebby and Jon just gape at the body. Even though I had told them about this strange, tragic occurrence, nothing could truly prepare them for the abnormalities in the Garden except for first-hand experience. I tap each of them lightly to break their spell.

"Are you sure you don't want to leave with us?" Luke whispers.

"Yes."

Luke knows better than to argue with me. "Well, go straight to the sewers now. I'll return as soon as I can."

We all hug good-bye. While the three of them are holding hands, Ebby in the middle, they step into the lightway.

I am rooted to the spot, contemplating if I should follow them after all rather than wait for Luke in the sewers. What if I'm caught on the way back? I feel vulnerable, even though I have a weapon. I lift a foot to step into the lightway, but am stopped abruptly. Someone is yanking my hair and pain shoots through the back of my head. I'm dragged backwards, screaming, and am forced to my knees. My assailant looms over me.

"You're not going anywhere," Cole says.

Chapter 14

Ambush

"PITIFUL." COLE STARES down at me with disdain.

Blood has soaked through the bandages on his hand and shoulder. He spits at me, misses, takes one step closer and brutally kicks me in the stomach.

The pain! And I'm weaponless—I dropped the electric prod during the ambush and it's too far away to reach. Wincing, I lift my head with great effort. "You don't have to do this, Cole. That person you pretended to be, that kind, gentle guy. That compassion is there, buried deep down."

"Cole was a lie! A pathetic puppy dog I created to gain people's trust. Everyone likes a puppy dog. My name is Coleus!"

He gestures an invitation to two Creeper birds. I scramble to my knees as they fly towards me, bracing myself for an attack. Instead, they swoosh over my head and land next to the mangled corpse.

"Bon appetite!"

The Creepers begin ripping the body apart. I bend over and vomit.

"Oh c'mon, Syn. This is the circle of life. Manna has fallen from the sky to feed these glorious beasts. Bet that when I'm done with you, they'll be ready for dessert." He whacks his good hand across my cheek.

"I just want my sister, Cole. Then you'll never see me again."

He grabs me by the throat. "You think you're ever going to get your sister back? Keep wishing. And, it's COLEUS!" He shoves me down again.

If I'm going to die, I'm going down on *my* terms. I cough repeatedly, forcing myself to stand. "C-Cole." The words barely scrape their way out of my mouth.

Cole smiles. "You've grown a spine."

More Creepers approach. An audience forms, like when a busker is juggling outside a market. I see familiar faces: Chameleon-Gal, now clothed, Lobster-Man, two Croc-Men, the Beetle-Man named Markus and Firefly-Woman, Katya, whose face is emitting a dim glow.

There are some Creepers in the group I haven't seen before. One has a feminine form but where her face should be is what looks like a bunch of tubes. The tubes separate and the young woman's face is revealed. The tubes are actually eight long tentacles that spring from the sides of her head, each one with a life of its own. She is surely the Creeper version of my old babysitter, Greeta.

"I appreciate the bravado. But Cole is my human name. The name of a being that does not exist. I am a Creeper, and proud of it. So you will address me as Coleus. If you breathe the other word one more time, I'll snap that hardened spine of yours in two."

"The last time I was here, you told me that you hated the Creepers!" I eyed our audience defiantly. "You insisted you weren't one of them."

"Though Synthia," he winks at the Creepers, "snapping your spine sounds like so much fun, I may do it regardless." He knocks me down and kicks me repeatedly in the stomach. The Creepers cheer him on.

I released these beasts. That is on me. This is surely one of my last moments on earth. So much pain. But then, peeking out of a bush to the right of "Greeta" is a familiar face. Flint. His sad expression confirms that he is still my friend.

Cole grabs a chunk of my hair and lifts me to my feet. "You know," he sneers, "the man who raised me, the man who was practically my father, told me that a gentleman never lays a hand on a woman. Then again, I'm not a gentleman. I'm a Creeper!"

He takes great pleasure punching me in the face and watching me collapse. Warm blood trickles down my neck. Phlegm has begun to build in my chest. As I lie on the ground preparing for my demise, to never see my sister or my aunt or my friends again, I think about how I've never met anyone so cruel in my entire life.

Then two things happen. A lightway appears behind the cheering Creepers, and for an instant, Cole is distracted. Then, in front of the lightway, a man dressed in a white tunic—could be a hospital gown—drops from the sky and lands with a thud, dead on impact, mangled like the other.

Flint takes advantage of this distraction and springs to action. The electric prod! He pushes it forward and it stops rolling mere inches from my reach. If I could only—

My breath is knocked out of me as Cole kicks me in the stomach, again. And again. "You killed my Syn. You don't deserve to share her name!"

The pain is so great, I barely feel the impact of each blunt force. Cole spins around and gallantly bows to the crowd of Creepers. They erupt into mad howls of encouragement. Because both Beth's and my life depend on it, I drag myself far enough to grab the prod. The Creepers see, but Cole mistakes their warnings as more encouragement. While he continues to celebrate, I fight every ache, gradually rising to my feet, suppressing a coughing fit. The will to survive can inspire incredible things.

"I dare you to call me Cole now!" Cole roars above the crowd and whirls around. What he doesn't expect is to see me triumphantly brandishing the electric prod.

"Cole!" I ram it against his chest.

As the electric current floods through him, he staggers backwards and seizes on the grass. Dead silence falls over the Creepers. They stand there, caught off guard. As the electric shock fades, Cole attempts to stand, awkwardly gesturing to the Creepers, not yet having control of his voice. Some charge forward eagerly, then stop in their tracks when I ram the prod against his chest again. "Cole," I repeat. He flops around like a fish that's been plucked from the ocean.

Despite the pain, I manage to grin and zap him again. As the electricity bolts surge his body, I say evenly, "Stay down. *Cole*."

Chapter 15

The Lion Weeps Tonight

YOU'D THINK COLE'S LOYAL MINIONS would try to stop me, yet, they can only stare with jaws dropped. Flint is gone and the young Croc-Boy he shared a room with is standing where he had been. Suddenly Greeta whistles. Two Creeper dogs dart from the crowd, running straight towards me.

Even if I had no issues tasering animals, I don't have time to zap them both before they reach me. Thankfully, I have a moment of déjà vu. These Creepers lunged at me the last time I was in the Garden and Beth stopped them. I recall what she did and hold up one hand like a traffic cop. "Stay!"

They stop in their tracks, tongues hanging out of their pointy, scaled snouts. I point to the house. "Go home!" They are defiant. I hold my ground—they take off in the other direction.

Cole attempts to stand, shaking like he crawled out of a frozen river. I step on his bloody, bandaged hand. He snarls with pain, yet still rises to his feet like some invincible monster. I shoot a dart into his chest. Then another. He's out again. I aim the dart gun at the Creepers and start backing away. "Do *not* follow me!"

All heads turn in the direction of high-pitched screeching. A Creeper bird is soaring across the sky. There is no time to run. Rooted to my spot, cowering, I expect it to lift me with its talons. Surprisingly, it circles over me and lands in front of the fresh corpse that fell from the sky. It digs in while yet another body bounces onto the lawn.

What the hell?!

The other Creeper bird is quick to partake in the buffet, rips the red leather jacket off the new body and tears into its skin. I feel like throwing up again, not only from the horrific sounds of tearing flesh, but from pain and the phlegm caught in my throat. As badly as I feel though, survival is foremost in my mind. Waving my dart gun at the Creepers, I back away. Without Cole barking orders, they seem less inclined to pursue me.

I honestly don't know if I've ever felt worse. I've never been beaten before. My head is throbbing and my stomach aches. I need to find a safe place to heal, but the spiral staircase would be the first place anyone would look for me. Plus, there is nowhere to escape if I'm cornered. Because I can barely move, running away is not an option. Since Cole is out cold and likely will be for a while, I decide to take a chance with the staircase.

It takes several minutes to climb the stairs. One at a time, stopping to clear phlegm now and then. Seconds after I climb through the cloud at the top, the pain fades. My lungs are clear. I take a deep, grateful breath and crawl to the middle of the platform. It is pitch-black from cloud cover. I lie on my back and close my eyes, finally at peace—safe, even if that is not entirely certain. *Rest for a few minutes. Just a few minutes.*

* * *

The sound of footsteps on the platform awakens me. It's still pitch-black and I can't see a thing. There is a long moment of silence. I don't dare move an inch.

"Synthia, I know you're here."

Instantly paralyzed, I couldn't move if I wanted to.

CLUMP. CLUMP. CLUMP.

Cole moves to the center of the platform, dangerously close to me. I feel around for the electric prod but can't find it. It's not safe to reach for the dart gun in my jacket pocket because any rustling noise will give away my whereabouts. I hope he doesn't have a flashlight.

"You have to be here. I *need* you to be here. I can't get by thinking you're gone."

Huh?

"I see that wretch's face and as much as I want to wring the life out of her, I can't help but think of you. That makes me want to kill her even more."

Cole doesn't know I'm here! He's talking to *her.*

"It should have been her that died and you who triumphed. She screwed that up and continues to breathe, to share your face, your name. It's only your dying wish that keeps her alive."

Even if I wanted to say something, I'd be speech-less.

"I hate that I pretended to be her friend. I hate that I flirted with her, kissed her. I hate that I can't kill her!"

Cole moves closer. He's standing beside me. His hands are probably clasped around the railing as he peers through the darkness. I wait for him to speak again so I can move farther away.

"I'll keep my promise, Syn. I won't kill her. But she will feel the pain of losing someone she loves. She thinks she can rescue her sister. Or trade her life."

Cole edges closer. His jeans graze my arm. I shuffle on hands and knees to the center of the platform as his crazed laughter echoes into the night.

"No, her sister's fate is sealed. Syn will watch poor Beth die, and will live the rest of her short, pitiful life knowing she couldn't do anything to save her."

No no no…

"If she finds comfort from believing that Beth's spirit lives on, I'll kill someone else she loves. Her aunt. Her friends. As long as she suffers, my pain has a purpose."

Cole moves closer yet again. It's like there is some magnetic pull coming from me. *Damn it.* I have nowhere to go now, pressed up against the far wall of the platform. He's going to bump right into me. His shoe touches my knee. He stops.

"Synthia, my dear."

I hold my breath.

"You gave Beth free rein of the Garden, felt like she was your own sister. Well, I have nothing now. So you need to let me have this one. If you look down on me with contempt, I am sorry. You are gone. I have nothing. Nothing but vengeance. And my lust for vengeance *will* be satisfied."

He's moving to the top of the stairs.

"And Syn?"

I don't dare move.

"No matter what, I'll always love you."

Clump. Clump. Clump.

He is totally bonkers!

My heart is pounding. Cole has no intention of letting Beth go. The only chance she has is for me and Luke to save her.

I unzip my backpack as quietly as possible and dig out my cell phone. I use its light to find the electric prod and tuck it close beside me. It is 4:38 A.M.

My symptoms will return right after leaving this platform. At least Cole doesn't know I'm up here so he likely won't return before sunlight. I need to rest before heading to the sewers, so I set my phone's alarm to wake me in an hour. Luke should have arrived in the Garden by then. Now that I know where Beth is and how to free her, we can work out a plan to save her. I close my eyes, hoping I don't sleep through the alarm. Within seconds, I feel myself fading away.

* * *

Horrific screeching sounds jolt me awake. It sounds like a giant crow cawing and scratching its talons on a chalkboard. As my eyes adjust to the light, another screech pierces my eardrums. My eyelids fly open. There is daylight, and several terrifying sights greet me.

Two Creeper birds are circling the platform. Two crocodile Creepers are guarding the stairway exit. And, Cole is standing next to me, pressing the button on my electric prod. Blue sparks are crackling inches from my face.

Chapter 16

Panic in the Sky

"Wakey, wakey," coos Cole sarcastically.

I scramble to my feet, narrowly dodging the shock from the electric prod. *My weapon!*

"Oh, you don't like that?" He zaps the electric prod in front my face, laughing as I cringe.

"I should be mad. Mad that you fried me with this." He threatens to zap me again. "Mad that you listened in on my private conversation with my love. But you know what? I'm glad you did."

I say nothing.

"Now we are on the same page. You know where I stand and what I'm going to do to your sister. That must tear you apart inside."

I clench my teeth and force myself to hold my tongue.

"And here you are, after a good old-fashioned beating, healthy as ever. Do you know why?"

I stare at his shoes.

"You destroyed the machine that made good health and eternal life possible for the people living in the Garden. Do you not wonder why those healing properties only exist up here now?"

I don't give him the satisfaction of a nod.

"My Syn," he says. "The one you killed. She provides healing, and for some reason I fail to understand, she doesn't retract it for you."

I can't think of any good reason why the platform would have healing factors. As far as I understand, it sits in the sky of another world, which is why the healing factors didn't apply here the last time I was in the Garden. So why now? One thing is for sure—I certainly don't buy Cole's *angel in the sky* explanation, that his Syn is watching over him from the afterlife to soothe his pain. Has he suddenly found God?

"Whatever reason my love has, I respect her wishes." He zaps the prod an inch from my face, then tosses it over the railing. "You heard loud and clear that I promised not to kill you. But your sister is fair game."

His fake smile twists into a sadistic smirk. "I'm going to drag you down from here, then beat her and slit her throat in front of you. My friends will hold your eyelids open so you don't miss a moment of her agony. Then you will experience the absence of her soul."

Tears threaten to flood down my face but I restrain them. "Do whatever you want to me, but let Beth go."

Cole leans against the railing. "How pathetic. You think you're so righteous? You'd trade your life for a girl you barely know? Well, I know better. You're scared of living with loss. You know that death is a quick escape from a lifetime of pain. You're right."

There is no way to get past Cole and the two crocodile Creepers. The Creeper birds circling above the platform are an extra layer of security. I'm trapped. Is death the only way out of this? The only way to save my sister? I don't want to die. But unlike Beth, an early death was written in my cards long ago. She could live to eighty or even a hundred. I'll be lucky to make it to twenty. As much as I want to enjoy every moment of every day until my time naturally runs out, her life is worth more than mine. I swore to protect it. One thing is certain. If I live, she dies.

I take in the bird's-eye view of the Garden. The view of one world from the sky of another. The Creepers flap their massive wings, circling nearer, my hair whipping across my face from the draft.

"It's a long way down, Synthia."

"That's one thing we agree on." I shrug into my backpack and face him. "Another thing we agree on is that some things are worse than death. Like losing a loved one."

"A loved one someone takes from you," Cole says, with malice.

"I am sorry about that. But you're not going to kill Beth for revenge."

"Oh? Why is that?"

"Because you can't make me witness something if I'm dead." With that, I whirl around and hop onto the railing, teetering forward, gasping with panicked second thoughts.

"No!" Cole screams.

Defiantly, I heave myself off the railing, and fall.

Chapter 17

A Leap of Faith

MY PLAN ISN'T TO FALL to my death, though the odds of avoiding that are not in my favor. Terror paralyzes me, numbs the shock even, but I don't fall far. A twenty-foot freefall lands me on the back of my intended target—a Creeper bird. I wrap my arms around its scaly neck, struggling not to slide off its slippery reptilian skin. I'm riding the beast!

I may have escaped Cole for now, but I'm not out of the woods. Maybe the Creeper will be distracted by my weight and pay no attention to orders from Cole. It nosedives towards the fog and a forest of trees it can't see! This can only end in disaster. Cole's howls of rage rapidly fade in our wake.

My lungs are filling with phlegm and the pain from Cole's beating returns with a vengeance. I must fight through this! I hold on for dear life as the Creeper U-turns away from the fog, swooping one way and then the other, zigzagging violently. My backpack jostles from side to side and my legs flap uncontrollably. *It's trying to throw me off.*

Again, the Creeper nosedives closer to imminent death. My stomach lurches as I'm lifted off its back, my legs flailing wildly behind me. Wind roars through my ears and takes my breath away. Rain pelts against my face. I can't even cough against the wind. I've never felt anything like this. But I've made it this far. I *won't* give up!

The Creeper zigzags and nosedives for countless long minutes before leveling off above the Garden's tallest trees. Several Creepers on the ground are pointing at us, shocked to see me of all people riding on the back of this reptilian beast. How do I get it to land so I can make it to the house before Cole does? We fly over the farm and the orchard, and then rise again. We glide over the house and head in the direction of the pond.

My lungs continue to fill with phlegm and a coughing spell invades, jerking my arms violently. The Creeper arches to the right, straight into a tree! Its reptilian beak crunches into the trunk, the impact jarring my grip loose. We tumble several feet before crash-landing on the hard dirt beneath the tree.

Muscles are throbbing. Unbearable pain clutches my stomach. A coughing fit is wreaking havoc. Still, I'm alive. *I've never even ridden a horse before!*

The Creeper is conscious though also dazed, thankfully. I want to lie on its back and curl up into a ball, but force myself to roll off and stand up. The Creeper snaps at my feet and I barely leap clear of its beak!

I limp across the lawn, the field of battle it seems, which is suspiciously quiet now. There is no sign of Cole. No Creepers guarding the house. *Should I be worried?* I make my way up the wooden stairs at the back of the house, gripping the banister. The steps are wet and slippery and I'm also not in the best of shape. As I reach for the doorknob, someone screams.

"Hey!"

A fully-clothed Chameleon-Gal is standing at the foot of the stairs. "He's going to kill you, you know."

"We'll see."

One swift turn of the knob and the back door swings open. I peek through the crack, half expecting an ambush. All is quiet for the time being. Glancing over my shoulder, I am startled that Chameleon-Gal has disappeared. I step inside, lock the door and secure the metal chain, then run to the front door and lock that too.

The house seems empty. There are no sounds to be heard other than my own labored breathing. Cole and the others will be here soon though. There is no time to lose.

Daylight streams through the doorway of the computer room, calling me to action. Racing forward with my arm across my face to muffle a cough, I plunk myself into an old leather chair. It rolls forward and I use my feet to brake. Rolling over to the same computer I used when Ebby was with me last time, I click the mouse. The screen lights up. Now, to follow Lundy's instructions and find that bubble! A loud cough surprises me as I'm intently navigating through files.

Suddenly, hasty pitter-patters scurry across the floor upstairs and race down the steps. I spin the chair around in time to see two Creeper dogs gallop through the doorway. I raise my hand. "Stay!" They screech to an abrupt stop and they gawk at me blankly, tongues hanging out of their scaly mouths. They'll be no bother. *Thanks again, Beth.* Now, speaking of Beth....

I face the computer again, tossing a warning glance at the Creepers. One has already laid down on the floor. Good. I click the mouse in the search bar and type "bubble." The screen immediately goes dark and my heart sinks. But, the power hasn't gone out because the computer is still running. The light on the monitor still glows blue. I'm about to freak out when text finally shows up on the screen. Phew.

Ten files are listed from *Bubble01* to *Bubble10*. I double-click the first one. A password prompt pops up. Lundy made fun of Cole for not knowing anything about password security. And why would he? He's lived here his entire life and probably has never even used the internet. I type in "synthia" just as Lundy said. Cole's Synthia, I'm sure. When I press "enter" there is a buzzing sound and a message in red pops up:

INCORRECT PASSWORD: USER WILL BE LOCKED OUT AFTER 3 FAILED ATTEMPTS

"Great." I didn't ask if it was upper case, lower case. I type "Synthia" with a capital "S" but in my rushed panic, type an extra "a" at the end.

INCORRECT PASSWORD: USER WILL BE LOCKED OUT AFTER 3 FAILED ATTEMPTS

Damn it! If the password is all caps, I'm screwed. No, Beth is screwed.

Carefully, I type "Synthia," one letter at a time. Before I can press "enter," I almost jump out of my skin, rudely interrupted by more high-pitched screeching. The Creeper dogs run to the front door barking. I ignore them—"enter."

At first, nothing happens. No buzz, no error message. Nothing. Then the screen abruptly turns white. The bubble! Same as the last time I was here and saw my parents. This time, no one is there.

Was Lundy wrong? Is Beth somewhere else? Or worse, could Cole have—. The thought is wiped from my mind by a reflection on the computer screen... a lightway has suddenly opened behind me. It leads right through the ceiling.

Outside, more Creeper bird screeches. Someone is determined to open the locked front door and the Creeper dogs are eagerly waiting there to greet that person. What I am about to do is risky, but it's necessary, for Beth. Without hesitation, I leap into the lightway.

Chapter 18

Enter the Void

WHEN I HAVE PREVIOUSLY ENTERED lightways time seems to slow, everything is blurred by a bright white light and when that clears, I find myself in a new world. This time, everything is immediately white. Not a white light. Just white. A seemingly endless white room. No walls or ceiling. Were my feet not planted firmly, I would have no idea where the floor is.

There is a half-empty bottle of water and some empty food wrappers in front of me—two from granola bars, one from a gummy fruit snack, and an empty Cheeto bag. It looks like they're hovering in the endless whiteness though they are at ground level, in relation to where my feet stand. Is this junk food all Beth has been fed?

Where *is* Beth?

"Beth!" No response. No echo. Nothing. "Beth!"

My worst fear hits me. Could Cole have already killed her? She is not here, and not with him. No, she has to be alive! When Cole didn't know I was listening, he said he wanted me to witness her death. So where is she?

"Beth!" I scream again, louder, bringing on another coughing spell.

It's obvious that my sister isn't here and staying won't get me any closer to finding her. Someone is trying to get into the house. Probably Cole.

There is no lightway in this bubble though. Was that lightway only an entrance? Did I trap myself?! I wave my hands through the air—up, down, around—panicking, looking for any glimpse of light. Suddenly, a voice drifts through the haze.

"Syn? Syn!"

"Beth!"

My little sister is gliding through the white space, looking like she is floating on a cloud. She breaks into a run and leaps into my arms, her feet dangling above mine.

"I knew you would come for me!"

"Oh Beth, it's really you. Are you okay?" I want to hold her forever. But there isn't a second to spare. I let go. "We have to leave. Now."

"He's coming?"

I nod. "Are Mom and Dad here too?"

Beth looks confused. "Why would they be here?"

"I'll explain later. Is there a way out?" How do you find a white lightway in a white cloud?

"How long have you been here?"

"About a minute."

"The voidway stays open for seven." Beth waves her hands through the white space. "Found it!"

From my perspective, there isn't anything special about that spot, but I trust my sister. She takes my hand. There is a sudden feeling of warmth inside and out, and suddenly we are back inside the house. The voidway is gone.

We're not alone. The back door is open. Snake-Man is glaring at us hungrily. His forked tongue slips out and flickers, then his mouth gapes open, the jaw dropping below his shoulders. Those fangs want blood. Another Creeper stands behind him—Greeta. She is on full alert, tentacles protruding from the sides of her head.

The Creeper dogs sprint over and I brace myself for the attack. Instead, they jump up on Beth and lick her face with their forked tongues. "It's good to see you, too." She smiles at Cole's pets.

Snake-Man grabs my arm, yanking me so close that my head is almost pulled inside his enormous gaping mouth.

"Sic 'em!" Beth shouts.

The Creeper dogs spring into action. One chomps down on Snake-Man's tail. He moans and careens backwards, tripping over his own tail and faceplanting on the floor. The other Creeper dog pounces on his back, growling and baring his sharp canines. Greeta hurries out through the back door.

Beth pulls me towards the front door but we don't get very far. A Creeper bird is trying to squeeze its oversized body through the doorway, snapping its fangs at us eagerly. There is no sign of fear from my little sister.

She releases my hand. "When the door is clear, run through as fast as you can!"

Beth charges the Creeper bird. Before I can protest, she has jumped through a gap between the Creeper's wing and one of its legs. She rolls and bounces onto her feet outside the door and leaps over all five steps onto the concrete. The Creeper darts from the doorway in hot pursuit.

"Run!" Beth screams. "Now!"

A wicked coughing fit causes me to lose my balance and tumble down the stairs. I force myself to my feet.

"Syn!" Beth shouts above the Creeper's shrill screeching. "Syn!"

I cough and cough. *Can't call to her. The Creeper is going in for the kill! Can't run any farther.*

"Hey birdbrain!"

Whose voice is that? There is no one else in sight. The Creeper arches its long neck in the direction of the voice. Beth ducks under its wings and races to me, slipping on the soggy grass.

Chameleon-Gal steps out from behind a tree, holding a spray can. She strolls up to the Creeper who is flapping its wings thoughtfully, not sure what to make of her. Chameleon-Gal sprays the Creeper in the face and retreats as it flails around, screeching in agony.

"Get out of here! *He's* coming."

I'd thank her if she hadn't promptly vanished. Beth and I run alongside the house. I am still coughing profusely.

"You're not doing so well, are you?"

I shake my head.

"You saved me. Now it's my turn." She takes my hand. "Stay with me."

This amazingly brave, spunky girl isn't like most ten-year-olds.

We are spotted by several Creepers as we hurry past the house by the back stairway. They give chase. One Creeper bird spreads its massive wings, lifts off the edge of the roof of the house and swoops right for us.

Beth darts to the right. Our escape route takes us past the pond. We zigzag between bushes and through poorly kept flowerbeds. The Creepers are getting closer and my condition is worsening.

"I can't run anymore," I choke, my knees weakening. "I'm sorry. Go!"

She pulls both of us into a protective bushy area. "It's okay. Look!"

A lightway has opened in the distance. There is movement and excited voices echoing across the pond. One voice in particular stands out.

"They're here somewhere," Cole shouts. "I need them alive!"

The lightway looks so far away. We'll never make it. They're all closing in on us. We're hidden from those on foot, but one Creeper bird is still on our trail and flying straight for us. I cover my mouth to muffle the coughing and with the other hand, point at the Creeper frantically.

Beth stays calm. "Wait for it."

Seconds later, another lightway opens directly in front of us, blocking the view of our winged pursuer.

"Come on!"

Beth takes my hand, helps me from the bush, and we leap into the lightway. As the light encompasses us, time slows. The confused Creeper bird is still flying towards the light but we both take great comfort in watching it fade as the lightway does.

Once the light dissipates, we find ourselves standing next to a near-identical bush to the one we were hiding in moments ago. It's a gray, cloudy day and isn't raining like it was in the Garden. We're on a property like my neighbor's back home. A sizable farm spreads out in front of us, but sadly, all the crops have been burnt to a crisp. Once lush-green fields are covered in dark ash. On the neighboring farm, two men wearing white hazmat outfits are burning the cornfield with flame-throwers.

These aren't the only things that differentiate this world from my own. Bugs are flying everywhere.

Everywhere! Flies, wasps, moths. We have to shield our faces from the insects. I want to celebrate our escape, but instead I'm hunched on the ground coughing and cowering from clouds of bugs.

We soon discover that the Eighth Plague and my deteriorating health aren't the worst of our problems. A menacing screech comes from above. That giant Creeper bird is nosediving straight towards us. It followed us through the lightway!

Chapter 19

Sects and the City

THE CREEPER IS COMING AT us so fast it's pointless to shelter ourselves. It could easily grab either one of us in its sharp talons, both of us at the same time for that matter. We cover our heads, close our eyes, and wait for the worst. Nothing happens. I open my eyes a crack. There is no sign of the creature.

Beth tugs at my arm. "Look. Over there!"

The Creeper is flying through a black cloud of insects, enjoying the smorgasbord. An insect buffet is a much more appetizing meal than we are. No argument there. The hazmat guys have dropped their flame-throwers and are running like hell away from the monster.

"This place looks like a war zone."

"We have to move," Beth says, offering me a hand up. "Before that thing comes for us."

Covering our faces with our arms to shield us from the bugs, we make our way through the field of burned crops. The ground is uneven and it's hard to see through the swirling black cloud. I can barely see my own feet in front of me. Beth saves me from falling numerous times.

The "Applegate's" house is boarded up, so no point banging on the door for help. By the time we reach the road, everything looks deserted. Even the hazmat guys are gone. We walk down the road to my house—my house in *this* world. I'm shocked to see that instead of the century-old Victorian-style home, there is nothing on the lot except a giant mound of sand. The house is gone. Torn down. So, no alternate universe parents to help us. If they even would help; my experience with parents from other worlds has been far from fantastic.

Beth is interested in a white, dust-covered Firebird that's older than I am. A large net covers it. I follow Beth's lead and help her drag it off. The coughing is escalating and my lungs are burning.

"You need to go to the hospital." Beth yanks on the door handle. It's locked. She scans the ground, picks up a rock from the side of the road and without hesitation, hurls the rock through the window.

I clear my throat.

"This is the only way to get my big sis to the hospital." Beth reaches through the opening, lifts the lock and opens the door. Then wipes shards of glass off the front seat and gets behind the wheel.

I roll the netting into a ball and slide onto the passenger's side, appalled that my little sister and I are involved in grand theft auto.

Beth rips out some wires from a compartment under the steering wheel and in no time, the engine roars to life.

"You're only ten years old!" I'm astonished.

"Buckle up." And keep an eye on the road. I can barely see over the dashboard." She grins. "Because I'm ten."

She releases the emergency brake, shifts the gears, and steps on the gas. We're moving! Beth has raised her head as high as possible and can barely see out the windshield. But she can still see enough to make a U-turn and get us onto the next street.

My chest feels like it's going to explode. My muscles ache. The pain in my stomach is torturous. As we cruise through an alternate version of my old farmland neighborhood, I take one of my inhalers from my backpack. I'm in such bad shape it doesn't do much good, but it's soothing enough to allow me some breaks from coughing.

It's obvious how much is different from my world after we arrive in the city. For one thing, even though my Redfern is far from a busy suburb, there are always a moderate number of cars on the road during the day. Here, so far it's just us. Probably a good thing, since a ten-year-old is driving the car.

The few people we see on the sidewalks are wearing surgical masks. And while the majority of buildings I'm familiar with are still standing, most of the businesses are different. Few are even open. Some are boarded up, while others are dark. All windows are screened and netting hangs over most doors.

"You okay?" Beth asks. "We're almost there."

Even though we're driving at a snail's pace, squished bugs are accumulating on the window. And in the rear-view mirror, a terrifying sight. An enormous black cluster of bugs like the one the Creeper dined on is pursuing us.

"Uh, Beth," I say, staring into the rear-view mirror.

"Crap! Hold on." Beth slams her foot on the accelerator and we blast down the street. The swarm stays with us. She whips the car around a corner and the swarm flies past. The accident happens in an instant. A tire explodes and we skid across the road in slow motion, slamming to a stop against something I can't make-out. I'm merely shaken up, but—

"Beth!" I gently shake her, but she doesn't respond.

Her head is leaning against the steering wheel. Blood is trickling down her forehead and dripping onto the seat.

Chapter 20

Dead Like Me

I'M FREAKING OUT! MY sister is knocked out cold with a big, bloody gash on her forehead, and I need to get to a hospital. I fumble to unbuckle my seatbelt and lean over, placing two fingers on her neck. She has a pulse!

We need help. I open my door and roll onto the street, squinting my eyes. Ashes are floating through the air. Behind the ashes, a man in a white hazmat suit is holding a smoking flame-thrower. He runs over. Another hazmat suit follows.

"What happened here?" The man's voice is muffled by his mask. "You okay?"

My lungs are so jammed with phlegm, I can't get any words out. I can only cough.

"Hailey, go check on the other girl."

I anxiously wait for Hailey to open Beth's door and examine her. Bugs are swarming inside the car, crawling on Beth's face.

"She's out cold, Frank."

"Help her," I manage to say in a raspy voice that no one hears.

"Should I bring the truck around?" Hailey asks.

"No, the hospital is a block away. Let's carry 'em." He hands Hailey his equipment. "Take this stuff to the truck."

"Right."

Meanwhile, Frank takes out a pocket knife and cuts the netting in half to cover each of us. It feels like forever, but we probably get to Redfern Memorial in less than two minutes. This place is very much like the hospital I have frequented many times in my own world.

"Car crash. Unconscious," Hailey tells the nurse at the front desk. "The other one doesn't look good either."

Beth is whisked from Hailey's arms and placed on a gurney. They roll her away and I try not to fear the worst. After spending most of my life not even knowing I had a sister, will she be taken away from me before I even have a chance to get to know her? Against all odds, I actually managed to rescue her from Cole, and now.... I can't even consider the possibility. Beth has to be okay. She just has to.

I'm seated in a wheelchair and rolled into the triage area, coughing continuously. After the doctor takes my temperature and checks my pupils, I manage to spit out "CF," barely loud enough for him to hear.

Ten minutes later, I'm tucked away behind curtains in the emergency ward, wearing an oxygen mask. It's impossible to wipe from my mind the image of my sister slumped over the wheel, bleeding. A giggle bubbles up in spite of everything, with the recollection of Beth sitting as tall as she could to see over the steering wheel. Feeling safe finally, and comfortable, I doze off.

When my eyes open again, I'm lying in my own room, receiving intravenous antibiotics. The nurse adjusting my IV drip tells me that the doctor will be in shortly. I lift the mask off my mouth and whisper, "Beth."

She breezes from the room, offering no response. Maybe she doesn't know that my sister is being treated here. Still, I fear the worst when she doesn't acknowledge me. I try again when the doctor enters and sits down in the chair next to my bed.

"I understand you were in a crash."

"With my sister," I whisper. "Beth. Is she..." I can't finish.

"Your sister is fine."

A flood of relief rushes through me.

"Beth woke up briefly. She may have a concussion, so we need to keep her overnight for observation."

"Now you, on the other hand, I'm very concerned about. I'm surprised you weren't already checked into the hospital."

"On the way here."

He nods. "Can you tell me your name and age?"

"Synthia. I'm sixteen." I don't see the point in telling him my name begins with an "S" like I usually do.

"And your sister's age?"

"Ten."

"I was informed that your sister was driving the car."

"No," I lie.

"That's good. The police will come in at some point to talk to you. And, we need to contact your parents and get them to fill out some forms."

Great.

"I'm a resident but Dr. Freeman, who treats kids and teens with cystic fibrosis, will come see you when he's done with another patient. He'll be giving you a thorough examination."

When the resident leaves, I try not to panic. Dr. Freeman is my doctor back home. Last time I went to another world, I pretended to be the Syn from that world and that had drastic consequences.

When Dr. Freeman enters and sees me lying there, he does a double take. He checks his clipboard, and then approaches with caution, like I'm a wild animal that might pounce if startled.

"Synthia?"

"Yes."

"I don't understand. This…I don't…."

What's going on? Either the me in this world is Dr. Freeman's patient or she isn't. And if she is, shouldn't I look like her? Shouldn't I...? Then it hits me.

I died.

Chapter 21

Eye of the Needle

THE ME IN THIS WORLD, my other, is dead. Either from CF or worse—murdered along with her parents, which was a common fate for many of my others, according to Beth.

Dr. Freeman takes a deep breath and exhales slowly. "Okay, I'm going to examine you. Then we will try and figure out what's going on."

As he conducts all the basic tests, I feel badly for the man. The Dr. Freeman in my world has been very good to me. Seeing him so confused and emotional is difficult. What should I tell the Dr. Freeman of this world? I decide to tell him the truth.

Dr. Freeman examines a chest X-ray I barely recall getting and asks me a few common questions. My stomach hurts at first touch. He jots a few notes on his pad. "Alright. I'll start with the CF. You have a serious mucus buildup. Your lungs are inflamed. You should have been in the hospital long before today."

I don't tell him I was recently released and have been doing a horrendous job of taking care of myself.

"But we'll get to that in a minute. First, I want to address the bruises. They cover a great deal of your body, your abdomen especially. Has someone hurt or abused you?"

I close my eyes.

He pauses, and then continues. "There is no internal bleeding from the blows to your abdomen."

I assumed he would take this more seriously. Ask if it was a relative, or if I am still in danger. He doesn't press.

"The bruises will be sore for a few days. Now…."

The doctor wants to address the elephant in the room. He sits down on the side of my bed.

Here we go.

"Can you tell me how it is that you're here? I can't wrap my head around this."

"I died. Right?"

"I saw your body in the morgue."

"You're not going to believe me."

"We'll see," he says, eager to hear my explanation.

"I'm from another world. Another version of the world we are in right now. A world where I didn't die. At least, not yet."

"Another world?"

"You've met my parents from this world, right? They're scientists. My parents from the world I come from, along with a colleague, created a way to travel to other realities. There are infinite versions of the original world. I've visited a few of them."

"Do you really expect me to believe this?"

"When did I die?"

The question jolts Dr. Freeman. I get it. It feels weird to ask.

"About two years ago. You were fourteen."

"How did I die?"

"She…you," he gulps, "choked on a moth."

"A moth?" *Not from CF? Not murdered?*

"Yes, a large moth blocked her airway. Though her CF was a factor as she already had difficulty breathing."

"Okay," I say after letting that settle in. "So, you know I died two years ago. You knew the other version of me. She didn't have a twin. And if she did, what would the odds be she also had CF?"

Dr. Freeman doesn't respond.

"That wasn't me who died. I'm alive in the world I came from. In that world, you can walk down the street without choking on bugs. This building is the same in my world except that there are no nets over the doors. In that world, you're my doctor."

"You're saying there's another *me*?"

"There are other versions of everyone. I know it sounds far-fetched. But you said I died and yet here I am."

"The younger girl," he says. "Your sister? The Syn I treated was an only child."

"Not to complicate things further, but she was born in yet another world. She was in trouble. The guy who beat me and caused these bruises held her prisoner and threatened her life. I barely managed to save her, but we ended up here instead of home."

Dr. Freeman is about to speak when there is a commotion in the corridor. Two security guards run past my room shouting into their walkie-talkies about a dragon.

"What the devil is going on here?"

"It's not a dragon," I say. "It's not like anything you've seen before. It followed us here."

Dr. Freeman shakes his head. "I need some air. Excuse me." He bolts from the room, sighing loudly.

I hope he doesn't return with the police. Or even worse, doctors from the psych ward ready to strap me into a straightjacket. I hope that telling the truth wasn't a huge mistake.

About five minutes later, Dr. Freeman returns to my room. "So, there is a dragon flying around outside. A dragon!"

It's no use telling him again that it's not a dragon.

"I've never seen a dragon before today. And *you* were dead. I saw your body in the morgue. So, while I am skeptical, I'm going to go along with your story for now and focus on your treatment. Who can the hospital contact on your behalf?"

"My Aunt. She is back in my own world though. And I won't be here long anyway."

"You need serious treatment. Regular antibiotics, therapy, rest. Two weeks minimum, probably longer."

"Dr. Freeman, we traveled to your world through something called a lightway. They only stay open for so long. If we don't leave before it closes we're stuck here. Forever. Two days is taking a bit of a risk. Two weeks and I'll never get home."

The doctor is clearly frustrated. "Syn, this is very serious. If you don't receive treatment, you will get worse. Much worse. You could die. And your sister needs to be monitored."

"I get it. But two days is as long as we can stay. As soon as we get home, we'll head straight to the hospital."

Dr. Freeman looks deeply into my eyes, like he can see through to the other side. "If I think you're a danger to yourself, I could have you restrained."

At that, I tear up. "If you don't allow us to leave, you're trapping us somewhere we don't belong. I'll never see my aunt again. Or my friends. Maybe there are versions of them in this world, but they are not *my* aunt. *My* friends."

"Synthia—"

"You're skeptical. I get it. But I'm not dead. I have a sister the Synthia you knew didn't have. There is a friggin' dragon flying outside for heaven's sake. If you tie me up, you're condemning my sister and me to a life sentence."

"Syn—"

"Dr. Freeman, I beg you. Please do what you can for me and Beth over the next two days. Then let us go. If you don't, I might as well be dead."

As if on cue, the Creeper bird flies past the window. Then Dr. Freeman does the unexpected. He laughs. Really laughs.

"I'll have your sister's doctor update me on her progress and will arrange for her to see you after you both rest for a while. Meanwhile, I have something in mind that might keep you alive for a few more days while you try to get home."

"Thank you," I say, relieved.

He smiles before leaving the room. "No matter who you are or where you're from, it's good to see you again, Synthia."

* * *

An hour later, Dr. Freeman returns. He approaches me with a syringe in his hand. He's going to sedate me! Keep me here after all. I won't let that happen! I rip the IV from my wrist and hold the needle tightly, ready to use it as a weapon.

Chapter 22

How to Tame a Dragon

"WHOA," DR. Freeman says, raising the syringe in the air. He sets it on the table next to my bed. "This is a treatment."

"What kind of treatment?" I ask suspiciously.

"It was concocted by your parents."

"What?" I lower the needle.

"Before your parents," he pauses, unable to find the right words. "When the other you was alive, your father gave this to me. It wasn't tested on human subjects so it was only to be used as a last resort."

"My parents created this…medicine?"

"They did. As crazy as it sounds, they were trying everything in their power to create a cure for your disease."

Knowing what I know, this doesn't sound crazy at all.

"Of course, two scientists alone in a lab aren't going to do what entire research teams have been trying to do for decades. Still, your dad gave me this.

He told me that if it works, it will clear your mucus. Temporarily."

Sort of like the former properties of the Garden. And now, the platform above the spiral staircase. A temporary reprieve of illness.

"Does it work?"

"After you…she died," I gave most of what I had to researchers. There have been positive results with lab rats but in some cases it has weakened their immune systems. I don't have to tell you how that could affect you."

He doesn't. I already have a weakened immune system and need to be extra careful not to catch colds, flus, and other ailments. But I can't worry about that now or I may never get home.

Dr. Freeman keeps pressing me, to make certain I am okay to accept the treatment, and that he has my consent. I have no choice. Who knows how many worlds we will have to travel through to get back to the Garden, and then we will have to face Cole while trying to escape. If I'm completely honest with myself, I am sort of excited to see the results of my parents' work.

"As far as I know," Dr. Freeman continues, "this still hasn't been tested on human subjects."

"Well," I say, grinning. "There's a first time for everything."

"Roll up your sleeve."

I feel a prick. Twenty minutes later there is no noticeable difference. An hour later, still nothing. Bored and tired, I allow my eyelids to shut. I wake up to a nurse changing my IV.

"How are you feeling?"

I breathe in and out. "Okay."

My chest is congested but not unlike any day when I'm at my best, when it feels no worse than a bad cold. My muscles are sore, but the CF symptoms are so much better. My parents did it! They suppressed the symptoms.

"I'm glad you were able to get some rest," the nurse says.

Dr. Freeman is pleased with my progress when he sees me later. "Don't dilly-dally when you leave the hospital. This treatment is only suppressing the symptoms, like a cold medicine. I gave you the only dose I had and when it's worn off, expect that you will be in as bad a shape as when you arrived."

I nod. "My parents in this world aren't alive, are they?"

"No, sadly they are not. How did you know?"

"I could hear it in your voice when you talked about them. What happened?"

The doctor is hesitant. "Are you sure you want to know? It's not pretty."

I think I already know.

"Okay," Dr. Freeman says. "Not that long after you, her, you know—there was a home invasion. They were both killed."

"Did they catch the murderer?"

"No. It was a real tragedy. No one knows what the intruders wanted. Money, jewelry and other valuables were untouched. It didn't look like anything was taken."

They obviously wanted my parents dead. Beth told me she went to several worlds where my family was murdered. But why? And by whom?

* * *

Later in the day, an orderly wheels me to Beth's room on the first floor. A bald girl not much older than six is resting in the bed next to Beth's. She reminds me of Janna and I offer her the brightest smile I can muster as the orderly wheels me past. So many people believe in God but what kind of God allows a child to suffer this way?

My sister is wearing a ghastly bandage around her head. I reach up and clasp her hand. "How are you?"

"Fine. How about you?"

"I'm good. No, terrific!" I tell her about the treatment.

I regularly visit Beth, who requires a couple days of bedrest. Fear that Dr. Freeman will have me strapped to my bed is gone. He has risked his job by giving me an experimental treatment that isn't government approved.

While Dr. Freeman is checking my vitals two days later, Beth comes into my room, unbandaged and perky. "We gotta go."

"I need ten minutes with your sister," Dr. Freeman tells her, "and then I'll go do my rounds. You'll have to slip out on your own. I can't be a party to that."

Beth sits down to wait, sweeps my backpack onto her lap and does an inventory of weapons, food, and supplies.

I close my eyes as Dr. Freeman checks the bruises on my abdomen. The pain has been greatly reduced. I feel pretty good, at least compared to when I got here. Hopefully this treatment will last until I get home. When I open my eyes, Beth is gone. So is my backpack.

"It was nice to see you again, Syn." Dr. Freeman pats my shoulder and moves towards the door. "Please, *please* take care of yourself."

"I will."

Beth meets him at the door and thanks him for taking such good care of me.

"Where'd you go?" I ask.

"Restocking our food supply." She holds up my backpack and shows me what's inside: granola bars, juice boxes, M&Ms.

I don't ask where she got them. Five minutes later, we're heading to a fire exit. Beth is wearing a jacket and shoes she wasn't wearing when we arrived. Again, I don't ask. Pausing at the door, we put on the surgical masks Beth "borrowed" from a storage room and eye each other silently, our eyebrows raised.

"Here we go." I open the heavy door.

We squint and shield our eyes from clouds of swarming insects, stepping on piles of dead ones on our way through the alley.

"Gross!"

"That girl I shared my room with?" says Beth.

"Yeah?"

"She told me about this bug infestation. It began about five years ago. The world's largest pesticide manufacturer's best-selling product unintentionally made bugs immune to the pesticides and amped up their breeding cycle. It has devastated the West Coast, affecting the food supply and the economy."

How terrible. Oh, the power scientists have. I think of our parents again.

We hurry through the alley to the main road, barely able to see anything through the haze of insects. I recognize a bank, which is a taxi hub in my world. At home, there would be at least six cabs parked here at any given time, but here there is only one. Beth tells the sad-looking cab driver where we're going. I recognize him as a teacher I've seen in the hallway at my school. In my world, anyway.

"Payment upfront," he says. "Eighty bucks."

Eighty dollars for a ten-minute ride! Not that it matters.

Beth hands the driver five twenties. "Keep the change."

I don't ask where she got the money. I don't want to know.

The driver takes the money and starts the engine. The windshield wipers rhythmically clear the shower of bugs. When we turn onto the first street of the Southlands community, there is quite a commotion in progress. The road is blocked off with orange cones and there are flares on both sides of the road. A police officer escorts a frantic mother and son past us. They're screaming, absolute terror in their eyes. There is a familiar screech in the distance. Then, gunshots. The Creeper bird, known here as the dragon, must be nearby.

"Gotta let you out here," the driver says.

Beth is determined. "We need to forget about that thing and get out of this place."

"Huh?" he grunts.

"We can't," I whisper, so the driver can't hear. "We brought that monster here. It's going to kill someone if it hasn't already. Or, they'll kill it."

Beth shakes her head. Either she agrees taking responsibility is the right thing to do or knows that I won't budge. She doesn't press the issue.

"What's happening?" the driver asks. "You getting out or what?"

"How much to get us where we asked to go?" Beth asks.

"Past the police barricades?" He laughs. "Two hundred."

I'm glad this greedy bastard was never *my* teacher.

Beth pulls out a stack of cash and hands him a hundred. I *really* don't want to know. "The other half when we get there."

The driver grabs the money and mumbles. He puts the car in reverse, it skids backwards, then makes an abrupt U-turn.

"This isn't the way," I tell him.

"Trust me, Kid."

While I'm relieved that the driver is taking us to the main road, he swerves and zooms onto the driveway of the first property. The cab careens off the driveway onto the grass next to the boarded-up house, and whizzes straight into the ashes of what was once a cornfield. We bounce and rumble across rough ground, past police officers with raised weapons who are chasing a dark shadow in the sky. Our dragon.

The cab crashes through a broken-down wooden fence into another burnt field, past the house, and onto the road where my house would be. There are flares on either side of this street too, and a police car with the trunk open. Two officers are leaning against the car, talking and batting at insects with their batons.

"This is the closest I'm getting, kids."

We unbuckle our seatbelts and Beth tosses the twenty-dollar bills onto the passenger seat.

The driver laughs as he gathers up the money. "Don't let the dragon getcha."

We can hear the Creeper, but don't have a visual. What we do see is an assortment of supplies in the trunk of the police car, including several flares and flare guns. Beth is a step ahead of me. As I approach the officers, she sneaks behind their car.

"You can't be here." The cop's voice is muffled by the surgical mask. "Where do you live?"

"Just down the road," I point at my old property.

"We'll escort you," the female officer says.

"That's okay," Beth says, reappearing. "We're good."

"We insist."

As we walk with the two cops, Beth catches my attention to show me what she swiped—a flare gun and a couple of flares. I don't like all the stealing, but I admire the kid's resourcefulness.

"Shouldn't you girls be in school?" The female officer asks. "They are on lockdown."

"I lied," Beth says to the cops. "We're not going home. We're going to lure the dragon away."

"What the hell are you talking about?"

"Syn, tell them."

Both cops turn to look at me and, caught off guard, I can't get any words out of my mouth. I don't need to. The cops collapse, first one, then the other. Beth puts the dart gun back in her pocket.

I shake my head.

"*What?*"

"These are police officers. Not killer Creepers."

"They would've gotten in our way."

I hate that she's right.

More gunshots go off and a woman screams in the distance. We need to do this. Fast.

"Let's go to the lightway before we get its attention."

"Good idea."

This lightway isn't hard to find. We can clearly see it shooting into the sky from a property three over from mine. The ominous shadow of the beast glides across the ground as we run for it.

At the lightway, Beth whips out the flare. "You sure about this? We could be out of here in seconds."

"It's our responsibility." I'm perfectly aware that this is a terrible idea. However, as much as I want to bring my sister home and return to my aunt, I can't live knowing we unleashed this beast in this world.

Beth hands me a signal flare, then takes aim and shoots one in the Creeper's direction. There is a popping sound and the sky glows red. It reminds me of the red sky in the apocalypse world I was trapped in a few months ago. Beth and I crack our flares and wave the glowing sticks in the air.

"Over here!" Beth screams. "The Creeper sees us."

"Hey, wait!" From out of nowhere, a young cop runs up to us. "What the hell are you girls doing?"

"Getting this dragon out of your hair!" Beth shouts. "You're welcome."

As the Creeper whizzes straight for us, the cop whips out his gun in a panic.

"Don't!"

The cop ignores my warning and fires countless shots. The Creeper heads for the cop. The cop freezes, his grip loosens around the gun and it drops. A wicked wind rushes past us as our Creeper swoops over and bunts him through the air. The young cop smacks the ground about ten feet away, rolls over, and lies motionless.

This wasn't supposed to happen. The Creeper was supposed to lunge at *us*. When we stepped aside, it would fly into the lightway. Now, the Creeper lands, beak open, about to dig into another feast.

"No!" I yell.

Beth makes a beeline for the Creeper and shoots three darts into its back.

I catch up to her right when the Creeper spins around, snapping its teeth. Its face is so close, its foul breath heats my cheeks.

Chapter 23

The Murder of Synthia Wade

BETH AND I HOLD OUR flares in front of us for protection, but they are of course useless. The Creeper snaps its mouth shut and stares into my frightened eyes, then at my sister. Its putrid breath nauseates me.

"We don't want to hurt you," I tell it in desperation, using the kindest voice I can. Perhaps it will recognize the tone of sincerity. The Creeper looks from me to Beth and back to me. Either this is working or he's trying to decide which one of us to eat first.

BLAM!

Blood from the Creeper's wounded shoulder has splattered my face. The cop is on his knees, holding a revolver with a smoking barrel. The beast faces him defiantly and I don't dare breathe. Before the cop can shoot again, the Creeper spreads its wings, flies high into the red sky, circles around, and descends back in our direction. No, I'm wrong. Not our direction. Straight for the cop! He digs his talons into the man's shoulders and whisks him into the sky. I close my eyes and cover my ears until his blood-curdling screams are out of earshot.

I can't speak. One minute passes. Then two. There is no sign of the cop or the Creeper. It's probably chewing on the poor cop who was just doing his job.

"I wanted to prevent innocent deaths and instead instigated one."

"We both know there is nothing we could have done," says Beth. "Let's go."

"Yeah. We've done enough damage here."

"And who knows how much longer the lightway will stay open."

On that note, we walk into the light without even taking one last look at the desolation we're leaving behind.

When the freezing of time ends and the light dissipates, we are in that field again. But rather than ash, we're standing on top of a plastic tarp that covers a line of crops. Rows of black tarp stretch across the property. There isn't one insect in sight.

"So far so good," I say.

We eagerly rip off our masks.

"How are you feeling?"

"Okay, I guess. Health-wise."

Whatever the doctor injected me with, it's working. My nose is stuffed up, worse than usual. My throat is sore. But considering I was at death's door two days ago, this is good. It won't last for long though. We need to find our way back to the Garden and then to our world so I can get proper treatment. While crossing the field, we scan for even the faintest glimmer of a lightway. This world looks very much like my own. All the houses seem to be inhabited.

As we move to the next property, Beth stops me. "When you found me in the bubble, why did you ask if Mom and Dad were there?"

"You don't know?" I ask, surprised.

"Know what?

"Synister imprisoned Mom and Dad in the bubble for years."

"They were there the whole time? If only I knew…."

"But you didn't."

"So where are they now?"

"I don't know. They were there when Cole was holding me prisoner in the house. But if they weren't there with you…"

"They're alive. They have to be," Beth insists.

"I'm sure they are."

It turns out that like the other residents of the Garden, Beth had no clue about Cole's motives or his alliance with Synister until it was too late. She had never seen Synister's face and had no idea who she was. I don't tell her the entire story because that would mean telling her what they did to Synister and my other doppelgängers. Beth doesn't know the horrible things our parents have done. What use is there in shattering her illusion? In many ways, I wish I didn't know either.

"Would you like a snack?"

"Yeah."

Beth takes my backpack and rummages through it. She tosses me a granola bar. We crouch down to eat, hoping the owners of the property won't see us. After finishing the granola bar, I'm parched.

We travel to the next property to search for water. There is a hose attached to the side of the house, so I duck down and trot over to quench my thirst. When I finish, Beth takes the hose. While she is drinking, I keep watch, listening carefully, always inclined to watch the sky for any sign of another Creeper bird. It's become a habit, no matter what world I'm in. I'm startled when Beth drops the hose.

"Listen!"

Someone is shouting. No, screaming. It's coming from the house next door, the duplicate of my home. *Our* home. And, the scream sounds like my voice!

I can't make out what the other me is screaming, but it sounds like she's pleading with someone. Then I hear my dad's voice. He's pleading too. My mom screams next. It's the most blood-curdling scream I've ever heard.

I sprint across the lawn.

"No!"

I ignore Beth. They're in trouble. I unhook the latch, race through the gate and across the lawn. I run past the black Jeep on the driveway and climb up the steps to the front door.

The door is ajar. I peek through the crack and see outdated yellow wallpaper, the same as what my aunt replaced years ago in my world. The screams have stopped.

Beth has caught up with me. "*Please* don't go in."

"Our parents are in peril. And so is the other me. If there's any chance I can help...."

Beth nudges my arm with her dart gun. I nod in appreciation and motion for her to stay where she is, then squeeze through the crack in the doorway, pointing the dart gun in front of me. There is a puddle of blood on the floor, flowing like water to a drain.

Then, I see an arm. And a hand. Motionless, outlined in blood. Then I see who they belong to. Mom, lying on her stomach with a wound that's severe enough for blood to be pooling under her. Dad is lying dead and bloody next to her. Hunched over the kitchen counter, like she is reading a book, is a girl who looks exactly like me. Eyes wide open, but lifeless. Blood has soaked through her sweater and streams down her legs to the floor.

I'm frozen with shock, fear, and sorrow. And with the realization that they were all alive a moment ago. That means—

CREAK.

Heavy footsteps thump on the basement stairs leading up to the kitchen.

Chapter 24

The Killer Inside

BETH AND I AIM OUR dart guns at the door that leads to the basement. What if we miss? What if there is more than one killer?

I grab Beth by the sleeve and yank her towards the den. When she hesitates, I tug harder. She gives in and we slip into the sitting room. We scamper over to the couch and duck behind it, gripping our weapons tightly. Each slow, mindful step through the kitchen brings the killer closer. Then, two steps into the den and a soft rustle as a foot lands on the wool rug. Did he hear us?

The footsteps cease. We don't dare move. I cover my mouth to muffle my breathing. The footsteps resume and travel in the opposite direction, into the kitchen, up the stairs.

Why is the killer still moving around the house? Wasn't this a targeted murder? Maybe it was a random robbery or home invasion. The footsteps continue up the stairs and along the hallway of the second floor.

"C'mon Beth, let's get outta here."

We tiptoe to the kitchen, gagging at the smell of blood. The eyes of my double are still wide open, staring at nothing. Bile crawls up my throat. I try to force it down but have no control. Vomit gushes to the floor, my repulsive act anything but silent. Footsteps thunder along the hallway upstairs.

Beth brushes past me. "Run!"

Into the front hall, down the stairs, onto the front lawn, heavy footsteps close behind. There is nowhere to hide now. The killer is too close for us to make a run for it.

"This way!"

We dash for the Jeep and scurry underneath, crawling to the center, holding our dart guns for dear life. Two very scuffed-up boots approach the Jeep. Well, this was a terrible place to hide. It couldn't be more obvious that if we're nowhere in sight, we're hiding under the Jeep. Duh. At least we have the dart guns.

The boots stop on the concrete about ten feet away. For a few agonizing seconds there is dead silence. Then the killer approaches the Jeep. The trunk is opened and then slammed shut. Could he be getting a gun? Our puny dart guns can't compete with that. We should have stayed hidden in the house until the coast was clear.

The killer moves away from the Jeep. I can't see his feet anymore. There is a rattling sound and then what sounds like air being let out of a balloon.

"It's a spray can," I whisper. "He's spraying something!"

We exchange worried looks while the spraying continues. Then the can is tossed away and rolls a short distance. The boots reappear and the shadow of the killer's legs stretches across the driveway in front of us. The driver's door squeaks open, then slams shut. The engine starts and the vehicle backs up. Beth and I hug our bodies together under the Jeep. As soon as we're exposed, we dash into some bushes, crouched as low as possible.

"He had to have seen us in his rear-view mirror," Beth wails.

Surprisingly, the Jeep speeds away.

"Phew." I drop my gun and take Beth in my arms. I don't want to let go.

"You still feeling okay?"

"Yes." I feel remarkably well. At least, no worse than when I left the hospital. "I wish we saw his face, Beth. I mean, who would do this?"

"It's probably the same person in every world."

The same person in every world? Or could someone be traveling from world to world, like we have? Kill my family in each world and then move to the next? What a terrifying thought.

What else is terrifying is what is waiting for us at the bottom of the front porch. Sprayed on the concrete, next to a discarded aerosol can is a messy red message.

HELLO SYN
SEE YOU SOON

Chapter 25

Scene of the Crime

BETH AND I ARE HIDING behind some bushes across the road from the crime scene. At least a dozen emergency personnel, mostly police, trample the property. Taping off the perimeter, going in and out of the house, barking orders, sharing theories and a few even making horrid jokes like there weren't three murdered people inside the house. I expected them to bring the bodies out on gurneys right away, but I guess crime scene photos and forensics procedures need to be completed first.

"Inside that house is an exact duplicate of myself. Dead. Only an hour ago, she was living her life like any other day and then it was all over." Like that poor nurse at the hospital. Like Wolf. Like Hopper.

"Who would do this?"

"The only person I know who hates me enough to want me dead is Cole."

While Beth contemplates things, I consider that our parents might have enemies here. Masie Winters could be alive in this world. Maybe they betrayed her here too, and she took out her revenge more viciously than the Masie in my world did. This might have occurred in other worlds too, where she is still alive. It's as good a guess as any.

In my world, Masie Winters banished our parents. She certainly didn't murder anyone though. And she didn't do anything to me, other than take my parents away. Why would she so viciously murder my family here? Plus, if they pissed off Masie so badly in my world, who else might they have betrayed in other worlds?

"Well, the killer sure knows who you are and that you were here. That message rules out a random home invasion."

"That's a chilling thought."

Beth is right. Since he killed my other yet knew I was alive, he must know I'm from another world. Yet he doesn't want me dead. The killer must be able to travel to other worlds. How else would he find me again and again? My world might be the next one he visits. What if this is someone from my own world? Someone I know? Someone whom I consider a friend? Cole certainly fooled me. If I get home alive, before long I will certainly find out.

I'll always feel like the killer could show up at any time. Am I putting my loved-ones in danger by going back? I'll never feel safe at home again. That was probably the intention of the message. The killer could have tried to murder me right then and there. Instead, he—or she—chose to taunt me.

A police woman enters the property next door and rings the doorbell, probably to ask the neighbors if they saw or heard anything. We need to leave before they cross the street. If they see a girl who looks identical to the victim, how could I possibly explain it? We sneak to the rear of the property and start searching for the lightway.

"What if the lightway is on the property of the crime scene?" asks Beth.

"Too late now."

Beth's expression is solemn. "I've seen these bodies once before. I knew this was happening in other worlds. The murders of your...our family."

"But you never heard the screams?"

"No."

We scour the property and find nothing. No lightway on the farms on either side. Either we've missed the lightway or it's on the property next to my house or—

"Maybe it's in the garden behind my house!"

"Could be," Beth says. "I have never seen a lightway more than two properties over from that house. And it's always been outside."

After the cop leaves, we cross the road and search the farmland behind the house. No luck.

"So the lightway is on my property."

"Of course it is," smirks Beth. "Right where all the cops are."

Police tape cordons off a good-sized area behind the house. Voices drift through the partially open back door, but there are no cops to be seen. While the house is an average size, the property is extensive, like a park. Though it was built on farmland, my ancestors on my mom's side created a botanical garden. I assume it's the same in this world.

We sneak to the back of the lot by the bordering farm we had already checked. Then we start searching. The lightway is most likely hidden by a bush or under something. While Beth looks under large stones by the pond, I crawl under trees and squeeze between hedges looking for a glimmer of light.

"So, what's your aunt like?" Beth asks when we regroup by the pond.

"She's great. Aunt Ruth moved to Redfern and gave up her old life to take care of me. Not out of obligation, because she wanted to. She's like a mother to me." I didn't appreciate that until recently.

"That's nice."

"She's your aunt too."

"She doesn't know I exist."

"She will. Aunt Ruth will take you in and love you as if she raised you herself."

Beth isn't listening to me anymore. "Beth?"

"Look!" She points at something shimmering in the water.

"Maybe it's—"

"No, that's it! That's definitely a lightway."

"Great," I say. "We're going to get soaked. Our supplies too."

"Looks like it."

"Hey, what are you kids doing here?"

Two police officers come up behind us. One is extremely fit and the other anything but.

"Shouldn't you be in school?" the heavy cop asks.

"We just finished lunch," I say. "We're about to head back."

"Hey, Eric," the thin cop says, gesturing at me. "Doesn't she look familiar? Like the...you know." They study what is likely a photo of my deceased other on his phone.

"Uncanny," Eric says, rubbing his chin. "Whaddya think, Rick?"

"You both need to come with us," Rick says.

"We have to get back to school," Beth says.

"We want to have a word with you. That's all."

I raise the electric prod, press the metal wand. The electric current crackles.

"Whoa," Eric says. "We just want to talk."

"And we need to go," I say. "Sorry."

I press the button on the electric prod again and as soon as it sparks, toss it between the cops. They leap out of the way. "Let's go, Beth!"

We dive into the water. I can barely doggie paddle, but only need to reach the lightway. Beth swims underneath me and draws my legs down. Time slows, and away we go.

* * *

When the light dissipates, Beth helps me to the surface and we hold onto the shore to rest. I gag and have a short coughing spell.

"You okay?"

"Amazingly, yeah. Though ask me again if a wave of locusts fly at us or Dad shows up with a shotgun aimed at our heads."

Beth giggles, her attention turning to several winged seahorses that are hovering a few inches above the water. They playfully dip out of sight and then resurface seconds later. Yes, we're back in the Garden. Though that is our destination, I feel tense knowing that we're surrounded by enemies.

"We have to be quiet now," I warn.

"Right."

My teeth are starting to chatter. I climb out of the water, wet clothes weighing me down. My soggy socks and runners squish with every step.

Beth scopes out our surroundings while I struggle to unzip the jacket pocket where I put the dart gun. The zipper is stuck.

"They're back!"

We whirl around and find ourselves face to face with a Creeper I haven't seen before. A man with translucent wings is hovering above the ground, his clothed butt pointing down with what looks like a stinger poking through the cloth of his track pants.

As we back away, Chameleon-Gal emerges from thin air. "Run. Get out of here!" She points to a pack of Creepers heading our way.

Chapter 26

Dead End

ZIGZAGGING BETWEEN TREES, WET clothes clinging, we race across once perfectly manicured flower beds and leap over shrubs. Our pursuers must suspect that we're heading to the lightway that will take us home. Instead of heading there directly, we race through the orchard and dart into the fog.

I catch my breath, cough a few times.

"You okay?"

I'm still shivering in these wet clothes, but… "Yeah, okay." I'll take "okay" any day.

"Good."

Carefully stepping with our squishy shoes, we move swiftly through the fog, side by side, arms stretched out in front of us.

"They're totally going to be expecting us," I tell Beth.

"I know. What weapons do we have left?"

I poke around my soaked backpack and hand Beth a plastic box of darts. "We have the dart guns, just need to reload. No more electric prods."

"Why'd you throw the last one at the cops? We could have escaped from them anyway."

"I had just used it and was afraid we might get electrocuted if we took it into the pond with us."

"Oh."

"I still have a couple of smoke bombs. Don't know how they will fare after getting soaked."

"Anything else?"

I shake my head.

We reload the dart guns and each find a thick branch to use to defend ourselves.

"All we need is to get past the Creepers so we can reach the lightway. Like a game of Red Rover."

"What's Red Rover? Beth asks.

"It doesn't matter. Just get past the Creepers and we're home free."

"It's not going to be that easy," Beth says. "You know that."

"Neither was saving you. Yet here we are."

Beth smiles.

When we reach our destination, I try to keep my composure. "We're almost home."

On the count of three we leave the fog and find ourselves in exactly the spot we wanted: in the Garden at the entrance to the bog.

Along with the sound of crickets chirping, frogs croaking, and insects buzzing (which makes me shiver after our time in Bugtopia), there is mumbling coming from the open green space on the other side of the bog. Right where the lightway home is situated. They are waiting for us, as we expected.

"Okay," I whisper. "We need to get to the lightway. That's it."

"Right. Red Rover," Beth says, smirking.

We march down the bouncy path of peat, breathless with anticipation. So far so good, by the time we arrive at the edge of the bog.

"Ready, Beth?"

"Ready, Syn!"

As we leave the protective tree-covered path, the open green space extends its welcome. There is a welcoming party too—Cole, and about twenty Creepers, including the remaining Creeper bird.

What is not here is the lightway.

What now? How do we get home?

As the Creepers begin to inch forward, Cole calmly holds up his hand. "No, that's fine. Let them join us."

I'm tempted to empty all of my darts into Cole, but even if I only shoot him once, there are not enough in both our guns to defend us against this many Creepers.

"You have never looked better, Synthia."

The monster who beat me to a bloody pulp in a rage of madness is so calm and collected, it's eerie. He's more than aware he has the upper hand.

"Wondering where your shortcut home has disappeared to?" He grins. "You know it was me who had that lightway opened in the first place, right? Now, why would I leave it open so your army of friends could return? Or, so you could leave us after such a short visit? That would be foolish!"

We aim our dart guns at Cole. The Creeper bird stands on its hind legs and screeches a fierce warning.

"Down!" Cole says. "Girls, my friend here is upset because you took his pal with you when you left."

Cole takes two warning steps forward and stops. "Shoot me if you want. My friends here will get ya. And besides that, I'd wake up eventually. So, you have only two choices. Let me lay them out for you.

"First, you can do this the easy way. Beth stays with me. We'll have a public execution an hour from now, torture her for a while, and then lop her head off her skinny little neck."

I don't give him the satisfaction of any response.

"And then Synthia, you can go home. It's a win-win. You get to live out the remainder of your short, miserable life, while I am satisfied you will forever feel the same pain you caused me. Trust me. You'll never forget the sight of your loved-one dying right in front of you. You won't ever stop feeling like you failed her."

I continue staring down Cole, avoiding eye contact with Beth.

"Your second choice? Shoot a few of us with your toy gun. You know, play hard to get. Either way, Synthia, your sister's head is going to be lopped off and you're going to watch it roll right in front of you.

For the very first time in my life, I truly want to kill someone. I hate—and uncomfortably cherish—the feeling.

"Is that what you want?" I scream to the Creepers. "To watch a ten-year-old girl being murdered?"

The Creepers exchange nervous glances.

Cole's rage finally surfaces. "They know what you did. They know you deserve it!"

"Maybe I do. But *her*?" I shriek. "She's never hurt anyone. Beth has spent most of her childhood alone because you held our parents prisoner. Then you kept her captive like a rat in a cage."

Beth whispers two words so quietly I can barely make them out. "Follow me."

Beth and I race through the open field. Cole follows. Ten seconds later, she stops and holds up her hand for me to stop too. Cole slows and his winged pet lands next to him. His minions, some beginning to question if they are on the right side of this, approach us carefully.

I keep the dart gun focused on Cole. Not that it stops him. He follows us step by step as we back away.

"You peons think you can get out of this? There is no way for you to get home. You realize that. I have the upper hand."

"Do you, now?"

Why is Beth smiling? Why so confident?

The answer is instantaneous. Nearby, a lightway flashes and then fades. Seconds later, another lightway pops up—right where Cole is standing! He freezes. The lightway flashes three times and then the beam of light remains static. Cole's face is full of rage as the beam of light grows brighter. The two-faced monster disappears into the light.

"Did I do good?" Beth asks.

Chapter 27

A Desperate Plea

BETH EXUDES SELF-SATISFACTION, her expression is colossal.

"I'm impressed." Did she memorize the pattern of lightways in the Garden?

"We're not out of the woods yet."

I follow Beth's gaze.

The Creeper bird has risen on its hind legs and stretches its wings, threatening to attack. Chameleon-Gal appears and holds up her hand like a traffic cop. The Creeper halts and lowers its wings.

Croc-Man steps forward. "Put your hand down! Let it rip them apart!" His order is followed by cheers, but not all the Creepers are on board. Something has shifted.

"We're not your enemy," I shout. "We just want to go home."

"Not our enemy?!" Croc-Man yells. "You kept us trapped underground for years until Cole rescued us."

"That's a lie!"

"That's what Coleus said you would say," Rat-Girl retorts.

"I'm sure he did. But I didn't even know this place existed until a few months ago. And news flash—it was *me* who freed you. *Me!*"

The Creepers mutter amongst themselves.

"We just want to go home," I repeat.

"So, you can let us go," Beth says, stepping forward, "or you can murder two children right now and be done with us."

My gutsy little sis.

"I say we kill her," the other Croc-Man shouts.

"That wasn't what I was going for," Beth whispers.

"Let's hold them until Coleus returns," Rat-Girl suggests. "Let him deal with them."

"But what if they're right?" asks Chameleon-Gal. "What if Cole has been lying to us this entire time?"

Croc-Man 1 glares at her. "When did you go soft, Crystal?"

"I never went soft. But, I questioned our dear leader when he burned alive several of our own. And then again when he beat the bloody pulp out of a teenage girl and savored every moment."

Silence falls over the crowd of Creepers. Her words are having an effect.

Something catches my eye. Something falling from the sky. A woman, writhing in a fit of panic. Everyone turns at the sound of cracking bones when she slams onto the ground. Eagerly, the Creeper bird flies over the crowd to feast.

"Go, Beth!"

With the Creepers distracted, we slink over to a row of blueberry bushes that borders the bog and duck under cover. We are scratched up, but that's the least of our worries.

Once we're safely hidden, I have an idea. "There is this guy named Lundy, living in the sewers. He might be able to set up another lightway to get us home. You know the secret entrance?"

"I know this Garden better than anyone. Even better than Cole."

"I'm sure you do."

Knowing there is a ladder that goes down to the sewers, I don't hold my breath for as long. I climb down, forcing myself through the sludge to the other side. By the time I have caught my breath, Beth is already standing behind me, caked in the tar-like mud. We splash puddle water over ourselves and pat down quickly, eager to find Lundy.

"Let's check the computer room."

Beth bends over and shakes some mud from her hair. "Okay, what are we waiting for?"

I grin as we sprint into our next adventure, racing through the watery tunnel corridors. Our splashing footsteps are halted abruptly around the first corner when we almost careen into Lily.

When she sees Beth, recognition flashes in her eyes. "Wow. You rescued your sister."

Beth starts to speak, but Lily raises one hand.

"Why did you come back, Syn? You got what you came for."

"I need to find Lundy. The lightway home has been closed."

Lily sighs.

"It's really important." I step around her. "We have to keep moving."

"I'll take you to him," she says, reluctantly.

Beth falls into step behind Lily and me.

"Did Luke ever come back?" I ask.

"No. But after you guys left, some Creepers came down here to see Lundy."

Damn it. The lightway must have closed by the time Luke tried to come back.

Lily stops at a metal door and knocks loudly.

"Yeah," Lundy's voice answers from inside.

We follow Lily into a concrete room the size of a parking space. Lundy is sitting cross-legged on a mattress, reading a *Walking Dead* graphic novel.

He stares at Beth. "You're still alive." He tosses the book aside and stands up. "You did it, Syn. You rescued your sister. But you shouldn't be here."

"That's what I told them," says Lily.

"We need your help," I plead. "So, Cole had you close the lightway that takes us home?"

"Yeah," he admits. "He can be very persuasive."

"You have to open it again."

"Wish I could. Really. He'll kill me. You know he will."

"So, come back with us."

"The police think I'm a murderer. They'll never believe that a two-faced lunatic from another world did it. I'm better off here. Cole won't kill me as long as I do what he says. He needs me."

"*We* need you," I beg.

"I don't want to see either of you get hurt. But I don't want to die either."

I can't argue with that.

"If you stop Cole," he says, "I'll do it, no problem. Until then—"

"I get it. And I don't blame you."

"Then what do we do?" Beth asks. "Cole will find his way back from wherever that lightway took him."

"You can't be here when that lunatic returns," says Lily. "If he or his posse see you down here, he'll know there's another entrance."

"She's right," Lundy says. "That entrance is the only way we can sneak out for supplies. Otherwise, we'll have nothing to eat except rats." He looks down at his graphic novel. "And besides, I need to get the next volume. Come to think of it, Negan and Cole would probably be best buds."

I have no idea who Negan is, and don't care. There's only one solution and that is to take down

Cole. I lower my head. "Can you guys round everyone up?"

* * *

Beth and I are standing in front of a group of thirty people in a long, narrow room. People are squeezed together on benches. Some I barely remember. Some I once called friends.

"Uh, thanks for gathering here," I say, projecting my voice as loudly as possible. Public speaking has never been my forte, but lives depend on this speech, so I give it everything I've got.

"Most of you know that I'm Syn. And you might recognize my sister, Beth."

The crowd stirs, then calms down.

"I know you're not happy I'm here. You want me to go back where I came from. Well, that is the problem. I can't leave with my sister without Lundy's help. And he isn't safe helping us as long as Cole is in charge."

"Get to the point," an older man I remember as Bear yells, followed by a chorus of discontented mumbling.

"The point is…as long as Cole is out there and in charge, we can't return home. As long as he is out there, you are all stuck down here. Eating rats, lacking supplies. Living without bright sunshine over your heads or warm spring rain misting your cheeks."

"And whose fault is that?" argues Bear. A chorus of supportive howls erupts from the benches as he angrily presses through the crowd and storms from the room. Lundy follows, desperately trying to reason with him.

"I'm sorry for everything that's happened," I yell above the commotion. I feel my throat stinging. "I didn't want any of this. But together, we can capture Cole. You can be free."

After a short, stunned silence, there is a roar of laughter.

"He has an army of freaks!" someone yells.

"You expect us to take them on?" shouts another.

The crowd erupts in chatter. Lily looks at me, then at Beth. She frowns. "I'm sorry Syn. It won't happen unless everyone agrees. Most are too scared to do anything."

The crowd begins to disperse, chattering loudly, tossing us sideways glances as they squeeze past.

I start to tear up. "Cole said he's going to kill my sister. I believe him."

"I wish there was more I could do."

The room is cleared. It's just the three of us.

"What now?" Beth asks. "You heard Lundy. We can't stay down here or these people are all in danger."

I wipe tears with a muddy sleeve. "Maybe we can spend the night in the fog. Rest. Come up with a plan."

"No," Lily says. "You're not sleeping outside. I'll find you somewhere discrete to spend the night down here."

"No!" Lundy runs into the room in a panic. "They have to leave now! Some Creepers just arrived. Cole too!"

Chapter 28

Bitten

HE'S BACK *already*?

"We can still hide them," Lily says. "He won't know they're here."

"He already knows they're here," Lundy says. "Bear told them about your big speech."

"Coward," Beth mumbles.

"They know where we are now?"

"Not exactly, Syn. I heard footsteps while trying to talk to Bear and hung back around a corner. Cole confronted the old guy, but he collapsed before saying anything else about the meeting. You need to head straight for the exit now. Cole will search every cranny. They'll find you eventually, no matter where you hide."

We charge out of the meeting room, but don't get very far before Beth stops. "The sound of our splashing footsteps is going to give us away!"

"I'll cause a distraction," Lily offers.

"No, you should—"

Before any of us can object, she splashes off in the other direction, without turning back. I stare after my friend with a heavy heart.

"Keep going!" says Lundy.

We turn a corner and find ourselves in the path of two Creepers I remember seeing a few months ago. Snakes with human-like flesh slithering in the shallow sewer water. They leap into the air, one whizzing past my head and the other sinking its fangs into Lundy's shoulder.

"Ahhh!" He grabs the snake with both hands and attempts to yank it off, but its fangs are buried deep in his flesh and it won't let go. I grab its tail and pull with all my strength.

A sudden flash of intense pain in my arm has me staggering. The other snake has a vice-like grip on me. "Beth. Go," I croak as my knees weaken.

"Not a chance." Beth yanks the dart gun from her pocket, presses the muzzle against the snake and shoots. The snake relaxes its grip and it drops into the water at my feet. As my vision blurs, there is another thwip of the dart gun and another splash. Lundy collapses. I crumple into a heap next to him.

"Syn, get up," Beth orders. "You have to get up."

"Go," I whisper.

"No."

There are voices in the distance. Commotion around a nearby corner.

"What about Lundy?"

"Listen. You don't get up, I stay with you and Cole finds us. Kills me. And you have to live with that."

Her words hit me hard. There is no way I'm letting Cole kill my sister. I fight the toxins swimming through my bloodstream and let Beth help me to my feet. Everything is a blur. "Lead me."

"Don't worry, your snakebite isn't fatal. You'll recover. Lundy too. Besides, we're so close."

Beth sure does know this place and its residents inside out. Amazingly, my vision is already clearing up. My strength is returning. There are still voices echoing in the distance though, so all our senses are on high alert. Beth yanks me backwards before I can turn the next corner.

"Shhh!"

One of the voices belongs to Cole. I realize where we are, and where the voices are coming from. Cole and his Creepers are blocking the secret mud entrance so we can't escape.

"Any other ideas for an escape route?" Beth asks.

"Yeah, I have an idea."

She lends an ear and I'm not surprised that she knows exactly where to go. At the T of a long corridor, Beth tells me we're turning.

"My vision is clear now. I'm almost feeling normal."

"That's amazing," Beth says. "Usually the effect of those bites lasts a good twenty-four hours."

"The injection Dr. Freeman gave me must have somehow protected me from the venom and helped me heal quicker."

Beth frowns. "Poor Lundy isn't so lucky."

"Listen! What's that?"

Echoes of something heading in our direction. Barking. Creeper dogs!

"I can calm them down," says Beth. "But they will give our location away for sure." She glances left, then right. "See that door?"

"That's it?"

"Yup."

We reach the door just as the Creeper dogs lunge from around the corner. We each hold up a hand in unison. "Stay!"

The Creepers sit, silenced, panting tongues hanging from the sides of their crocodile-like snouts. Beth grins at me, impressed. Together, we slide open the door and as soon as it clicks shut, the Creeper dogs start barking again. We don't have much time before more Creepers arrive.

"Look! There's a latch," says Beth.

I click it and there is a buzzing sound behind us. Bolts of electricity are crackling from the floor to the ceiling through a black tunnel. The portal Lundy calls the voltway has opened directly in front of us.

"No!" Beth is showing real fear for the first time. "Not through there. Tell me that's not your plan."

"It's not." I place my hand on Beth's shoulder. "You trust me?"

"Of course," she says without hesitation.

"Follow me." I guide her around the voltway and sit down at the computer. The screen lights up with a click of the mouse. That page Lundy showed me is still open! I double-click the fourth file in the second column.

DebWade9997465

"Mom!" Beth exclaims in surprise.

Nothing changes with the voltway. The Creeper dogs have stopped barking. There are voices in the corridor and someone is frantically rattling the door handle.

Did I do this wrong? Should I have tried to close the voltway first?

The door handle continues to rattle. The voltway emits smoke. No, not smoke. Fog. The tunneled black abyss fogs up. When it dissipates, in its place is a good old reliable lightway.

"Let me try the handle!" A Creeper's voice is muffled through the door.

I grab Beth's hand. "Ready?"

"Let's go."

We walk into the light. When the light dissipates, we find ourselves in a concrete room identical to the one we left, except for one thing. Three wooden crates are stacked in place of the computer.

"We gotta keep going in case they follow," I say.

The door here is open and we promptly exit.

As Beth leads us out of the sewers, she turns to me. "The file. That was Mom's name."

"Yes, and the others were Mom and Masie Winters."

"What does that mean?"

"I don't know."

The exit is an exact duplicate of the one Maya led me to. It takes great effort to hang off the ladder and pipes and drag away the lid. When it's done, Beth sighs with relief. I cough.

"My lungs are clogged up again."

"The injection is starting to wear off?" says Beth, concerned.

"I hope not."

It's nearly pitch-black outside, but I make out that we are on a property like the one behind "home". "I'm sorry, Sis. I wanted to get you back to our real home. The odds aren't great that this is it."

"It's not your fault."

"I don't know what to do next." I rub my eyes. "I'm tired. You good with finding a place to hunker down for the night?"

"Yeah."

We don't want to bump into any version of our parents, or even worse, find them dead. So we decide to cross the property adjacent to home and look for a shed or an empty house. As we near a farmhouse, I notice a bright red light up ahead on the road. At first, I think it's a car's brake lights, but as we get closer, I see that it's lighting up a wooden sign. This sure isn't here in my world.

Curious, we cross the road to read the sign. There is nobody around, though the lights are on in some of the surrounding properties. The glazed oak sign is twice my height and the width of two cars. At the top is written:

The Children Will Be Found, The Children Will Return, June 14, 2003

Beneath that are at least a hundred names, each one accompanied by a photo. Some faces I know well.

Sylvia Dubois (Fern)
Gwendolyn Dubois (Lily)
Allison Fraser (Rose)

And one I sure as hell can't miss: Synthia Wade, with a picture of me when I was about three.

Two more photos stand out, posted side by side:

Darren Silva
Bryce Stevens

The boys are young. Darren is seven or eight, Bryce a few years older. With their photos next to each other, there is no doubt in my mind. *Cole.*

"What is this?" Beth asks.

"These are residents of the Garden. Their real names."

"I don't understand."

I stare at my sister in awe. "This is the world…. The world where the people in the Garden…. No, not only people—*everyone*—were taken from."

Chapter 29

The City of Lost Children

"TAKEN? WHAT DO you mean, *taken?*"

Beth has no clue what Mom and Dad did. How much do I tell her?

"What do you mean, *taken?*" she repeats.

"Let me ask you this, Beth. To your knowledge, what exactly is the Garden?"

"It's a world that Mom and Dad discovered. A world where no one gets sick. They were researching it so they could create a cure for you."

A world they *discovered?* Is that what they told her? She was only five when Synister captured them, so maybe that's all she remembers. It's time she knows the truth.

I take a deep breath. "Mom and Dad didn't discover the Garden. They created it."

"*What?*"

"Cole told me. So did Synister. When they had me tied up. Cole said that our parents ripped out part of another world to build the Garden."

Beth is shocked.

"Hey, I don't know if it's true for sure," I try to reassure her, though looking at Darren and Bryce's photos it's almost certain that for once Cole was telling the truth.

"Cole's crazy! I wouldn't believe anything he says."

"Right. Still, I'm certain that the people in the Garden were taken from somewhere, and their memories wiped. Look at this sign. These are the people who live in the Garden. You recognize most of them, right? So Cole and Synister weren't lying about that. They were taken. And this is the world they were taken from."

"But the Creepers. And Cole?"

I point to a picture of a middle-aged man with long, greasy hair. "Troy Gallagher. Do you recognize him?"

Beth examines the photo. "That's the Creeper we met. The one with butterfly wings."

"Darren Silva and Bryce Stevens," I say, pointing at their photographs. "Two completely different boys. A little older now, they are one. Cole."

"I...don't understand."

"You've been to so many other worlds. Have you ever seen anything resembling a Creeper?" I ask.

"No."

"Something went wrong. Animals, humans, even insects, and in the case of Cole, two humans. They were somehow conjoined and brought to the Garden."

"Mom and Dad did this?" Beth is on the verge of tears.

"They did some things that weren't very good."

And the winner for 'Downplay of the Year' is...

"Their intentions were good but—"

"So, all these people," Beth hiccups with tears, "were kidnapped by Mom and Dad? Their minds were erased?"

"Yeah. They were."

"Maybe you're wrong?" she says, unsure of her words.

"It's possible."

But unlikely.

"Let's find a place to sleep. I need to take my pills."

Lights are on in the first three houses we pass. The sheds are locked. We even try opening the doors of a few cars parked on the road, but they're locked as well. Eventually, we arrive at an old house that is in desperate need of repair. It's in complete darkness. The shed behind the house is locked, but we find something even better. An old red barn with both doors open wide.

We creep closer and pause at the doors, listening carefully. It's dark inside and all is quiet. I shrug out of my backpack and rummage around for flashlights. Beth raises her dart gun as we sneak inside.

There are enough stalls for two dozen horses. Each stall is completely bare. Hay is piled at both ends of the structure. Our flashlights reveal a loft and Beth climbs the ladder to check it out.

"It's perfect," she reports after climbing down. "Hay to sleep on. Clean."

Beth shines the beam of light at the ladder and I climb up. Accustomed to sleeping in a comfortable bed, "perfect" might not be the word I'd use. But for one night, it will suffice. I toss my backpack on a pile of hay. Beth is already on her way to the door.

"Where are you going?"

"To get water. Food—something nutritious with lots of calories. You need that, right?"

"Yeah, but—"

"You can join me in my pillage if you want." She grins, obviously aware that I have been uneasy about her "borrowing" things. "I'll be in and out. They won't even notice that someone picked the lock or that anything's gone."

"Okay." I sigh.

As soon as she is gone I regret not accompanying her. What if something happens? Though, she has been doing this for years apparently. Less than fifteen minutes later, the barn door creaks open.

"It's just me," Beth whispers, peeking over the top of the ladder.

"That was fast."

Beth smugly empties a shopping bag of food and blankets. "Nobody was home."

"You went all out, Sis."

She got a few bottles of water and a paper cup, half a loaf of bread, cheese slices, two apples, a bag of carrot sticks and packaged cookies She even heated up two TV dinners in the microwave; a chicken fettuccine alfredo and a beef lasagna.

We share the TV dinners, eat all the carrots and cheese, pig out on the cookies and save the bread and apples for breakfast. I dig my pills out of my backpack. Somehow the inside of the pocket that held my pill container didn't get too wet after we jumped into the pond in that other world, so my pills are still intact. I drop some enzymes into a cup of water and take the pills like Dr. Freeman instructed. I have to skip the therapy vest but will do the inhaler treatments. My chest is congested and my nose is runny, but considering that I was released from the hospital early this morning, I'm not feeling too shabby.

Appetites satisfied, we lie on the hay under our blankets and turn off our flashlights. Cold night air stings my cheeks and I tug the blanket farther over my face. I'm tired and can't help but wonder how we're going to get home.

My ears are ringing from the silence. "You awake?"

"Nope," Beth replies, giggling.

I shuffle closer. "I can't sleep."

"Why not?"

"I can't get the image of those people falling to their deaths from the frickin' clouds out of my head.

Don't suppose you know why people fall from the sky in the Garden. I mean, how is that even possible?"

"The people there didn't think much of it," Beth says. "But I've been to hundreds of worlds, maybe more, and have never seen anything like it. It's weird."

Not much scares this girl. Then I recall the fear in her eyes when she thought I was going to take her through the voltway. "How about the voltway?"

"What about it?" she asks, hesitantly.

I immediately regret bringing it up, not wanting to keep her awake either. "Have you gone through it?"

"Kind of."

"It's okay if you don't want to—"

"A couple of years ago, I ended up in another world. Kind of a world, anyway. Different than what I was used to. It was the most beautiful place I've ever seen."

"But?"

"But there was something there. Something…terrifying."

I can't help myself. "What was it?"

"Some kind of creature. I only saw a glimpse of it." She pauses. "But that was enough. It was so big, the ground rumbled when it moved. I ran for my life, and that's when I came across the voltway."

"Wait, the voltway was in that world?"

"Yeah. The beast was getting closer, so I took a chance and ran right through it."

"It transported you someplace?"

"Yeah. To the sewers in the Garden. Back when the Creepers were living there. Creepers don't scare me. This thing though…."

"Whoa." I told her what Lundy had shared about Jade, and how his severed arm was all that returned after he and Mackie ventured through the voltway.

"Yeah. If I didn't know better, I'd say that the voltway transports you into *Jurassic Park*."

"Wait, you've seen *Jurassic Park*?" This is almost as interesting as the unseen monster.

"Of course. Who hasn't?"

"In another world?"

"Yeah. I watched movies while staying in abandoned houses. *Jurassic Park* is one of my favorites. The sequels sucked though. Harrison Ford only starred in the first one so no surprise there."

"Wait. You saw *Jurassic Park* and it starred Harrison Ford?"

"Yeah, of course. He was the paleontologist who didn't like kids."

"Wow. Wait until Ebby and Jon hear that you saw a version of *Jurassic Park* starring Indiana Jones."

"Huh? Christopher Walken was Indiana Jones."

"Oh my God. They're going to flip."

We spent a long while talking about movies. I have seen tons with Ebby and Jon is a huge film nerd. I can't wait to listen while Beth tells them about all the differences in the movies she has seen in other worlds. They're going to love her, I am sure of that. And wait 'til she tells them she saw *Beetlejuice* with Bill Murray as the Ghost with the Most!

All the chatting soon tires us out. I fall asleep, forgetting about bodies falling from the sky and the monster on the other side of the voltway.

* * *

When I open my eyes, Beth is sitting cross-legged, watching me.

"Morning," she says.

"How long have you been up?"

"A while. You know you totally snore?"

"Yeah, I know."

"Oh, of course you do. You're stuffed up because of your CF. I'm sorry."

"Hey, it's fine."

I can't wait to get this girl home to Aunt Ruth and have a family snuggle. I swallow twenty or so pills for the zillionth time and puff my inhalers. We munch on bread and apples, and stuff the remainder of the loaf in my backpack.

"Let's get out of here before someone finds us," Beth says.

"No argument from me."

We return to the property of my duplicate house and are strolling along the road when my chest begins to feel congested. I start coughing.

"Syn?"

"I'm okay."

My hacking continues and a man approaches. "You girls okay?"

I step back, startled by his face.

"Synthia?" He cradles my cheeks.

I gaze into familiar eyes.

Beth says it first. "Dad?"

Chapter 30

Taken

DAD SQUEEZES MY SHOULDERS FONDLY. "Syn. It's you. It's *actually* you."

His hair is salt and pepper and he is clean-cut, unlike the last time I saw my real father in the bubble. He had a long, straggly beard then.

He turns to Beth and holds her at arm's length. "And you. You look so much like her. How…?"

This was what I was afraid of. I wanted to leave this world without coming across alternate versions of our parents. What do we tell him?

"Masie's behind this, isn't she?"

Beth and I glance at each other, unsure of what to say or do.

"I know you're not *my* Syn. You're from another world."

"We are," I tell him, coughing again.

"And what's your name?"

"Beth," she answers nervously.

"You're mine, aren't you? My daughter. From someplace else."

"Yes."

"Wow," he says. "All these years of Masie's mad attempts to travel to other worlds and what do you know? In some other reality, she actually did it. And now here you are."

"We need to leave," Beth says. "We have to return to our own world."

"Oh, I understand," he says disappointedly. "Would you like to come inside for a few minutes? I have so many questions."

"Thank you, but we've gotta go."

"You're coughing. Come in for a cold drink. I even have…*my* Syn's equipment. All of it. You can use it. Or take whatever you need."

He's desperate for our company. And answers. But Beth and I have run into a version of our parents before. They also acted kind at first, but ended up having dark, ulterior motives.

"Okay," Beth says, surprising me. "Half an hour. Then we have to go."

Dad nods excitedly. "Okay. Half an hour."

As we walk towards the duplicate of my house, I glance at Beth curiously. She avoids eye contact. I gather she needs this as much as he does.

The house is the same as the one where we found the bodies. Old yellow wallpaper. No recent renovations. Newspapers are strewn across the kitchen table

230

so that its color is anyone's guess. Dishes are piled high in the sink. A large photo of the family—this world's Mom, Dad, and me when I was maybe two years old—hangs on the wall of the kitchen next to the back door.

He ushers us into the den and we take a seat on the sofa, dust stirring from the cushions. Dad brings us each a cold glass of lemonade and sits down across from us on a green leather chair. This paints a comforting picture from my childhood, of my real father sitting on that very same chair reading the newspaper, although this dad smiles at me in a way that makes me uncomfortable.

I clear my throat. For now, the coughing has subsided.

"Is, um, your wife here?" Beth asks, trying to break the awkwardness.

Yeah, what about all those questions he had?

Dad's face drops. "No, she's not. After Syn was…well, taken…things were hard. She left. Made a new life for herself."

"I'm sorry," I say. "And your Syn?"

"Of course, you don't know," he began. "A long time ago, there was a multitude of abductions on the same day. Even pets went missing. Rumors were that they vanished into thin air, but no one knows for sure what happened."

"My Syn," he pauses. "My Syn was playing outside with a hula hoop. Deb had her nose buried in a book. We never saw Syn again."

"I'm so sorry." I discretely shake my head at Beth, warning her not to tell him what we know.

His Syn was most likely one of the many my parents abducted and experimented on—murdered. The Syn from this world could even have been Synister herself. I'll never know, and certainly won't share any of that with the man sitting across from us.

"What's your world like?" he asks.

I take another sip of the lemonade, studying him over the rim of the glass. "In my world, it was my parents who disappeared. My Aunt Ruth raised me."

"Ruth. Haven't heard that name in a while. How is she doing?"

"Good. But I've been gone a few days and she doesn't know where I am. She must be terribly worried."

"Of course. Finish your lemonade and you can be on your way shortly."

At that, Beth gulps down half her glass.

"How about you?" Dad asks Beth. "In your world, your mom and um, your dad. They had a second kid?"

"They did." Beth is smart enough not to mention the Garden. It's better that he thinks we come from the same world.

"I would have loved nothing more than to still have Deb in my life, and two wonderful children. How is your health, Synthia?"

"It has its ups and downs."

"You said you have your daughter's equipment," Beth says. "How about the therapy vest?"

"That's not necessary," I interject. "We'll be home soon."

"Can you get it?" Beth asks, ignoring me.

"Of course." He hurries out of the room and we listen to his footsteps clumping up the stairs.

"Why?" I ask. "We need to go."

"You're coughing again. That serum is wearing off and the doctor said to continue all your treatments. You haven't cleared your lungs with the vest since we left the hospital in Bugtopia."

"But—"

"No buts. We don't know how long it will be before we are back in your world and you can receive medical treatment. We may need to face off against Cole. You take care of me, and I take care of you. Right?"

"Okay. Then we leave."

"Right."

Dad returns, toting a dust-covered vest, the machine under his arm, wires dragging on the floor. He plugs it in and slaps some dust off the vest. As he places it over my head, I help adjust it. He turns it on when I'm ready. As I sit there, awkwardly, my chest vibrating, he watches us.

After another awkward silence, he speaks. "Wait 'til Masie hears about this. That somewhere, in some other universe, she's achieved what she's been trying to do for years."

"Where is Masie, now?" I ask.

"Living in Massachusetts. She leads the Physics Department at Harvard. We keep in touch occasionally, through email."

"And Mom?" Beth asks.

"Last I heard she was living on a remote island in British Columbia. We both took it hard when our Syn went missing. I never blamed her, but things between us were never the same."

Dad helps me take off the vest when my session is over. I do feel better. He tells me he also has a nebulizer but it's useless without the medicine, and my inhalers will do the trick.

"Thank you," I say. "We should go now."

Dad turns around and closes the double glass doors that separate the den from the kitchen. "I'm sorry," he says. "I truly am. But I can't let you leave. I can't lose you again."

Chapter 31

Daddy Issues

I KNEW THIS WAS A BAD IDEA!

We could knock him out with a dart gun and make a run for it. Beth's eyes don't show any fear. I'm pretty sure she's looking for guidance. If I wasn't here she would have already taken action, but we're in this together. Dad looms before us.

"What do you think is going to happen?" I ask. "That we'll willingly stay here with you? That we'll all be one big happy family?"

"We can be."

"Not going to happen," I tell him bluntly. "So, now what? Are you going to lock us up in the basement? Come down a few times a day to feed us and spend quality time with your chained up sorta-but-not-really daughters?"

It's obvious he's conflicted. Our showing up here was unexpected and his only plan is for us to stay. "This isn't the answer. We're not going to be the family you want. I'm sorry, but we're not your daughters."

He fidgets, grinds a stale breadcrumb into the carpet with his shoe. "You're right. I can't force us to be a family."

"I know this is hard," I say.

"You have no idea."

"I do, actually."

"So, can we go?" Beth asks. "Or do I kick you where it hurts?'

Whoa, Sis.

He steps back to provide us a path. We hurry past him to the kitchen, grab our jackets and my backpack.

"Where are you going to go?"

"Somewhere nearby there is a, well, a type of portal," I explain. "It will either take us to another world or the one we came from."

"Where is this portal?"

"No clue whatsoever." I hoped he'd be wary because of this and have no further interest in us, but…

"You know what? I'm going to come with you. Maybe I will find another version of my family…one that wants me."

After an awkward pause Beth says, "Okay."

Only those who travel through a lightway can move from one world to the next. Beth and I are the only ones who will be able to see the lightway because we traveled through the one that brought us here. I guess humoring him won't hurt though, and we'll leave as soon as we find it anyway. The poor man doesn't have much to live for if he's willing to leave everything behind in an instant and come with us into the unknown.

I trot after Beth, down the steps overlooking the garden. Dad stands on the landing thoughtfully, taking one last look inside. He brings no belongings, no keepsakes to remember his life. He doesn't even bother to shut the door. I feel sorry for him.

"Let's split up," I suggest. "We'll have better luck finding the lightway."

After he walks away, Beth and I start searching in the garden behind the house.

I feel guilty. "He'll be confused when we're gone."

Beth stoops to examine a shiny object that's lying next to the hedge. "Don't worry. At least he's excited about something and," she crunches the beer can flat with an air of disgust, "he's not staring at us. That was making me nervous."

"It was pretty weird." I focus on parting some long grass, only to reveal a shiny hubcap. "Nothing here."

"Girls!" Our dad is calling. "I found it!"

Beth raises her eyebrows. We follow the sound of his voice around to the pond, past an overgrown flowerbed. Sure enough, light is streaming from under a large ornamental rock.

"Look at that!" He lifts the rock and a beam of light shoots into the sky. "Stunning! Absolutely stunning!"

How does he see this? Only Beth and I have been able to see the lightway in any of the other worlds we have traveled to. I try to wrap my head around why this time might be different. Then I understand.

I traveled to other worlds through lightways in the Garden. This lightway is different. We opened a file of my mom's on the computer in the sewers. It took us to a specific world rather than a random one. It took us to the world where the Garden's residents were taken from. Somehow this is different. Other people can see the lightways here.

This is *not* good.

"So, do we step into it?"

Beth and I are lost for words.

"Yeah," I finally say.

He smiles. "Fantastic. Let's do this!"

And with that, he steps into the lightway.

"I'm worried," Beth says. "Now what?"

"Um, wait a few minutes before going through. Maybe we'll end up in a different world than him."

"Unlikely."

"You have a better idea?"

"We can stay here. Move into his house. Start a new life."

I gawk at her.

"No, think about it," she says, and I realize that she has been doing that since we arrived. "We'll never have to fear Cole again."

"But my aunt—no, *our* aunt—is family. I can't turn my back on her. Plus, I have friends. I'm in school. And besides, if Cole hasn't already discovered the lightways that can be accessed through the computer, he will eventually. He'll find us, especially if we don't return to the Garden."

"Fine. But if we see Dad again, we need to ditch him somewhere. He's dangerous."

"I agree we need to lose him. He's lonely though, not dangerous."

"I don't know…."

A few minutes later, we're holding our dart guns tightly, in case we end up in the Garden with Cole or any of his Creepers in our path. We step into the lightway. When the light dissipates, we're standing in the exact same spot. The only difference is that our duplicate dad is waiting for us.

"I was afraid you weren't coming." He surveys the new surroundings. "So, this is another world? Like my own?"

"No. There are always some differences."

At the sound of a car engine, Dad takes off in the direction of the house.

"Wait!" I yell, as we dash after him.

By the time we find him, the car engine has been turned off. Dad is standing behind some bushes, spying on the carport. He raises his hands to his chest and tears stream down his face.

Exiting the gray Volvo is me, Mom, and Dad. We crouch so they won't see us. My second dad pats his Syn on the back as they climb the stairs. As my mom and my other enter the house, this world's Ian Wade pauses and tells them, "I forgot something. I'll be back in a minute!" He returns to the car and pops open the trunk.

The dad we brought through the lightway wipes tears off his cheeks and faces us. "Don't try to stop me," he whispers firmly.

"What?" we chorus.

"Shhh! If you try to stop me, if you warn them, I swear to god I'll kill you both." He brushes past us like we're nothing to him, pushes through the bushes, and sprints to the carport.

I yelp when he slams the trunk door down hard on the head of his unsuspecting double. He slams it down repeatedly. When he drags him away from the car, this world's Ian is still alive, although injured and confused. The Ian we brought with us secures his victim in a headlock, and—

SNAP

Beth yelps with me. The body thumps to the concrete. Horrified, we watch the killer undress his doppelgänger and change into the dead man's clothes. Tossing his own clothes in the trunk, he piles the body on top of them. The victim's foot hangs over the side and with absolutely no emotion, he flips it inside like it's nothing but a window scraper, lowers the trunk door, and slams it shut.

Beth and I are in shock, shivering, completely forgetting that we are armed with dart guns. Stiffly, we step back as he approaches.

"How could you?" I whisper.

"This is the closest I'm ever going to be to getting my family back."

"No."

"You have no one to blame but yourselves. If you hadn't been so selfish, if you had stayed with me in my world, it would never have come to this."

My poor sister, who is scared by so little, is shaking like a teacup on the side of a highway. I wrap my arm in hers without taking my eyes off this man.

"My warning stands. Don't blow my cover. This is my world now. Go home to yours."

He backs away and with one final warning glance, casually strolls to the foot of the stairs and makes sure his shirt is tucked in. Satisfied that he's an exact match for the dead man, he climbs the stairs and opens the door.

"Did you get what you needed?" I hear Mom ask.

"I certainly did," her husband's killer says as he closes the door behind him.

Chapter 32

Guilt Trip

"IT WASN'T OUR FAULT," Beth insists.

"Right."

We're standing in a cornfield two lots over from where we watched our dad murder another version of himself.

"There's nothing we could have done," Beth says. "You saw what he did to...to himself!"

"They'll figure it out. If not soon, eventually. What will he do to them when that happens?"

"I've traveled to so many different worlds and seen some terrible things," Beth says. "Interfering with other people's lives, trying to help, always makes things worse. Remember what happened to that cop when we tried to get that Creeper to follow us through the lightway?"

"How could I forget?" The memory of the cop becoming Creeper food will haunt me forever.

"The worlds we travel to aren't our own. We're only visitors. We can't get involved."

"We *can* get out of here though," I say, pointing to a glowing cornstalk. "I'll race you there!"

I rip it out of the ground and a lightway streams upwards.

Beth and I leap into the light with our dart guns poised and exit into what seems to be a duplicate cornfield.

"Did we even go anywhere?" I do a 360. "Are we still in the last world?"

"Look behind you."

Sure enough, the house of the property we're on has been painted with a fresh coat of blue. Not peeling beige like the last house. Greatly relieved, we begin to scour the cornfield for any sign of a lightway.

Beth grows thoughtful as we search and finally, my curiosity won't rest. "What are you thinking about?"

She parts a couple of cornstalks and flips over a large rock with her shoe. I wait.

"What else did Mom and Dad do?" she finally says. "What haven't you told me?"

"Perhaps it's better you don't know. That you remember them in the best light."

"I have good memories of them from when I was a little kid. But what we just saw? And in that other world when they tried to shoot us?"

"Let's put it this way. They did bad things. Very bad things. They had good intentions. But still…."

"Good intentions?"

"Like you said before, they wanted to cure my CF."

Beth is apprehensive. "What did they do?"

"Be careful," I warn. "Are you sure you want to know?"

"I'm sure."

So, I tell her everything. What bothers her the most, and understandably so, is that our parents took versions of me from other worlds and experimented on them. That they tortured and killed them.

"Do you think they're still alive?" she asks, trying her best to stay strong.

"They were in the bubble when I left the Garden a few months ago. Now they're not. Either Cole killed them—"

"Or they're still alive!"

"Somewhere."

"They're our parents," Beth says. "I love them."

"Me too." Though I don't know if that's true anymore. Any positive memories from my childhood have been overshadowed by the graves of my others, by their voices that I heard in my head before they were finally set free.

* * *

We travel to two more similar worlds, despair intensifying. It's been two days since Dr. Freeman gave me that treatment and there is no telling how much longer it will last. On the bright side, we manage to avoid those worlds' versions of our parents, and even find a place to rest in a duplicate hayloft. We're low on food and are nibbling on granola bars when the barn door creaks open. We duck as heavy footsteps stomp down the length of the barn. They stop.

"I know you're up there," a man yells in a deep voice. "I saw you kids come in."

We exchange worried glances.

"I'm going to leave. If you're not gone in five minutes, I'm calling the cops."

The police are the last thing we need.

"You hear me?" He stomps out.

Beth shrugs. I frown and throw the granola bars in my backpack. His two-minute warning comes as we're climbing down the ladder. As we warily approach the exit, I glance at his shadow stretching across our path on the dusty barn floor.

"One minute!"

We step outside. Standing beside the door is a heavy-set man. Not the man who lives on this property in *my* world.

"You girls planning to smoke dope up there?"

We shake our heads.

"Sorry, Mister."

"We'll leave," says Beth.

The man watches us head down his driveway.

Beth points straight ahead. "Syn, do you see that?"

At first, I don't see anything other than tall buildings in the distant cityscape. I squint to make out what Beth sees. In the darkening red sky there is a beam of light. Most people would identify it as a searchlight.

"I see it."

"See what?" the man says. "You know? I don't care. Scat!"

"Mister, I'm sorry we trespassed. But please, can you do us a favor?"

"Seriously?" the man asks with raised eyebrows. He crosses his arms over his chest. "And what would that favor be? Not calling the cops?"

"Yeah, that," I say. "And maybe calling us a cab?"

* * *

The sun has gone for the night as we enter downtown Redfern. Ahead of us, the beam of light shines brightly into the sky.

"Do you see that light?" I ask the cab driver.

"What light?"

"The searchlight straight ahead."

"I don't see no light. You kids on crack?"

I shake my head as he glares at us in the rear-view mirror.

"Where you wanna get out?"

"Denny's," Beth blurts out before I can open my mouth.

* * *

We exit the restaurant after an incredibly satisfying, much needed calorie-filled feast. Beth is carrying a paper bag containing two extra meals to save for later.

The lightway is about five or six blocks away. As we walk in that direction, I feel my chest getting congested again. A couple of blocks later, phlegm has accumulated in my throat. I cough. And cough. And cough.

Beth pats my back. "Are you okay?"

Unable to answer, I cough for a spell, fearing the quick fix has finally worn off.

"Syn?" She waits for my answer, trying to console me.

While still full of phlegm and with my nose stuffed up, when the coughing subsides my chest feels less clogged.

"Are you okay?"

"I think so. Let's keep moving."

Beth keeps a close eye on me as we press on towards the beam of light. For the most part, this world is similar to my own. If it weren't for little things like Draper & Son Furniture being renamed Draper Furniture here (did Mr. Draper not have a son in this world or did his son decide to pursue stand-up comedy instead of work in the family shop?), I might have thought I was finally back home.

We turn right and there in the center of the street is the lightway. A car drives right through it with no effect.

"I have money for a hotel room," Beth suggests. "We can rest and do this in the morning."

"No. This is an abnormal lightway. Have you ever seen one as far out as the city?

"No. Never."

"So we can't count on anything normal. Who knows, it could disappear in five minutes."

"Good point."

"And, we have to be prepared that it will take us somewhere…different."

"They're all different," Beth says.

"We just have to be prepared. For anything."

Keeping that in mind, I take my evening pills earlier than I normally would. Then I breathe in through my inhalers and gulp down more water. "Whenever you're ready."

"Let's go."

One more time, we walk into the light.

When the light dissipates, we are standing on the same street. Yet everything is so very different.

Chapter 33

Apocalypse Now

STOREFRONTS AND OFFICES ARE DERELICT. Some are boarded up, others have smashed windows. Many resemble a meth house after a police raid. Graffiti is spray-painted on all the buildings, streets, and sidewalks. So much so, there is no room for further "artistic expression". Much of the spray-painted graffiti consists of one word:

DOOM

Other messages are for the most part, doom-related:

> GOD DOOMED US ALL
> DOOM IS ETERNAL
> DOOM SHALL REIGN UPON THE MASSES

Lovely.

Tattered banners hang from one broken window to another. They all say the same thing:

DOOM

Other than us, there isn't a single soul on the street, although chanting can be heard nearby.

"Doom. Doom. Doom."

I'm sensing a theme here and don't like it. "Where the hell are we?"

"I've seen weirder," Beth replies, smirking.

The chanting sounds closer. A block away now, though sound echoes off buildings in unpredictable ways, so who knows? I've rarely been in the city at night in my hometown, and never alone. So being out here in this messed-up version of Redfern, with a very real sense of doom beyond the graffiti and chanting is totally freaking me out.

"What do you think about hunkering down somewhere safe for the night?" I suggest. "Get off this crazy street. Search for the lightway in the morning?"

"The lightway will be easier to see at night."

The kid is braver than I am. She is right that the lightway will be easier to find at night. I would also prefer to return to the Garden at night when we can use the shadows to our advantage. But this world is so different. We don't know if the next lightway will show up in the city, in the vicinity of my duplicate house, or even somewhere else entirely.

Before I have a chance to respond, four guys and a girl turn onto the street. They're wearing ripped jeans and leather jackets. None of them look like they have showered or groomed in a week, something I can unfortunately relate to. They are passing a bottle of liquor around, taking swigs, and it's obvious from their staggering that this isn't their first bottle of the night.

"Doom for all," one guy slurs.

"And all for Doom," a girl mumbles. She and her pals burst into laughter.

Beth and I back up to the building behind us and enter through the paneless door, trampling over shards of glass and crumpled trash. We stand on the inside of the shattered window. As the group nears, I recognize a face. No, two faces.

"No way!"

"What?"

"The girl. That's Lily, from the Garden. And the blonde guy…."

"I recognize Lily. Not the guy though."

"Look closely."

Beth peeks out a bit farther. "Oh!"

He is one half of Cole.

"Bryce something, according to that sign we saw."

As they near our hiding spot, we move from the window so they won't see us. They joke around as they pass. Lily's double, this world's Gwen Dubois, has an acid tongue. They mockingly chant Doom-related expressions, each one followed by bursts of laughter.

They are out of sight and yet more echoing Doom chants are heard. There is a commotion of some kind, angry shouts from the hoodlums that have passed us.

We peek outside, careful not to cut ourselves on the jagged edges of broken glass. A dozen or more people have lined up to face the hoodlums, each holding a flaming torch. They're dressed all in black; jeans, leather jackets, and masks that reveal only their eyes.

"Doom! Doom! Doom!" they chant non-stop, as if in a trance.

The hoodlums swarm them, screaming obscenities. Bryce smashes a bottle over one of their heads. A masked man swings his torch at Bryce. Bryce ducks and the clothing of a pal beside him ignites. The marchers and hoodlums leap out of the way as blood-curdling cries fill the air. He rolls around in agony, flames encompassing his body. I try and look away but I catch a peripheral glance of his blazing figure rolling around on the street, surrounded by a black sea of onlookers. After a hellish minute or so, he is still, like a burning log in a fireplace.

"I'll kill you!" Bryce raises a fist in the air, clutching a nasty-looking shard of glass. Gwen and one of the guys try to hold him back, pleading with him to leave, but he breaks away from them. Beth gasps as he viciously swipes the jagged edge of glass across the throat of the man who lit his friend on fire. The man drops his torch and falls to his knees, frantically gripping his throat in a failed attempt to stop blood from gushing out.

Bryce picks up the torch and lights the nearest marcher on fire, sending him hurtling to the ground, shrieking. His torch is snatched from his side by Gwen who lights another masked man on fire. An out and out riot is in progress. The marchers taunt, "Doom, Doom, Doom" as the hoodlums continue their attack, lighting one marcher at a time on fire until only one is left standing. The only two surviving hoodlums are Bryce and Gwen.

Bryce gazes at his dead friends, and at Gwen kneeling beside them in tears. In a final moment of rage, he drops his torch and lunges at the last marcher, forcing him down, pummelling him into a bloody pulp.

I don't know who the bad guys are. The marchers? The hoodlums? All of them? But the rage I see from Bryce is clearly the same rage I have seen from Cole. Calm as the sea, laughing one minute, and then a towering inferno of anger the next. And Gwen— Lily—burning people alive?!

Even Beth is affected by what we have witnessed. After Bryce and Gwen leave the scene, she says, "Let's search for the lightway tomorrow."

* * *

I wake up coughing, curled up on a dusty couch. Beth is sitting on a chair next to me and hands me a bottle of water. I gulp half the bottle down and wipe my mouth. My chest is more congested than yesterday, but still not nearly as bad as when I went to the hospital in Bugtopia.

This office on the top floor of a building was the best place we could find to settle down for the night. It wasn't crawling with squatters. The two old couches we slept on in the reception area are worn from years of use, torn, splattered with coffee stains, and littered with cigarette butts. Gross, but we didn't have the luxury of being picky.

Beth hands me my pills. "There are only enough left for tonight and tomorrow morning."

"Guess we have to make tracks then, huh?" I try to sound cheerful.

Beth frowns. "At least you will get some exercise while we search for the lightway.

We are gorging on stale Denny's takeout when I am startled by the sound of loud static and a voice booming over a loudspeaker.

"Damn the souls the Lord has taken."

"Damn the gluttony that preceded the Doom."

"Damn the Lord that doomed us all."

Then a chamber of voices chant, "Doom! Doom! Doom!"

After a minute of doom chants, there's more static and all is quiet again.

"What the hell?"

"That's the third time since dawn," Beth tells me. "You slept through the other choruses. Lucky you."

I go to the window and look out over the city, but can't see any loudspeakers. The streets are deserted.

But, something beyond the city limits causes my jaw to drop.

Beth joins me at the window. "Weird, huh?"

"Weird doesn't even begin to cover it."

Disbelief numbs me at the sight before us. A wide strip of the Southlands farming community…is gone! The road in front of where my house should be is cracked as if damaged by an earthquake. It looks like a section of the land was literally ripped apart and taken away. All that remains is a giant crater—a pitch-black hole—and what looks like metal platforms or bridges that have been built above the hole.

While staring at this bizarre sight, everything becomes clear. "Beth, I know what this is. I know where we are."

"What do you mean?"

"This world is different. Different from all the others. That crater. That was the Garden. Before…."

Beth looks confused. Maybe even scared. Or both.

"Cole told me about this when I was his prisoner. This is the world where it all began. The world where Mom and Dad ripped out the Southlands community to create the Garden. This is it, Beth. This is ground zero."

Chapter 34

Harbingers of Doom

Cole had said that whatever world my parents had ripped apart to form the Garden was destroyed. That they eviscerated an entire planet, committed mass genocide. He was wrong. This world is still intact. Royally messed up, but intact. And we're here right now.

"Are you sure?" Beth is skeptical.

"Look at the land that is missing. That is the Garden. The borders match up and the missing section of land looks similar in size to the Garden. It makes total sense."

"How's that?"

"Think about it. On the computer in the sewers, I clicked on the fourth of Mom and Dad's files. There were ten listed. I bet that each one opens a lightway to a different world. The first world we went to was where the people were taken from. We didn't thoroughly explore the others, but there was probably something in each world that links it to the creation of the Garden."

"Like what?"

"Maybe they're where my duplicates were taken from. It seems like we've been traveling to each world in the column of Mom's and Dad's files. This is the sixth we've been to in that list, making it, if I'm right, the last world. This world is different from the others because the lightway to get here was in the city, not in the area surrounding my house. You said it yourself, that you've traveled to hundreds of worlds and never saw that before."

"I dunno."

Beth still doesn't buy it. Perhaps she's in denial about Mom and Dad's crimes.

"It doesn't matter," she says. "Our goal is to find the lightway and get back to the Garden."

"Well, whether I'm right or not, we still have a big problem."

Beth turns her back to the bleak cityscape. "Finding the lightway."

"Where do we even start? Obviously, the area around my house is out. So that leaves the rest of the Southlands area and the city. Every street, every alley, assuming it's not inside a building."

"I've never come across a lightway in an enclosed area," Beth reminds me. "No house, no shed, no barn. It's always outside. Though like you said, this world is different."

"How about this? We get a cab and have it drive down each block while we keep our eyes peeled. You have enough cash?"

"Yeah, but—"

"If that doesn't pan out, we ask the cabbie to drive us to Southlands and search the remains. If we don't have any luck by sundown, we use the darkness to our advantage and scour the city on foot."

"Among the crazies?"

"Let's hope it doesn't come to that. What do you say?"

Beth nods, but her mind is clearly elsewhere.

We slide our dart guns out from behind the cushions, snatch the rest of our things, and head down the stairs. It's drizzling. I clear some phlegm from my throat and raise my hood. There is nothing to see except for a couple of cars parked at the curb and a cat hunting for prey. Chanting in the distance sounds like it's coming from all around us, hopefully the echo of only one crazy group of doomsdayers.

We pass one of the parked cars on the street, an old banged-up Volkswagen Beetle that is so filthy we can barely make out that it was once red. Beth opens the driver's door.

"Whoa, we're not stealing another car."

"You think we're going to find a cab in this ghost town?"

"Good point."

"And look at it. It's abandoned."

"Fine, but I'm driving."

"You know how to drive?"

"How hard can it be? At least I can reach the pedals and still see over the dashboard."

Beth giggles. "I'll walk you through it."

She hotwires the engine, then instructs me how to coast down the street. It's important to move slowly so we don't miss the lightway. After treating us both to minor whiplash at an intersection, I drive to the end of Fifth Avenue, barely missing a fire hydrant, turn left onto Francis Road, then right on Sixth Avenue. We cover all of Redfern's downtown. Redfern is a small suburb—an empty suburb in this world. We haven't seen one single person all day. Not one shop or restaurant is open and we're both starving.

Where is everyone? It's been hours!

I drive to the residential area on the outskirts of the city, gaping at the deserted urban wasteland. Shopping centers, housing complexes, and schools— windows smashed, some boarded up with plywood. Rotting garbage is strewn about like no one here has ever heard of a trash bin. We're driving down Gilmore Crescent when the distant chanting we have become accustomed to grows noticeably louder.

"Pull over here."

I turn the wheel and the car comes to a jerky stop.

"I meant beside the curb, not *on* it." Beth is trying to tease, but looks worried. "Listen."

The chanting sounds like it's no farther than a block away. But that's not all we can hear now. Shouting and screams of terror turn me to ice.

"We need to get outta—"

Suddenly, a man rushes past the Beetle, fear plastered across his face. I check the mirrors. More people in a panic. Men, women, kids, climbing over fences and hedges, running along the street. We lock our doors, although with all the windows smashed, we're still vulnerable. Surprisingly, they run past the car in droves without noticing us.

A figure rounds the corner behind us, dressed in black. He's wearing a mask like the marchers from last night.

The chanting grows louder. "Doom, doom, doom!" A hoard of masked doomsdayer marchers is inching our way.

Beth and I duck in unison. The chanting draws closer, along with heavy footsteps. It's not only the marchers we can hear now. There is a woman. No, at least two women are screaming over the chanting. Screaming for their lives.

"Doom! Doom! Doom!"

The high-pitched terror in the women's voices pierces my eardrums. I'm trembling. They can't be any more than thirty feet away. I rest my foot on the accelerator, ready for instructions. If only Beth was in the driver's seat.

"Doom! Doom! Doom!"

They're right beside us.

"Doom! Doom! Doom!"

Chanting. Footsteps. Maddening fear tearing its way to my bones.

One of the women slaps a hand down where the driver's side window once was, dirty, matted blonde hair tousled every which way, eyes wide with astonishment at the sight of us cowering inside. She wrenches her other hand free of her captor and clamps it down on the car door.

"Help!" she screams. "Help me!"

A gloved hand yanks her back by her hair, but she braces herself against the car. As the masked man grabs her shoulder, he spots us. "Sinners!"

Another masked man gapes through the window. Then another. Now, the entire posse is staring into the car. The woman is finally pried away from my window and a pair of burly hands grabs me.

Chapter 35

The Black Hole

THEY SAY SEATBELTS SAVE LIVES. Well, the car I'm in isn't even moving and the only thing keeping me from being dragged out of it by masked maniacs is the fact that I'm strapped in.

Beth releases the emergency brake and turns the key in the ignition. "Hit the gas!" The engine roars, sputters, dies.

Son of a…. It ran perfectly fine a few minutes ago!

"Doom! Doom! Doom!"

Three masked men race to Beth's side of the car.

"Watch out!"

I'm too late. Two filthy hands grab her around the neck. I manage to shoot a dart into his shoulder. He collapses, giving Beth a window of opportunity. She shoots the man who has a strong grip on me and attempts to start the engine again. It roars and then sputters.

"Hit the gas again!" Beth shouts. The engine is silent.

An arm reaches through the broken window in the back, unlocks the door and someone climbs in. He leans between the seats and grabs Beth's wrist, as she attempts to start the engine.

"Hit it!" she screams as soon as the engine roars. The car lurches forward just as the man in the back seat grabs me. Beth raises her dart gun and rams the barrel into his eye. He falls back, screaming.

"Buckle up, Buddy," she sneers.

I zoom ahead, zigzagging down the street. Glancing in the rear-view mirror, I see the blonde woman trying to escape again, four hooded men on her tail. They overtake her and drag her off her feet. I brake.

"Keep going! We can't save her."

I feel terrible. There truly is nothing we can do though. I pry my eyes from the horrible scene behind us, lose control of the car, and veer left. Beth grabs the wheel to stop us from hitting a tree. The car comes to a stop with a jolt, our passenger pitching forward. He reaches for his neck, grimacing.

"Didn't I tell you to buckle up?" says Beth, raising her dart gun again, ramming the barrel into his other eye.

I hardly recognize my sister.

"Syn, take off his hood," she orders.

I slip shaky fingers under the bottom of the hood and lower it, but the reveal is anti-climactic. This is a guy I've never seen before. Maybe in his mid-forties.

The word "DOOM" has been carved into his forehead.

He is enraged. "Sinners! You will face the wrath of doom. You will fly into the abyss."

"Okay," Beth says, nonchalantly, still holding the gun on him. "Thanks for the warning."

I glance in the rear-view mirror again. The doomsdayers are far behind and staying put, tending to their fallen. I can't see either of the two women and hope they somehow got free, but doubt the creeps would let that happen.

I unbuckle and face our passenger. "What the hell is going on here?"

"Doom."

"Have you seen a strange light? A light that comes out of nowhere?

"Doom!"

Great. He's only fluent in Groot.

Beth releases her seatbelt and smacks the butt of her dart gun across his face. She presses the barrel against his chest. "Get out!"

He feels around for the door handle, squinting puffy red eyes that are watering profusely now. I actually feel smug. As Beth screams another warning, he finds the handle at last, and stumbles out of the car.

"Survival isn't pretty," she says as my brow furrows. "Let's go."

I start driving again. "We're never going to find the lightway like this. It could be anywhere. In any of these yards, in any park or playground, under a garbage bin in an alley."

"Just keep going."

"Where?"

The street comes to an end. With Beth's assistance, I make a hard left, but slam on the brakes as I notice what lies ahead. One block away, marching in our direction is another group of hooded doomsdayers. These guys are dressed in red leather and are wearing matching red masks. Another group of leather-clad masked men are marching behind us, wearing green attire.

"Doom! Doom! Doom!" The group in red spreads out so we can't drive around them.

"What now?" I ask, more to myself than Beth.

"Drive right at them."

"What?! I can't kill anybody!"

"They'll move."

"What if they don't? These people are insane."

"Then some of them die so we can live."

"No! That isn't right. There must be another way. There's always another way."

"No, not always. I've been on my own since I was five and have survived worlds as cruel as this. I've had to do things to survive. Things I didn't want to do."

"But you've never killed people."

Beth doesn't answer.

"Beth—"

"If this is the only way we can live, and very bad people want us dead, we don't have a choice."

"But—"

"You risked your life to save me. Are you going to let these nuts take my life now? Or yours?"

"Of course not." I have nothing else to say.

"Doom! Doom! Doom!"

We don't have much time.

"They'll move. You'll see."

Keeping the wheel as straight as possible, I accelerate. The red-hooded men stop, determined. They're not going to move! But Beth is right. This is about her life too, not just mine. I have to do what I have to do.

I'll hit them in about ten seconds if they don't move. Stay focused. Don't brake. Nine seconds. Eight. Seven. Keep breathing. Five. Four. They aren't budging. Two. Suddenly, the wall of red doomsdayers parts like the Red Sea.

"Yes!"

We screech past them and down the hill. Several blocks later I try to brake, but the old Beetle keeps zooming ahead at full speed.

"Slow down!" screeches Beth.

"It won't stop!"

At the bottom of the hill, we fly through an empty intersection into the Southlands area where another group of doomsdayers is marching. I swerve and smash through the wooden barricade blocking Balaclava Avenue. A shard of wood rockets through the broken windshield and impales my cheek. I don't even have time to scream. There is another group of doomsdayers ahead.

"Look out!"

"Hold on!" I swerve straight into a hedge and we're thrown forward. "Let's get out of here," I shout above the revving engine.

I manage to open my door against the network of branches and climb through sharp twigs. Beth follows my path because her door won't open. We're surrounded by doomsdayers.

"Hurry!"

In the time it takes for Beth to join me, I notice a metal platform on the adjacent property. I am familiar with this area and have never seen this before, but it's the only way to avoid the doomsdayers.

We run for it, but our feet are sticking to the driveway. There is a light coating of the same mud-tar combo that is in the bog area of the Garden. It's not sticky enough to stop us but does slow us down.

I'm out of breath by the time we reach the platform, and phlegm is building up yet again. We are approaching a fork in the road, with three options to choose from. While studying our options, I yank the shard of wood from my cheek, wincing.

We choose the path straight ahead which seems to be clear of doomsdayers. We're surrounded by a freeway of metal platforms leading every which way, chanting doomsdayers marching upon many of them.

Now it's clear exactly what the metal platform is for. What I saw from the window of the office where we slept isn't a platform at all. It's a bridge. A bridge over the pitch-black abyss.

Hanging from the sides of the platform railings are banners that all say one thing: "Doom". That seems less like a statement and more like a fair observation now. This whole damn place is doomed, and we will be too if we don't escape.

I study the bridges ahead like I'm playing Pac-Man, trying to avoid the paths where we'll run into the red, green, or whatever color doomsdayers. Unless the player is a world champion, Pac-Man rams into his enemies at some point. And like often happens with Pac-Man, we discover we have made a wrong turn. We're surrounded by "ghosts" that may end our game. Permanently.

Ahead, a group of green-attired doomsdayers awaits. A group of red baddies are not far behind us. They have all stopped in position, knowing we're cornered. The repetitive chants have evolved.

"Doom. Doom. Doom. Doom. Into the abyss. Into the abyss. Doom. Doom. Doom. Doom. Into the abyss. Into the abyss."

"Oh my God!" says Beth. "They want to throw us over! Into the black hole!"

Suddenly, things start to piece together. I dare to lean over the railing, squinting to try and see through the black nothing below. "I know where the lightway is!"

"That doesn't help us now!"

We're surrounded by more doomsdayers than we have darts. They are moving in on us like the walls of a garbage compactor.

"Quick, Beth. Figure out where we are. Exactly where we are. And where we need to be." I quickly untie one side of a banner. It flutters to the platform while I untie the other side. I hand Beth one end.

"No good." She points to a platform about fifty feet away. "We need to get over there if we have any chance at all."

"There is always a chance. Now, do we let them choose our fate? Or do we make our own?"

Beth's lips show the hint of a smirk. She steps onto the lower railing and sits on the edge of the top railing, gripping it with one hand and the banner with the other. I do the same. The doomsdayers speed up their pace, muttering, the chanting quickening.

"Thank you for coming back for me, Syn," Beth says, tears brimming. "I love you."

"I'll share my sentiments when we get there." I wink and climb onto the railing, stretching the banner taut. "Whatever you do, no matter how hopeless it seems, promise you won't let go."

"I'll never let go."

Tears streaming down our cheeks, our eyes locked on each other, we leap off the railing. Gloved hands claw the air behind us as we fall…into the abyss.

Chapter 36

Journey to the Center of the Earth

"SYN! BETH!"

Did I imagine it or did someone call our names as we fell into the pit of darkness? That voice.... Clinging to the canvas banner with one hand and with Beth a few feet away, thoughts of what I may have heard are replaced by intense fear.

The last time I took a literal leap of faith wasn't long ago. This is scarier by far. So much more is unknown this time. The odds of survival are even slimmer than during my last jump, which landed me on the back of that Creeper bird. Plus, this time, my life isn't the only one at risk. Whatever fate waits will be shared by my sister. The sister I came to the Garden to save.

I had thought that the black hole was directly below the platform, yet we fall for what seems like forever. I feel the rush of the plunge, my backpack suspended above my shoulders, my hair streaming after me. The banner is flapping wildly, threatening to be snatched from my hold. I clutch it desperately, like a security blanket. It offers comfort because I know that Beth is holding the other end.

Even if I wanted to scream or call out Beth's name, that's not possible. The air pressure from the fall is intense and I can barely breathe! Suddenly, everything goes black. Not pitch-black but *nothing* black, as though I'm blind.

We continue to freefall through nothing when vertigo hits. Everything is spinning. All around me, within the dark nothing are images like 3D projections at the planetarium. Events from my life, good and bad, flash before my eyes:

My first memory of coughing blood into the sink.

Hospital visits that followed and meeting Janna there.

My parents in a yelling match with Masie Winters, which I'm listening to from the top of the stairway.

Mom waking me in the middle of the night; the last time I saw her.

Aunt Ruth embracing me for the first time after my parents disappeared

Aunt Ruth visiting me at the hospital.

Defending Ebby from a bully in French class.

My first date with Jon, watching the Annie remake at Redfern Cinema.

My awkward but special first kiss with Jon.

Mom jabbing my thigh with a long needle as Dad holds me down. Wait, that never happened!

Being pushed into the pond in my garden at home.

Meeting Rose, Flint, Lily, and Cole.

Someone slicing my bare chest open with a scalpel. That never happened either!

Hugging a maskless Synister. That certainly never happened!

Beth defending me from the Creeper dogs.

Hugging Beth after realizing she's my sister.

A dozen shadowy figures standing outside my house at night. What?!

Cole smashing my face against the stairwell landing inside the house.

Being tied to a chair, seeing my defeated, aged parents on the computer screen, captive in the bubble.

Smashing the blue dome in a rage.

Witnessing Synister's death.

Kissing a tall, blonde boy at the beach. A boy I've never seen in my life?!

Cole holding Beth captive.

Aunt Ruth…In the Garden?! I lean close to tell her something. She looks terribly concerned.

Rescuing Beth from the bubble.

Beth and I jumping off the railing of the metal bridge, hearing our names being called.

Falling through the black abyss, watching the projections I'm seeing right now.

Suddenly, there is a flash of light below. I see Beth! She's still holding tightly to the other side of our lifeline, her head bent down to see what waits below. The light grows brighter. So bright, I have to squint to see Beth. Gradually, the light eats up the darkness. Time slows.

I was right! Now I know where the people falling from the sky came from. *The abyss!* Not that this bit of knowledge will help us now.

Time speeds up again, returning to normal. I manage to catch my breath in the nick of time. The lightway disappears and we drop from the sky, freefalling through the clouds. My lungs are taking a beating. Even if by a miracle we survive, I may not have any life left in me.

We plunge below the clouds, getting a bird's-eye view of the Garden, fog borders, bog, cabins, and all. The platform above the stairway is hovering at our level. Just floating there. How bizarre! The banner is billowing above us like a parachute, our legs are swaying from side to side. We are not slowing down! My lungs are clogging up. It feels like they are on fire.

Everything below is rapidly growing larger. I try to clear my mind and figure out where we are going to…land…and am pretty sure it's near the Square. A patch of grass that in a minute will be our deathbed. I begin to feel lightheaded. Close to passing out.

"Syn! Hold on!" Her voice trails to nothing.

I can't. *I must.* Hold on to that banner. Stay conscious. Not much longer.

Closer. Almost there. There's the Square, the well. Something moving. Maybe Creepers. Bushy treetops. Closer. We sway again from a gust of wind, which directs us straight for a tree.

Don't sway. *Don't sway now.* That tree could be our salvation. *Or it could impale us.*

Almost there. Sway to the left. *Damn it.* Only grass below again. Right when we're about to sail past the tree, the wind swings us over it again.

My clothes are torn. I'm whacked in the face by branches. The banner shreds the instant it connects with the tree. I hold on for dear life and try to breathe, but my lungs are so full of phlegm!

The banner feels less resistant, and not because it has been shredded. Beth is no longer holding the other end!

Beth!

I fall. Either to my end or breaking every bone in my body. *Or not.*

The remainder of the banner is clinging to a branch. My arms are yanked almost out of their sockets as I bounce up a few yards, then down again, dangling from the canvas about ten feet above ground. The banner tears again. A piece no larger than a glove is all that remains clutched in my fist. The canvas stretches, tears, lowers me a few more feet. I meet the ground in a flash, coughing non-stop, muscles ablaze.

Chapter 37

The Astonishing Ant-Man

I CAN BARELY BREATHE AND am at risk of being captured by Cole or one of his Creepers, yet only one thought fills my head.

Beth!

Wincing from pain, I manage to twist around. She's nowhere to be seen. Someone might hear me coughing, but my lungs are seriously gunked up again. The treatment is wearing off. Not that the fall helped. I've never heard of anyone with CF going skydiving. Essentially, that's what has happened. *Without a friggin' parachute.* And I survived! My dart gun is gone though.

I lie on the ground for a few more minutes, giving myself a chance to recover. As badly as I feel, the Dr. Freeman I met in Bugtopia said that all my symptoms would return when the injection wore off. I'm not quite there yet. But it's coming—it's been three days since the treatment. I struggle to stand. Nothing is broken, yet I ache with every movement.

A rustling sound tears my attention away from my predicament. Tentatively, I crane my neck to see what's causing it. Beth! She's climbing down the tree and miraculously, seems to be fine.

When our eyes connect, I remember the promise I made right after we jumped. "I love you."

Beth smiles, relieved to see that I also survived our descent. I can't wait to hug her, but our family reunion is short-lived. Her smile fades. "Behind you!"

I twist around too quickly, grimacing from pain, and at the sight of the Creeper who greets me. There is no doubt what animal was amalgamated with this man—tall, lanky with a hunch. I'm staring at a giant ant. While he mostly resembles an ant, his scaly arms, legs, and fingers are shaped like a man's, and he's wearing loose-fitting gray sweats and a Nike sweatshirt.

Beth scuttles down the tree and rushes over, ready to fight for me, even though she has clearly lost her dart gun too.

The Ant-Man raises his hands like he's surrendering to the police. "Hey," he says in the voice of a dorky college freshman. "I won't hurt you. I swear."

"If you try to hurt either of us or yell for backup, I'll squish you like the bug you are."

"She's fierce," he says to me. "Don't worry, it won't come to that." He lowers his hands and looks around to see if anyone is listening. "I'm Larry." He politely extends a hand to Beth. She warily shakes it, and then he shakes mine. His scaly skin surprisingly feels no different than a human's.

I cough again. Man, it's painful just to cough now.

Larry looks around nervously. "We can't stay here. Let's move into the fog."

As soon as Larry sees me limping, he gently wraps my arm around his shoulder, allowing me to use him as a crutch.

Beth's suspicion of him has not faded. "My warning still stands."

"Fair enough," Larry says. "Many Garden residents have sided against you. Please know that you also have friends here."

"Why would you want to be our friend?" I ask. "Hasn't Cole convinced everyone that we're the enemy?"

"Not everyone. I'll admit that many of the Creepers would kill you on sight if Cole hadn't demanded that you are brought to him alive. Most would do it out of loyalty. They need a leader. After years of chaos underground they crave one. But some of them do it out of fear. Cole is only one man, yet they fear him. I fear him."

"Then why are you helping us?" Beth demands.

"Because I owe her everything."

"Owe me?" I ask.

"I know the truth. That it was you who helped us escape our prison. I know Cole trapped us there in the first place."

"Why do you know this and others don't?"

"Again, some doubt Cole yet fear him. Even the ones who let you escape a few days ago will remain loyal to him. We have some mutual friends here though."

"Maya."

"Yes, I'm friends with her kids. Well, only Jeremy now." His voice quivers.

"I'm sorry."

"That is all on Cole, not you. Still, I pretend to pledge my loyalty. I've seen what Cole will do to those he considers traitors. But believe me, that is all an act."

"Where are Maya and Jeremy now?" I ask.

"I've only seen them once since that horrible day. They're mourning. Maya doesn't want to see anyone. Not after what happened to her family."

"I understand."

The sound of voices and footsteps crunching on fallen leaves interrupts our conversation. "Did you hear that?" someone says.

"Time for me to go," Larry whispers. "Take care of yourselves." He promptly exits the fog, leaving us alone.

I take Beth's hand and point to the border of the fog. We walk in the direction of the bog. Probably not a place we can go now that Cole is aware of our secret entrance, but we need to get away from whoever is out here with us and have easy access to the Garden. I can't suppress my coughing much longer.

"This way!"

Still holding hands, we burst through the wall of fog and into the Garden, about two minutes from the bog.

I start coughing again. "Ow."

"We have to hide," says Beth. "This way!"

She leads me toward a group of trees and bushes. We're racing across the grass when Beth yelps and yanks me to a stop. Her head is tilted up and both hands are covering her mouth in horror.

Hanging from a tree, not more than ten feet above us are Teng and Tian, that nice Chinese couple. Dead.

Chapter 38

The Hanging Garden

TENG AND TIAN'S LIMP BODIES sway from side to side, the ropes squeaking against a branch.

"Why?"

"Why?" a voice mocks. "You know perfectly well *why*. This is on you."

Beth and I spin around and face two Creepers. A Croc-Man I've seen before, and a man who looks human except that his legs arch back like a grasshopper's.

"No need to run or try to knock us out," Grasshopper-Man says. He hops closer with his arms raised. "We're not here to hurt you, we just have a message."

I gesture at the dangling bodies. "That message?"

"No, that is a peek into the future," Croc-Man says.

"You have a message? Get to it," Beth orders.

"Coleus strung up those two," Croc-Man says, "to give you a taste of what will happen if you leave the Garden again."

"A taste?" Beth says.

"Yeah, a taste. Coleus will kill every human being here if you leave the Garden again. Every. Single. One."

"It's by his mercy that they are still live today," Croc-Man says.

"Cole's *mercy?*" snarls Beth.

"And that's not all," Grasshopper-Man says, ignoring her.

"By Coleus'…generosity," Croc-Man continues, further provoking Beth, "he is giving both of you twenty-four hours to turn yourselves in."

"If you don't," Grasshopper-Man adds, "before he hunts you both down, he'll kill every human hiding below us."

"What's wrong with you?!" I shout. "These are people's lives. Children's lives!"

"Like we said," Croc-Man replies, "this is on you. If they die, it's because you put yourselves before the people you say you care for so deeply."

"That's bullshit, and you know it!" I lunge at him and Beth grabs my arm.

"Be that as it may," Croc-Man smirks, "Cole will remain in the house and you may turn yourselves in at any time."

Both Creepers turn to leave, Grasshopper-Man leaping ten feet at a time.

"This is *not* on you," says Beth. "Not on either of us. You know that, right?"

I don't reply. "Now what do we do?"

"We sure don't turn ourselves in to that monster."

"Of course not. I'd never let anything happen to you."

"I know," Beth says with affection. "We go to the sewers now. That's what we do. We have twenty-four hours to convince the people down there to fight for their lives."

"Right. Their lives are on the line now, not just ours. Hopefully that will motivate them. There's no other way."

With my lungs still feeling weak, we decide to go to the grate entrance rather than climb down through the mud. Cole has given us time because he wants to play with us, to bait us into turning ourselves in. That means we should be able to get through the Garden without being hunted. My assumption is confirmed when the few Creepers we do see on our way to the other side of the Garden do nothing but stare. Only one calls out a warning that gives way to evil laughter, "Hey kids! Your time's running out!"

The sound of our names echoing across the Garden jogs a memory. "Beth!"

"Yeah?"

I have to cough again and Beth waits. "When we jumped, did you hear someone call our names?"

"I did!"

"Was that—? Could that have been…Dad?"

"It did sound like it. Do you really think so?"

"If he only called my name, I'd have major doubts. But he called your name too."

"He did." Beth's eyes are twinkling. "Yes, he did."

"It had to be our real dad. None of the doppel-gängers would know your name!"

"Right! We have to go back!" Beth declares.

I don't tell her I'm never going back to that horrible place. The chances of making it out alive a second time are minuscule. "First we need to get out of this mess."

"No kidding! We can't leave the Garden again until Cole is dealt with."

I remember something else. "When we were falling through the black hole, what did you see?"

"What do you mean?"

"Well, images were projected in the dark. Events from my life."

"Ok."

"You didn't see anything before we entered the lightway?

"No."

My head must have been playing tricks on me. Or maybe the images were conjured up by fear. That would explain those visions of events in my life that I've never experienced.

There are no guards on duty at the grate entrance. Beth helps me lug the grate cover to the side and climb down. We amble through the sewers for several minutes. The place appears deserted. I fear Cole might have already killed them all, that the ultimatum was a cruel joke. But then, we finally see someone.

"Syn, look. It's Lundy!"

"Lundy!"

He waves excitedly and runs up to us.

"I'm so sorry about everything," I say." And for leaving you after that thing bit you."

"You had no choice."

"Where is everyone?" Beth asks.

"They're congregating in the meeting area. Follow me...or...all that shouting."

"What's going on?" asks Beth.

"This is because of Teng and Tian," I say.

"Yeah," Lundy replies, frowning.

"Lundy, I need to talk to everyone. We have to fight back."

"I agree. Right now, he's trying to convince them that's the only way for us to survive."

"Who's he?"

The answer to my question arrives seconds later when we step into the gathering space.

"Syn!" Luke rushes through the crowd.

Chapter 39

The Calm Before the Storm

LUKE SCOOPS ME UP INTO a hug. "I was worried about you."

When he pulls away, he eyes Beth. "You must be Beth," he says and then slides his eyes in my direction. "You did it! By yourself!"

"We're not out of the woods yet," I tell him.

"We're getting there," Luke says. "I have a plan, but everyone has to be involved. And some still need convincing."

"Let me talk to them," I say.

"Alright," Luke replies, without hesitation.

He escorts me to the front of the crowded space, past threatening faces. Even Lily can't force the semblance of a smile.

"What's she doing here?" one woman shouts. "They're dead because of her."

"She's the reason we're trapped in this dungeon," another yells.

"Hey!" Luke intervenes. The chatter subsides. "Hear her out."

I look at the despair in everyone's eyes, cough a couple of times, and clear my throat. "You're right. Two good people are dead because of me. You're all here because of me. I can keep apologizing, but it won't change the truth—the only way to get out of this is to fight back."

Murmurs of disapproval erupt again.

"You're all going to die!" I scream above the uproar, then pause to catch my breath.

The voices fall silent. Faces turn towards each other, questioningly.

"What did you say?" Dawn asks.

Beth places a hand on my back. "I said that you're all going to die. Tian and Teng's murder was a warning. If Beth and I don't turn ourselves over to Cole in twenty-four hours, he will kill every single one of you."

It takes a few moments for my words to sink in before chaos explodes. "So let's turn you guys over! End this now!"

Luke whistles to silence the crowd. "You'll have to go through me. And that won't end well."

"Besides that," I say, "the Creepers could have easily captured us on our way through the Garden. Cole wants me to make a choice. A sacrifice—my sister and me, or all of you."

"This is your fault!"

"Do the right thing for once!"

"Hey!" Beth shouts. "This is not her fault. It's not my fault either! I'm not surprised that you want to throw me to the wolves. I've been alone since I was five. My parents disappeared and I was all alone, yet no one would even look my way after Synister gave her orders. You listened to a woman you didn't even know. You're all cowards. I was a kid, alone and afraid. You threw me to the wolves a long time ago!"

Silence. The room is laden with guilt. I can't help feeling guilty for not being there for my sister, even though I didn't even realize she existed.

"Now you're willing to condemn me," she continues "and the only person who ever did anything to help me. You cowards are no better than *him*."

I pull Beth close, tears forming in my eyes. Beth's eyes, however, are as dry as kindling.

She moves out of my embrace and eyes the crowd. "If you ever want to see daylight again and not have your necks roped to the branch of a tree, you have to fight back. Listen to what Luke tells you. You might earn more than your freedom. More than your lives. You might even earn some redemption."

My ten-year-old sister never ceases to amaze me.

"Let's go." She takes my hand and we press our way to the exit through the chastened crowd.

"So, everyone," says Luke, "are you ready to talk about how we do this?"

* * *

The thin layer of cardboard shifts under my feet as I lean against the corridor wall where I slept not long ago. That was when Beth was still Cole's prisoner. Now she is with me, her head resting on my lap. *We will survive this.*

After a short rest, Beth leaves in search of food. I put in a request for *anything but rat*. I'm preparing the vest for another treatment when Luke enters.

"Knock knock." He grins.

"Hey." I try to stand.

"No, stay." He squats to my level. "How are you feeling?"

"Been better. Been worse. Where were you? How long have you been here?"

"I returned about an hour after I left. And then, accidentally stepped into one of those light portals and ended up someplace else. At first, I thought I was home again. But there were a few things that didn't seem right. Then I ended up in another world—someplace totally bizarre. I was stuck there until yesterday. You wouldn't believe that place."

I smile. "I'm sure it was nothing like the world I fell from."

"What?"

"Oh, nothing."

Luke shrugs. He then proceeds to help me on with the vest.

"So, you told everyone your plan?" I ask in my familiar vibrating-vest voice.

"I told them *a* plan."

"*A* plan?"

Luke peeks outside the corridor and then sits down next to me. "The thing is, we need to think like Cole. He knows you're going to fight back. He can't expect that after all you did to save Beth, you're just going to hand her over to die. He wants you to fight back and knows you may very well have backup. Because of that, he needs to have an ace up his sleeve."

"Right."

"There's no way he can have this entire place wired. I searched up and down. Plus, Lundy told me that Cole doesn't have surveillance equipment. So, he's got to have at least one mole."

"You think someone down here would betray everyone?"

"I do. Cole could have agreed to spare them. People are built to survive, no matter what it takes."

He's right about that.

"So, anyway," Luke continues, "I spit out a plan that resembles a standard military drill I know all too well. I'll be giving everyone instructions on what to do immediately before they're deployed—when it's too late to pass on a new strategy to Cole."

"Makes sense." I hate that he used the word *deployed*, like we're heading into a war zone.

"The real plan involves everyone down here getting into place before we do. They are going to be our cover so we can get to Cole. Ideally, I'd like to take care of the guy myself, but I know you'd never submit to sitting on the sidelines."

"Never," I concur, coughing up phlegm that's already been loosened by the vest.

"So anyway, we get to Cole, capture him, and hold off the Creepers. Lundy will set up the lightway that will get us home. I brought some weapons. Real weapons. Plus, I'm making tools with stuff they have down here."

"Good."

"You rescued Beth all by yourself. So, I'm optimistic that together we can do this. I'm sure of it."

"That's what I want to hear."

"Of course, not everything will go according to plan. It never does. So, I have a plan B."

"Good."

"And a plan C."

"And no one dies. Right?"

"Syn, I have no intention of killing anyone. I've seen enough bloodshed overseas. But, if innocent lives are at stake, especially yours, I'll do what's necessary."

"Hopefully it doesn't come to that." There's a smudge of dried mud on his cheek that's been bugging me since I first noticed it in the meeting area. I reach over to wipe it off and Luke misinterprets the gesture.

"Syn," he says, gently moving my arm away, "I think you're great but—"

I can't help laughing. Luke is totally clueless. "There's mud on your cheek. I want to wipe it off."

"Oh," he says, instinctively touching his cheek, which is now turning red from embarrassment.

"You thought I was making a move?"

"Ebby does seem to be pushing for that."

"Luke, besides the fact that you're considerably older than me, I know you're not interested in girls."

Luke is speechless. "How…how do you know?"

"Just do. I've known for a long time. There's no reason to be embarrassed."

"I'm not. But…does Ebby know too?"

"No. You should tell her. Ebby would never judge you. She's not like that."

"I don't know," he says wearily.

"Oh, come on, it's 2016. I know Ebby. She'd be immediately trying to introduce you to available guys at school."

He laughs. "Yeah, you're probably right."

"I am right."

"The thing is, it may be more accepted than it used to be, but not everyone has come around. It's been…." Luke is lost in thought.

"What? You can talk to me."

After careful consideration, he says, "My dad's as big a homophobe as they come. He's aware I'm gay, but he'll never admit it. And then…."

"Yeah?"

"In Afghanistan, everyone in my squadron knew. They were totally cool." He lets out a long sigh. "Before things went haywire."

Luke stares at the tattered piece of cardboard we're sitting on, fingers the rough edge absentmindedly. Finally, he looks at me. "I joined the Armed Forces to help people, plain and simple. Some didn't want us in Afghanistan, but the villagers we protected from attacks thanked us daily. We did a lot of good and I was thankful I signed up.

"My unit consisted of young men from all parts of the US who wanted to do good. No trigger-happy jerks. They wanted to protect their country, to save lives. We all got along. Like I said, they knew I was gay. They chided me like guys do in the Marines, but it was all lighthearted and everyone got it for some reason or another. Some guys get paranoid and worry that gay soldiers might hit on them. I didn't experience any of that." He gazes at nothing in particular.

I let him take the time he needs. Ebby said he never talked about his experiences out there or why he was discharged, so I'm touched that he feels he can talk to me.

"We were stationed in a village, two hundred miles from Kandahar. It was quiet there. No action. I was playing soccer with the local kids and a few other soldiers when we received intel that there was a suspicious vehicle approaching. We were getting the last of the villagers into their homes when a beat-up cab sped our way. The driver, a father of six, lived in the village. He must have been driving a hundred miles an hour and was headed straight for us. We aimed to fire, but the car screeched to a halt forty yards away. The driver got out and put his hands up. He kept glancing at the car nervously. I knew then that the car was loaded with explosives. We all knew. Regardless, our captain ordered four men from our unit to approach the vehicle."

"Why? He didn't see the signs you did?"

"He saw them. His intentions were good, if not misguided. He wanted our men to check it out, possibly disarm the vehicle. Yet the car was far enough from any homes that we could have blown it up from a distance. He made a bad call. But, orders were orders. Jameson, Attica, Singh, and Forster approached the cab."

I dread hearing the part of the story I know is coming and try to distract myself with the task of removing the vest.

"Attica looked through the back window. He must have seen a timer or a blinking light. He yelled a warning, but it was too late. The car blew up. The driver, Attica and Singh all died instantly. They were the lucky ones. Jameson had burns over his entire body. Even with painkillers, he was in agony for two days before he died. Forster also suffered extensive burns, plus he lost both legs and the sight in one eye."

"Jeez."

"As I assumed, the Taliban had forced the driver into the village. They had his son. We didn't even know he was missing. So, two strikes against our captain. And guess what he said?"

Luke continues before I can answer. "He was distracted because I hit on him that morning. That his judgement was impaired."

"That's crazy."

"Totally. Not only did I not hit on him, but how could anyone buy that as an excuse? His father was a general, so they did the easy and cowardly thing. They demoted the captain and discharged me."

"I'm so sorry, Luke."

"The captain's rank was reinstated within a month. I was still out. You're the first person I've shared this with. Maybe because we'll be going into battle together," he says with an awkward laugh. "Anyway, I wanted to do some good, to make a difference. Because of a coward attaching an unfair label to me, I never got to finish the job."

"If it's any consolation, you have a second chance to make a difference. To save Beth and me, and give everyone living in this putrid place their lives back."

He nods, though I know that even if we win the battle against Cole, the experience Luke had will weigh on him for a long time.

Just as I'm wondering why Beth is taking so long, she storms into the room in a panic. "Creepers are here!"

I toss the vest aside and jump up.

"You should stay here," says Luke.

"Fat chance." I'm the first one through the door.

As we charge to the mud wall entrance, panicked voices echo off the tunnel walls. Rat-Man and one of the croc-men, two of the Creepers from the cheering crowd who watched Cole pummel me, are standing in front of the mud wall. Rat-Man disappears through the wall, while Croc-Man begins to claw his way through, shouting, "We know what you're planning! Coleus will soon know too." He slides out of sight as if sucked through the mud.

"Son of a—"

The sound of a muffled gunshot coming from where the Creepers have escaped startles us. There's another. And another. Something is inching back through the mud into the tunnel. Croc-Man drops onto the cement, covered in muddy tar, blood spurting from his chest. Then Rat-Man slides out, also bleeding.

We're all staring in disbelief at the sewer water that's turning red when two more figures thrust their way through the wall. They're people, not Creepers, and each one is holding a gun. As they wipe the guck off their faces, Beth and I gasp.

Standing in front of us are the last two people we expect to see—our parents!

Chapter 40

Meet the Parents

AFTER AWKWARD, QUICK INTRODUCTIONS, Luke leaves Beth and me alone with our parents.

My parents! How strange to see them standing across from me right now. Not other versions of them, not in a bubble on a computer monitor—in real life— the two people who gave birth to me and raised me until I was five, and then vanished.

As they wash the muck off in the shallow pool of sewer water, I notice how jubilant Beth is. Why am I not overjoyed too? After they're cleaned up, I notice they are dressed in very familiar black leather jackets.

"Deb," Dad says, lightly stroking a finger across Beth's cheek. "Both our girls, together. Would you have ever believed it?"

"And they've grown up so much," Mom says, unable to take her eyes off of us. "You grew into such beautiful and amazing young girls."

Beth hammers them with questions on the way to the room where people congregated earlier. I have a ton of my own questions, but let her have the first go.

"Something happened," Mom says after Beth asks how they escaped. "One minute we were in the bubble and the next we were in front of the house."

"We were hungry and weak," Dad says. "There was a commotion inside. The rain was hammering down on us and we weren't feeling well. The Garden's properties weren't doing anything for our pain and discomfort. That two-faced maniac was screaming inside the house so we made our way into the sewers, avoiding the Creepers, and went to a world we were familiar with. We had to get away before our disfigured captor and her Creeper boyfriend realized we had escaped."

That must have been after I smashed the blue dome. This happened as Synister died in Cole's arms, right before he chased me and kidnapped Beth. They were there, outside the house, and had no clue their daughter was inside.

"The captor," I say. "You mean Synister."

"Is that what she calls herself?" Dad asks. "Whatever her name is, she's a psychopath."

"She *was* a psychopath," I correct him.

"She's dead?" Mom asks. "Good riddance."

"Good riddance? No!" I glare at my mother. "She was a girl. Like me."

"She wasn't like you at all. She imprisoned us for years, kept us away from family."

"Because you held her captive, tortured her, made her what she was."

"We did it for you Syn," says Dad gently. "To give you a better life."

"You tortured and killed girls for *me*?!"

"Was that you who yelled our names when we jumped into the black hole?" Beth asks, eagerly changing the subject.

"It was," Mom replies. "After we regained our strength, we wanted to return to the Garden. We had no idea that Syn was here but wanted to at least find you."

"We looked everywhere, but couldn't locate the lightway in that world," Dad adds. "To stay alive while searching, we stole some outfits from those nut jobs and infiltrated one of the factions."

"Did you kill anyone?" It's an accusation more than a question. "Did you throw anyone into the black hole?"

"Syn, we're not monsters," Mom says.

"Isn't it your fault that Doom World is in utter chaos to begin with?"

"Syn," Beth says, "they just got here. We haven't seen them in years."

"How *did* you get here?" I ask, ignoring Beth's plea.

"We saw the two of you jump and realized that was the lightway," Dad explains. "Fearing the worst, we had to get to you both as soon as we could. We found some parachutes at an abandoned military base and came as soon as we were able. Perfect timing too, if you ask me."

I don't even bother asking how they knew where in the Garden to find us. Instead, I pelt them with more accusations. "So, you were in Doom World for what? Weeks? Months? Neither of you could figure out where the lightway was? We figured it out in two days!"

Beth tries to calm me down.

"It's okay, Beth," Mom says. "Syn, we're scientists. Scientifically, it didn't make sense that the lightway would be where it was."

"How so?"

"That empty black nothing in the crater…. Well, it's hard to describe. We call it Oblivion."

"Oblivion?" Beth asks, as confused as I am.

"Yes. Oblivion is the core of every universe, every timeline in history. It's not a substance. It's not an element. It wouldn't take us anywhere because it's not anywhere to begin with. It just is."

"That was Masie's area," Dad pipes in. "As are the lightways, travel through the multiverse and such. These are things we've played with that we were not as knowledgeable about as we had thought."

"Masie," Mom says, suddenly on alert. "Have you seen her, Synthia? Has she hurt you?"

"I haven't seen her. She's dead."

Our parents are astonished.

"Not long after you went missing, the police found three bodies, burnt to a crisp. One was identified as hers."

"Who killed her?" Mom asks. "And who did the other bodies belong to?"

"They never found out who did it. The police assumed that the other bodies were yours. They were too charred to identify."

Mom covers her mouth in horror. "All these years you thought we were dead?"

"No." Tears are forming in my eyes. "I always believed that you were out there somewhere."

"Oh, Sweetie," Mom says, clasping my hands in hers. "Who took care of you?"

"Aunt Ruth."

"I'm so glad. She never wanted kids of her own."

"She's been like a mother to me." I add, knowing that would be painful for Mom to hear.

"Who took care of you, Beth?" Dad asks.

"She took care of herself," I answer before Beth can. "She had no one."

"But I do now," Beth says quickly. "A real family."

"You do," Mom says. "You both do."

As we near the meeting room, Beth walks sandwiched between our parents, holding their hands. For the first time since I rescued her, she comes across as a little girl, vulnerable and innocent. I'm happy for her, but wish I was as happy to see Mom and Dad as she is. I've waited for this for years. But the things they did. The kids they tortured, the people they killed. How could I ignore all of that?

By the time we reach the meeting room, I'm coughing again.

"How are you feeling, Syn?" Dad asks.

"I've been a lot worse."

"You shouldn't be here." He frowns. "The healing factor doesn't work now. You need to be where you can receive medical care."

"I didn't have a choice."

We approach one of the tables. Beth and I sit on one side, our parents on the other.

"What do you mean you didn't have a choice?" Mom asks.

"I had to come because Cole kidnapped Beth."

"What?!"

"Mom, Syn saved me." Beth is beaming. "She was really sick. But she still came here, got past Cole, and saved me."

"I'm proud of you, Syn," Mom says. "But we've got to get you home."

"We can't leave," Beth says. "Cole closed the lightway to our world."

I fill them in on Cole's threat and Luke's plan.

"This friend of yours," Dad says, "Luke. You trust him?"

"Yes."

Our parents agree to work with Luke. They can help because they know this place. They *created* this place.

They are also responsible for all the death that has occurred in these worlds. I can't let that go. "What made you do this? Why did you create all of this?"

"You know why, Syn," Dad says. "We did it for you. So you could have a normal life, grow up, and have a family of your own."

"You should have let me be."

Mom glances at Dad, trying to make sense of my words.

"You should have let me live with the disease I was born with, have a normal life with my real parents. Terminal illness or not, it would have been a happy life. Instead, I grew up without parents, with no clue what happened to them, and with so many questions. Part of my heart was always missing. I had a sister I didn't even know about."

"Syn..." Mom starts.

"You did this all for me?" Angry tears are streaming down my cheeks. "Well, I'll tell you what. You shouldn't have bothered."

"We couldn't do nothing," Dad says. "We had to try."

"All you needed to do was be there for me and support me. Like the parents every kid needs." I am coughing again.

Mom reaches a caring hand across the table and I refuse it.

Dad speaks when my coughing subsides. "When does this rebellion go down?"

"1 A.M."

"It was still light outside when we came down. Why don't you two get some sleep? We're going to talk to Luke."

I reluctantly agree, only because my body needs rest if I'm going to have any chance in this fight. Soon, Beth and I are back in our corridor, lying under ragged blankets. We never did eat anything, so we nibble on some munchies Luke brought. I'm relieved to be feeling okay and hope the treatment Dr. Freeman gave me in Bugtopia will hold back the worst of my symptoms until after the upcoming ordeal.

"I know they've done bad things," Beth says, "but they're still our parents. And they're finally with us again."

"I know." I wonder if that's a good thing or a bad thing.

Chapter 41

Of Course You Know…

FOR THE PAST ELEVEN YEARS, I have struggled through life, growing up without my parents. Now, they are sitting by my side as I swallow my pills. Mom takes the bottle of water from my hand when I'm done and twists the cap back on. They are being overly attentive, like I'm a baby who needs help with everything.

We fill up on packaged foods Luke brought. It seems like he raided a vending machine. Chips, brownies, pretzels, oh my. I have managed to go through my entire stay in the Sewers Apartment Complex without sampling their famous rat dish. The food energizes me. Hopefully, this isn't my last meal.

The corridors are empty as my parents and I head to the mud wall where Luke and Beth are waiting. Where my parents made their "killer" entrance earlier. I wonder if the bodies of the dead Creepers still lie there, which reminds me of something.

"I need you to make me a promise."

"Anything." Mom takes my hand.

"No one dies."

Moms hands fall away from mine like she truly doesn't understand the request.

"You killed two Creepers yesterday. That can't happen again."

"Syn," Dad says, "we'll do whatever it takes to protect you and your sister."

"That's what I'm afraid of. Listen, if it's a matter of life or death, I won't fault you. But if there is any other option, please go with that."

"What about Cole?" Mom asks. "You surely can't expect us to let him live after everything he's done?"

"I absolutely expect that! Don't you think you've killed enough people? Luke promised to capture him unless there's no other way."

"This is war, Synthia," Dad says. "People die in war."

"When I leave here, I want to know that the Garden will be a world where people and Creepers can live in peace. If you start shooting and kill Cole, who the Creepers see as their leader, he'll become a martyr to them. The Garden will be in worse shape than it is now. So we capture him. Alive."

"The Garden isn't a society," Dad says. "We brought people here so that if we weren't able to find a cure, you could still grow up in a community. But as long as there are no healing properties, this is nothing more than a failed test site. The people here, and the Creepers, are just lab rats."

"What's wrong with you?! These are human beings. You kidnapped them, wiped their minds as if their lives meant nothing. Can't you take any responsibility for what you've done?"

Dad shakes his head. "Syn—"

"You stole everything from these people! You owe every person here, every Creeper, the best life possible. Maybe you created the Garden, but you don't get to label it as a test site. It is a society!"

Mom looks defeated.

"I swear to you both. If you kill anyone when there is another way, Cole included, I'll never talk to either of you again!"

Leaving my parents in the shadows, I storm off, coughing my way down the corridor. When I reach the mud wall, I am comforted to see Luke and Beth, and relieved that the bodies of those two Creepers are gone.

Luke seems anxious. "Please stay down here, Syn. Until this is over."

"Not a chance. This is my battle. I'm sure Beth told you she won't stay behind either."

"Six times," Beth says with a smirk. Her smirk vanishes suddenly when I have another wicked coughing fit.

"That treatment you got in Bugtopia is wearing off. You should stay down here."

"What treatment?" Luke asks.

"Our parents in another world developed it. Syn got really sick in one of the worlds we ended up in and had to go to the hospital. The treatment helped suppress her symptoms, so we could find our way back to the Garden. It's like a miracle drug."

"Wow!"

I can hear my parents coming.

"Hey, you should tell them, Syn!" exclaims Beth. "That would mean the world to them."

"Shhh!" I give her the eye, and then Luke. "Please don't. Not now."

I don't give our parents more than a glance when they join us at the mud wall. Luke hands everyone weapons. My parents and Luke are already wearing artillery belts, and each of them is armed with two shotguns.

Luke straps an artillery belt around Beth's waist and then mine. Unlike his, ours aren't equipped with revolvers. We are armed only with a dart gun, an electric prod, and a couple of smoke bombs. If everything goes according to plan, we won't need them.

"Okay, stay where you are for ten minutes, while we get into position," Luke tells us.

"Make it twenty," Mom says.

Mom is planning something. Wish I knew what.

Luke hugs me, lifting my feet off the ground. When he lets go, my parents are waiting to do the same.

I back away, eyeing their weapons. "Remember what I said."

"I love you both," Mom says.

"Ditto," says Dad.

I want to reciprocate feelings of love for my parents but because of what they've done, I decide to remain silent. They pause expectantly, their hearts breaking. After they have exited through the mud wall, deep regret about not returning their affection claws at my heart.

* * *

I push my head through the mud surface and gasp for fresh air, coughing as dirty water trickles into my mouth. I wipe a sleeve across my lips to get rid of the mud and to muffle the coughing. We can't alert any Creepers to our presence. I'm still splashing mud off my weapons with bog water when Beth whips out her muddy dart gun.

I freeze. "What is it?"

"Shhh, listen!"

There is rustling in the bushes. I draw my dart gun and glance every which way. We seem to be alone. The rustling ceases. All that's left to hear is frogs croaking, bugs buzzing, and crickets chirping, and my own heavy breathing because my nasal passages are blocked.

Beth switches her flashlight on at the lowest level, but after leaving the bog we realize we don't need it because there is adequate light from nearby lightways. We dart past the spiral staircase, across the farm and into the orchard. We exit the protection of the orchard, lights from the house now illuminating our path.

The field next to the house is empty, except for two figures. Snake-Man is standing behind Rose, pressing a dart gun against her head. One we dropped while falling through the abyss, probably. Even just a tranquilizer dart will do serious damage being shot point-blank into her head. It might even kill her.

It doesn't appear Snake-Man has spotted us. "Get down, Beth! Follow me."

We crawl across the grass, the two long shadows before us growing ever closer. Snake-Man's tail stands straight up and starts to rattle when we're barely six feet away.

"Don't come any closer!"

Slowly, we rise to our feet.

"Okay," I tell him.

"Put your weapons down."

I lay mine down. Beth keeps aiming hers.

"You'll hit Rose!"

"I told you to put it down!" Snake-Man bellows.

"Put yours down first," Beth orders.

The Creeper presses the dart gun forcefully against Rose's head. She winces yet avoids eye contact with me.

Then it hits me. Luke was sure there would be at least one mole. Rose wouldn't want to hurt me, but Cole has leverage on her. Flint. Cole would love to see me betrayed by a friend.

"Beth," I whisper.

"I'm not standing down, Syn. Sorry, but you're not going to like this."

"No. Do it anyway."

My words startle Beth, but she isn't distracted for long. She shoots a dart into Rose's shoulder. Rose looks shocked, possibly even relieved as she collapses. Snake-Man is stunned. I yank the electric prod from my belt and charge, aiming for his belly. He convulses from the shock and collapses to his knees, tail rattling non-stop.

Applause rains down from above. A familiar silhouette is standing at the edge of the roof. "Bravo, Synthia! I didn't think you'd ever consider that a Judas was in your midst. Hey, since you brought backup and came prepared for a fight, I am revoking my offer to turn yourselves in."

BLAM!

The rooftop silhouette staggers.

BLAM!

The silhouette falls two stories.

"No!" I run to the body. There are two bloody bullet holes in Crystal's naked stomach. Blood flows from the chameleon girl's mouth as she attempts to speak. The sound of liquid gurgling in her throat is all that is audible. Cole's unwilling shield goes limp.

Cole is still standing on the roof. "Surprise!" he sneers and applauds again.

Seething with more contempt than I've ever had for anyone, I watch him scamper across the roof and fade into the shadows.

"Syn!" Beth is alarmed.

Creepers are appearing from the shadows one by one. We're surrounded. Some are holding weapons, some are using fear-stricken residents of the sewers as shields.

"Alright then!" Cole's voice projects like he's using a megaphone. "Synthia. Remember how I gave you a chance to turn yourself in? To spare the lives of everyone? Well, I'd say the clock is still ticking but clearly you have decided to reject my offer. You have put yourself above everyone else. So know this—you alone are responsible for what happens next."

I stare into the petrified faces of the prisoners. Dawn, Bear, Fawn. Nell looks like she has accepted that this is the end of the road. Poor Lily is shivering like she's been pulled from a frozen lake, desperate for me to do something, anything.

I feel helpless. I clear my throat and ask, "What happens next?"

Cole's lips twist into the sadistic grin that has become all too familiar. "Because of you, Synthia Wade. Because of you, *everyone* dies!"

Chapter 42

This Means War

WHEN LUKE SHARED HIS PLAN with me, it seemed solid. People were to sneak into the cabins in the dead of night and subdue the Creepers so we would face less resistance when we went up against Cole. Rose was one of the people on that mission. Luke didn't think she was right for the job. However, she insisted on going to her old cabin to reunite with Flint. And now, an ally is dead. Poor Crystal.

Nobody else can die.

As I reach for my belt, a metal canister flies from the bushes and lands on the ground in front of the Creepers. On impact, smoke billows from the canister and blankets the area. From within the smoky cloud erupts screaming, the smacking sound of fists hitting flesh, bones cracking. No gunshots—Luke and our parents are on this!

A glimmer of jubilation sparks inside of me. I grab Beth's hand and we race around the smoky battle cloud, take cover behind some bushes, and wait for the smoke to clear. While the fighting continues, I let out a few overdue coughs that no one will hear over all the noise, and try to pinpoint where Cole might be.

As the smoke dissipates all I can hear is whispering, wheezing, and coughing. It thins enough to reveal shreds of clothing strewn about, stained with blood, and seven motionless bodies on the ground—five are Creepers, two are human. One of the humans is a man I don't know, the other is Nell. I run to her, Beth to the man.

"He's breathing!"

I gently lift Nell's head, relieved as her breath brushes my cheek. Her eyes flutter open, and then close.

"The Creepers are all unconscious," Beth says. "I'm going to move this guy to the side, so he doesn't wake up surrounded by the enemy." She drags him about twenty feet, even though she's only half his weight. I feel guilty not helping, but don't have the strength. A gunshot echoes in the distance. Then another, followed by screaming.

"Damn it," I mutter. "Beth, help me get Nell someplace safe so we can join Luke and our parents."

We prop up Nell, so she's mostly leaning against Beth. Three excruciatingly long minutes later, a cabin comes into view. So near and yet so far. I am out of breath and can't even muster the energy to cough. We balance Nell against the outside wall of the cabin.

"Let me go in and check it out," Beth says, her dart gun raised.

Just as Beth enters the cabin, there is a strange buzzing noise behind me. Another Creeper.

This one has the body of a human, but his head is extra-long, oval shaped, with six fly-like eyes alongside his nose. He's holding a sharp-edged stick. Before I even have time to let Nell slip from my arms and defend myself, a dart whizzes past my shoulder and lodges in Fly-Guy's chest.

"I can't leave you alone for a second," Beth teases.

We're both startled when another gunshot as loud as thunder cracks through the air.

"Quick, let's get her inside!"

"Ugh." Beth gags. "This place is a sty."

The air is thick with a putrid, rotting smell. The floor is littered with dirt, discarded food, and garbage. Four filthy mattresses are spread across the floor, strewn with food wrappers.

I'm about to puke. "Let's try the other room."

While lacking the décor of a two-star hotel, it's an improvement. We ease Nell onto the bed. I sit down beside her for a minute to rest and clear some phlegm from my throat. "I hate to leave her here."

"We have no choice. You okay now? We need to keep moving."

We face an unwelcome but familiar Creeper when we return to the main room. Rat-Girl is holding the second of our lost dart guns from the abyss freefall.

"Now it's my turn," she says.

"Get down!" Beth flicks off the light so that all we can see is Rat-Girl's silhouette in front of the window. From a crouching position in the corner, I listen to Beth's footsteps charging across the room, followed by several thumps and a few yelps—thankfully not my sister's—and then one loud thud on the floor. Now, Beth's silhouette is standing at the window in place of Rat-Girl's.

"Let's get outta here!"

"You're amazing," I say when we meet at the front door. "You know that, right?"

"I know."

I bump into someone while opening the door.

"Flint!"

"Syn! Where's my mom? Is she—"

"She's okay, just knocked out."

"What! Where?"

I barely get the words out and Flint charges off, flinching as two more gunshots pop.

"He'll probably never speak to me again when he finds out we're the reason Rose is unconscious."

"Let's get moving!"

We press off in the direction of the house. Our path takes us around a lightway. It disappears and the flash of another replaces it. We approach the house cautiously, following the perimeter alongside the bushes.

Beth nudges me and stops. From where we're crouched we can easily make out the shape of the head and wings of the Creeper bird. It's on guard, perched on the roof above the back door of the house, ready to attack and indulge in its next meal. There are traces of a fight on the ground below its perch. No visible victims, but shreds of clothing and broken sticks, and voices coming around the corner of the house.

We adjust our path and manage to get to the empty carport without the Creeper bird spotting us. It's quiet. Too quiet.

Beth inches towards the other end of the carport with me following closely. Suddenly, I'm grabbed from behind. One arm clamps around my waist and lifts me into the air; a large hand covers my mouth. I sink my teeth into the hand, but whoever is holding me doesn't loosen their grip. The faint taste of blood in my mouth makes me gag. My captor spins me around and races with me down the driveway. There are footsteps running behind us. Are they in pursuit or do they have Beth?

A voice bellows behind us. "Over there!"

There is a dull thud to our left. Smoke clouds our path and I fight to see in front of us. Still, we're on the move. I can barely breathe now, from the exertion, the hand pressed against my mouth, and from the smoke that's growing thicker. Just when I think I'm going to pass out, we've reached the fog.

I'm forced through a winding path past trees, footsteps still on our tail. I bite down hard on the hand again and this time I'm freed.

Before I have a chance to scream, my captor whispers, "Syn, it's me!"

Dad!

"Be quiet and hang on while we lose them."

"Where's Beth?"

"Behind us. With Mom."

"This isn't helping my congestion," I wheeze.

"We're almost there."

When we stop, Dad lets me down and investigates the bite on his hand.

I cough freely and after clearing my throat, confront Dad angrily. "What the hell?"

Mom touches my shoulder. "Syn, there were threats you and your sister didn't see. You were walking right into them."

"You were being followed," Dad adds. "Luke handled them while we got you to safety."

Dad hands me a puffer. I inhale the vapors and hand it back as he hands me the second one. When I'm done, I don't feel any better. My lungs are clogged big time and getting worse.

Beth is by my side. "What's happening?"

"Your friend Luke has impressive tactical skills," Mom answers. "But the two-faced tyrant has been ahead of us every step."

"Luke insists on helping the injured before we break into the house," Dad says.

"Good," I reply. "How are they?"

"Two causalities. Everyone else we found is safe now."

"Casualties. Who?"

"No idea," answers Dad. "A man and a woman. For now, we have to get you to safety and make a play to take out Cole."

"Take him out?" My temper is fired up again. "Like you tried to do when he was on the roof? That was you, right?"

"It was. I had an opportunity to end things right then and there."

"No, you didn't. You killed an innocent girl!"

"Calm down, Synthia," Mom says. "And lower your voice."

"She was not innocent," insisted Dad. "She was one of them."

"No!" I hiss. "There is no *them*. She was a good person. She stood up for Beth and me. You killed her!"

"I was aiming for Cole."

"But, you promised. You swore you wouldn't."

"Syn," says Dad, "My priority is getting you home to a doctor. My priority is to protect you. It always has been. That's what your mom and I have been doing since the day you were born. Good parents do whatever it takes to protect their children."

"Good parents? Good parents don't kill innocent people. They don't torture and kill children!"

"Please," Beth whispers. "Not now."

"Not now? Then when? Dad says he is a good parent. He may be that in your eyes." I face my dad. "But to me? You're not a father. I have no father."

"Syn!"

"And you're not my mother," I say, hating the tears forming in my eyes. "My mother's name is Ruth. She's been there for me, like a mother. Being the best she can be, even if one day she has to let me go. Killing someone would never have crossed her mind."

I whirl to face my dad again. "Besides not being a father, you're not even close to being a good person. You justify your sins by claiming you're protecting your kids, when all you are is a sad old man who wasted his life trying to save someone who never even knew him."

There is dead silence. I study my father through hateful tears. His eyes are empty. Expressionless. Like a man who has nothing left worth living for.

Why doesn't he say something? The answer to that is soon apparent.

I gasp. Blood has begun to trickle from one corner of his mouth. The sharp point of a machete is protruding from his chest. The blade is retracted without a sound, and my father's body falls forward. Mom yanks me out of the way.

I'm paralyzed, wrapped tightly in Mom's arms. Beth kneels over my dad's lifeless body and screams. And then I see Cole, standing where my father had stood seconds ago, grinning sadistically, primed for another kill. I pull my eyes away from his, only to be transfixed by the sight of his fingers tenderly tracing the bloody blade.

"One Wade down," Cole snarls. "Two more to go."

Chapter 43

Casualties of War

MOM IS IN A STATE of shock. No longer registering that Cole is standing next to us brandishing a bloody knife, I wrestle from her arms and sink to my knees, cradling my father's face in my hands. "No!" Then, sobbing, take his hand in mine and gently kiss where I had bitten him. His hand is warm. I look up at Mom. Then at Beth.

She is motionless, detached—will not look at me. Her attention is fixated on only one thing and before I can stop her, she has drawn the handgun from my father's holster.

BLAM!

I jump at the sound of the gunshot.

"I'm going to kill you!" Beth fires another shot, but Cole has vanished into the fog. Stiffly, she goes over to where he was standing, shoots off three more rounds before the gun only clicks.

I leap to my feet and wrap my arms around her. She fights me at first but then a whimper of despair sends her burrowing into me. We both break down. I watch Mom from the corner of my eye. Finally able to process what has happened, she pulls out her gun.

"Cole won't return," I tell her. "This is a game. A game he's playing with me." He said *Two to go.* Not three. *Two.* He plans to let me live so I can suffer as my family is taken from me, one by one. Cole intends to kill Mom next because killing Beth will be like stabbing me in the heart. Yes, he will save Beth for last. *I won't let that happen.*

Mom is stoic. She tries to console us. "Mom," I sputter, "the things I said…right before—"

"You didn't do this." She gazes at me intently. "Understand?"

"But, the last thing Dad experienced…the daughter he had dedicated his entire life to save…condemned him for it. I broke his heart. I know I did." The fact that I said it during the last moments of his life is too much to bear.

"It was Cole," Beth says. "It was all him!"

"I won't kill him," Mom says. "You have my word."

"I *will* kill him," seethes Beth.

A part of me wants to kill Cole too. I hate him for making me feel that way.

Mom promises that we'll give Dad a proper burial. For now, all we can do is move on. She leads us through the fog for about five minutes, each of us cloaked in grief, one foot in front of the other, one breath at a time.

"I think this is the spot." She pokes her head through the misty wall. "It's clear. How are you feeling, Syn?"

I know she means physically, beyond my grief. The thing is, though my mind has obviously been elsewhere, when I take a few seconds to think about it, I'm not feeling too good. The effects of the treatment Dr. Freeman injected me with are definitely wearing off.

"I'm okay." It's not a lie. Relatively speaking, I am okay. The question is, how will I feel in ten minutes, or twenty, or in an hour?

Mom takes the gun from Beth and reloads it like she's done it a million times. She hands it back to Beth.

"Mom, seriously?"

"We're fighting for our lives, Syn."

It's awful to see my ten-year-old sister armed with a loaded gun, although the thought of her unable to protect herself is even worse.

"Now, neither of you will agree to sit this out," Mom says, "but I've seen what's out there. That bastard intends to pick us off, one by one, and you guys must stay hidden until I find Luke. We'll come for you and make a new plan to get into the house. Once I'm in the house, I can fix this whole mess."

"You really will come back for us?" I ask. "You're not going to handle this yourself? If you'd let me—"

"No." Beth is firm. "Syn, you should stay here and rest. I know how to take care of myself. I'm an excellent shot."

"Yes, you are. Still, if you're out there, I should have your back. Even if I suck at it."

"You should stay, Beth. Take care of your sister."

Beth seems to be considering it. But then, "No. I have to take care of you both. After Dad…."

Mom rests a hand on Beth's shoulder. "Beth, there's a cabin right outside—you and Syn hide there and I'll be back as soon as I find Luke."

Beth shakes her head firmly. "No, we go—"

Her words are cut short when Cole's face appears through the fog, hovering like the Cheshire Cat. He wraps his hands around Beth's neck and they both disappear. *This can't be happening!*

Mom and I chase after them. A steady, warm rain is falling in the Garden, where we find ourselves face to face with Cole and a small army of Creepers: Butterfly-Man, Lizard-Man, Snake-Man, and Turtle-Man, who I assumed was burnt to a crisp. His shell is charred black, but the man inside looks no different.

Beth, the ever-defiant prisoner, tries to kick the gun she dropped across the grass to us and curses when it's scooped up by Butterfly-Man. He holds the barrel to his face curiously, like he has no clue how to use it. The other Creepers snicker and then duck when he points it at them.

"Knock it off, you morons!" Cole's outburst is cut short when Mom aims her gun at him. "Go ahead. Try to shoot me, Debra. See if you can do it without hitting your daughter. Even better—why don't you trade places with her? You're next on my list anyway."

Mom lowers her gun. "I'll lay down my weapon. You release my daughter."

"No!"

"Shut your mouth, Synthia!" Cole's relaxed but sinister composure has shifted to anger. "This isn't just about you and me anymore. You may have taken my love from me, but your dear old mom and dad kept her captive. They tortured her!"

"I did it for my child." Mom tosses her gun to the ground and takes me in her arms. "Take care of your sister...when I'm gone."

"Mom, don't!" Beth struggles to escape.

The Creepers are ready for Cole's orders. I can only stand there feeling helpless as Mom approaches Cole. Even if Mom could be stopped from making this sacrifice, Beth will still die.

Then it hits me. I was originally the primary target of Cole's revenge. But who would he want to suffer the most? The person who unintentionally killed his girlfriend? Or the people who tortured and disfigured her? Killing Dad stung me and Mom. Killing Beth would hit us both too.

"Mom, Cole's lying! He's going to kill Beth!"

"You're a smart girl, Synthia," Cole says evenly. He motions to Snake-Man, whose tail is rattling with excitement.

Eager to comply, Snake-Man whacks Mom in the face. She staggers and falls backwards. Cole thrusts Beth into Lizard-Man's clutches. Snake-Man slithers out of the way.

"Hey!" I rush to Mom's side, sliding to my knees on the wet grass and taking hold of the gun at her feet. "Don't even think about it!" I scream, aiming it at Cole's chest.

"Well now, isn't this interesting," Cole purrs. Beth stops squirming as Cole raises the gun to her head. "But I doubt that the girl who values life more than anyone would actually be willing to take the shot."

"I swear, I'll do it!"

"Give me the gun, Syn." Mom is on her feet again.

I won't take my eyes off Cole. "No! I have to do this."

"Do it then!" Cole taunts, his eyes piercing through me. "If you don't, guaranteed, I will put a bullet in your long-lost sister's head."

Is this how my parents felt when they decided to do anything to save their child, no matter how horrible?

Cole laughs wickedly. "You know, the best re-venge would be to steal your innocence. To turn you into the kind of monster you despise most—a killer. You have two seconds to decide." He presses the gun against Beth's head. She closes her eyes.

I pull the trigger.

CLICK.

Beth's eyes fly open.

Cole bursts into laughter. "Looks like I'll have the last laugh after all. I brought you over to the dark side and yet you still have to watch your sister—"

Mom tears the gun from my hand and pulls back the hammer. Cole braces himself, pointing his gun at Mom.

Before Cole and Mom can have a shootout, Turtle-Man slams his shell into Cole, knocking him off his feet. Beth takes the opportunity to chomp on Lizard-Man's hand and is freed from his grasp. She catches Snake-Man off guard, kicking him in the shin and diving for Cole's gun. Cole's Creeper goons hold up their arms in defeat as Mom waves her gun at them. "You're all done here."

The cowards race across the Garden, slipping and staggering on the slippery grass.

Beth leaps to her feet and points the gun at Cole. "Now who's gonna have the last laugh?"

"No!" Mom stops her. "Nobody is going to kill anyone!"

"He killed Dad! He'll come after…us…."

She trails off when Mom holds the gun to Cole's head.

"Mom!" I plead, coughing again. "You promised."

"Yes, I did." She lowers the gun and shoots him in the kneecap.

"That should slow him down," Turtle-Man says, with the hint of a smile. "If he tries to get up, I'll slow him down even more. Slow is what I do."

I wince as Cole's anguished howls rise above the drumming sound of steady rain.

"Our work is done here," Mom says. "Now, let's go find Luke."

The grassy area behind the house looks like a war zone. Luke is barking orders while he and a dozen sewer residents are fighting Creepers. The grass is scattered with the injured.

Mom fires a bullet between some charging Creepers. They dive for cover, giving the humans an edge. Half of the Creepers have already been knocked unconscious.

Luke whacks another Creeper over the head with a shotgun. "Both doors are guarded," he shouts as the Creeper's knees buckle.

"And from above too," notes Beth.

The Creeper bird is pivoting on the roof, watching both entrances of the house.

"The basement window!" I shout.

"There's a thick layer of concrete behind the glass," says Mom.

"Give me a minute!" Luke punches the last Creeper out cold. He gives his head a good shake, water spraying everywhere.

"You guys okay?" Luke asks. "Where's your dad?"

Beth and I frown. Mom looks away, pretending to watch the Creeper bird on the roof.

"Oh no. I'm so sorry." He hugs me.

Mom gently interrupts. "Save your condolences for later. Cole is injured and under guard. This is our chance to get inside the house so I can open a lightway and send my kids home. Front or back?"

"Front," Luke says. "Here's the plan."

Luke and the six people with him move around to the back of the house. Two Creepers are guarding the door, four more are blocking the stairway. And of course, there's the remaining winged Creeper looking down on us. Hungry, yet patient.

"New plan," a voice shouts from behind. We spin around and see Turtle-Man's blackened shell. But this isn't the Turtle-Man who helped us. It's Cole. The shell, stolen from its owner, is now being used as Cole's oversized shield.

Cole aims his gun at Beth, but before he can shoot, he topples forward. Standing where Cole had been are Ebby and Jon, with their arms outstretched.

"Oops," Ebby says with a smirk. "I'm such a Klutz."

Luke is shocked. "What the hell are you doing here!?"

"Saving your asses."

Jon is eyeing the Creepers still guarding the back door and the Creeper bird on the roof. "Or being really stupid."

Cole takes aim from where he lies sprawled on the grass.

"Luke!" Mom shouts.

Luke doesn't hear. He's running to greet his sister.

BLAM!

A gunshot rings through my ears and I gasp as Luke tumbles and rolls to a stop, blood already staining his shirt from the bullet hole in his stomach.

Chapter 44

The Lawnmower Man

"NO!" EBBY RUSHES to her brother's side and kneels beside him.

Mom and Beth are transfixed. Then, a sudden movement from the corner of my eye. Cole is crawling back to retrieve the turtle shell. Mom and Beth spring into action simultaneously and shoot multiple rounds into Cole.

I have no time to think about the fact that my sister might have executed a man in cold blood, or that Cole is likely dead. My focus is only on Luke.

"No no no no no no no no no," Ebby rambles.

I put my arm around her. "Let's turn him over, okay?"

Ebby takes a minute to contain herself and then she, Jon, and I turn Luke onto his back. The hole in his stomach is larger than a quarter. Blood is flowing from it like a fountain.

"No, no, no!" Ebby cries. "Luke—"

"This is my fault," Jon says flatly. "It was my idea to come back."

"No," Luke sputters, blood trickling from his mouth.

"We've got company!" Mom announces.

I glance up, not at all surprised that the Creepers who were guarding the house are charging. The Creeper bird on the roof is flapping its wings eagerly, about to take flight.

Mom leans into the turtle shell where Cole is lying and lifts out his shotgun. She shoots a round into the air. "Don't come any closer!"

They don't.

Mom takes out a pocket knife. She rips a sleeve off Cole's jacket and presses it against Luke's wound. "Press down on this to stop the flow of blood."

"We have to get him to the staircase!" I plead in between coughs. "It's the only way we can save him now."

"We can't carry him," Mom says, eyeing the Creeper bird. "Even if we could, he's bleeding out and the platform is on the opposite side of the Garden. It will take at least twenty minutes to get him there. He's lucky if he has five."

The Creeper bird glides down from the roof. Mom aims the shotgun, but the Creeper is not coming to attack. It approaches the bloody body still lying on its back in the turtle shell. Cole's arm twitches.

"You kids need to say your goodbyes. And fast."

"No!" Ebby wails.

"Yes." Luke manages to lift his head. "Go home. Be safe."

"This is my fault," Ebby sobs, desperately stroking Luke's hand.

"I'm so sorry, Luke. I never should have—"

"No, Syn. No one's fault. Go home. Ebby, tell Mom and Dad...." He rests his head on the ground.

Ebby and I lean over Luke, our tears uniting with the raindrops. I try to accept reality. To be there with Luke in these last moments of his life, but my heart is heavy with feelings of guilt. If this is anyone's fault, it's mine. Luke was fighting for me. First my Dad. Now, Ebby's brother. A friend.

As I'm staring at the rain-soaked, bloody piece of cloth I'm pressing against Luke's stomach, I become aware of a faint rumbling sound, which steadily grows louder. A ride-on lawnmower rounds the corner of the house and sitting on top is Larry, the lanky Ant-Man we met yesterday.

He leaps off the mower. "Oh my, this looks bad."

The Creeper bird screeches and takes flight, but Mom holds it off with the shotgun.

"He probably won't make it," says Larry, "but we should try. Help me get him on this thing."

We lift Luke by his arms and legs and with Larry's help, heave him onto the mower, laying him down below the two front seats. Larry slips behind the wheel and Ebby sits in the seat beside him, leaning over Luke.

"Hang in there," she says. "We're gonna take care of you."

Larry revs the engine and turns to the rest of us. "Hop on!"

Mom holds the shotgun steady at the Creeper bird. "Hurry. There's no time to waste!"

We jump onto the metal platform along the side and hang on. Larry takes off around the side of the house faster than I've ever seen a mower go, past the house, across the open field. Smooth sailing.

"We've got company," Jon yells in the wake of two gunshots. The Creeper bird is flying over the roof of the house.

"Keep going, Larry!" I try to shout above the engine but to no avail. My lungs are too weary.

Larry doesn't falter from the task at hand, but still the Creeper bird catches up in the orchard. Beth screams. We're about to crash into a tree. Larry swerves left and we rumble across puddle-ridden mud that used to be viable farmland. The Creeper is flying next to us now. Larry ducks out of the way of its wing and Ebby tries to stop him from falling off his seat. Too late.

"Larry!"

"Keep going!" he yells.

Beth makes a gymnast-like leap into Larry's seat and veers the mower to the open field.

"How's Luke?" Jon shouts.

"I don't know," Ebby says hopelessly, peering up through strands of soaking wet hair. The Creeper bird slams against the mower and Ebby clings to her brother, still pressing that blood-soaked piece of cloth against his wound.

We are heading straight for the stairway. Beth's eyes are wide with panic. "It won't stop, it won't stop!" She frantically tries to turn the key.

We don't have time to leap before—SMASH! The mower crashes into the stairway and we're all knocked off except Luke and Ebby. The front of the mower is crushed, yet amazingly there isn't even a dent on the stairs. The engine sputters and dies.

"There's a pulse!" Ebby shouts. "He's still alive!"

Jon helps me off the ground. "We need to get him up there now!"

The four of us have positioned ourselves to lift Luke when the Creeper bird lands on the grass in front of us. It screeches through barred chompers.

"No!" Ebby shrieks. "What are we going to do now?"

Another Creeper circles overhead and glides down. *The dragon! It found its way back!*

"Oh great," says Jon.

The faint hope I had for Luke's survival fades. Until—

The second Creeper bird faces the other, advances on it, and our about-to-be attacker retreats. Is the dragon on our side now? While it hovers above the ground screeching at its compadre, we use the distraction to lift Luke off the lawnmower and lay him on the grass.

I put my hand on his chest. No heartbeat.

"Syn?" Ebby squeals with worry.

Blood seeps through parted lips. I hover. No breath!

"Syn?"

"He's not breathing."

"No…." Ebby bows her head.

I take Luke's hands. "We have to get him up there!"

"But he's gone," says Jon, eyeing the Creeper birds again. They are circling each other now.

"He was alive a minute ago," I insist. "Maybe…."

"Let's do it!" Ebby takes one of Luke's hands from me. Jon and Beth lift his legs. We hoist him up with everything we have and step onto the first step, then the second. One step at a time.

"Be careful," Ebby says.

"We don't have time to be careful," I say. "We have to move fast."

We're all sweating profusely—Jon especially—and I feel like my chest is going to explode, if I don't pass out first. But as I've learned this past week, when the life of someone close is at stake, it's amazing what the human body can handle.

My head finally peeks through the cloud. When my eyes rise above it, I'm startled to see about a dozen people lying down or leaning against the railing. The platform is splattered with dried blood. But there's no time to think about that.

"Help!" I yell. Everyone runs over and gets behind Jon and me. We tug with all our strength until Luke is fully lying on the platform.

His chest is still. I lean over him, listening for any sign of breath. Nothing. My bruised body is already healing. My clogged lungs are beginning to clear. I put two fingers on Luke's throat. No pulse. Nothing but the lifeless body of a good friend. A hero.

Jon turns away, biting his lip.

"Luke!" Ebby screams. "Wake up! Luke!"

"I'm so sorry." Tears explode as my friend and I bury our faces in each other's embrace. "I'm so sorry."

The only sounds on the crowded platform are from us sobbing. But then I hear another sound—a wet cough.

"Guys," says Jon. "Look!"

We turn around. Luke coughs up some blood.

"He's alive!" Beth wipes her eyes excitedly.

Jon lifts Luke's head so he doesn't choke.

Ebby moves closer. "Luke?"

His eyes flutter open and he meets Ebby's concerned gaze. "Hey." He takes in our surroundings, the others on the platform. "Where? How?"

"Does it matter?" I ask.

"It doesn't," says Beth.

Our war might not be over. But this is a win. A huge win.

Chapter 45

This is Not a Test

I KNOW SEVERAL PEOPLE WHO are sitting with us on the platform. Lundy, Bear, Dawn, Fern. Even Crystal, discreetly wrapped in a towel. I was certain she was dead and yet here she is. Another win.

During the battle, Larry had taken it upon himself to gather the wounded and bring them up here. Luke had put Lundy in charge of that same task, and he and Larry have been working together.

Larry pokes his head through the cloud at the top of the stairs. Ebby runs over and throws her arms around him. "Thank you!"

I suddenly remember something. "Nell! I left her—"

"We got her," Lundy says. "She's fine. She's below with friends."

"How about the wounded Creepers?"

"I couldn't have humans and Creepers up here together, Syn. They'd be at each other's throats."

"With one exception," Crystal says. "I promised to behave."

"I've tended to the injured Creepers as best I could in the Garden," Larry says.

"Why'd you choose humans over Creepers?" Luke asks.

Larry lowers his head. "My kind have been on the wrong side, blindly following a lunatic who's out for revenge."

"Thank you," Luke says. "You're a lifesaver."

Ebby lifts the blood-saturated piece of cloth from Luke's stomach. The bullet hole has already started to close. As soon as Luke steps off this platform though, the healing will reverse. This fix is only temporary.

For a moment, I revel in the feeling of being healthy again. A feeling experienced for the first time in my life after entering the Garden. Before I ruined all of that.

"Luke," I say, "I know you feel better now, but you need to stay up here or—"

"I know. I'm not going anywhere. And neither should—"

"Ha! Nice try," I say. "Ebby, Jon, stay up here with Luke, okay?"

I don't exactly have to twist their arms after what they've been through.

One thing has been nagging at me. "How did you guys get back to the Garden?"

"The lightway we came through before has been gone for a week," Ebby says. "But this evening Jon spotted one of those light portals through the window in your shed. And somehow convinced me that we might be needed."

"That was me," says Lundy. "When I was tending to the wounded, I had a brainstorm. A way to link to the network in the house through the computer in the sewer. I placed a new lightway in the chicken coop that links back home."

"We can go home, Beth."

"Mom can't return though, right?"

"No. Masie made sure of that."

"We have to make sure Cole is really down," Beth says. "And that Mom is safe."

"Of course," I reassure her. "It didn't look like Cole had much fight left in him though. I don't even get how he's alive after you and Mom, you know...."

"Mom did promise she wouldn't kill him. Guess I missed his heart," Beth says, sounding disappointed in herself.

As I say my goodbyes, a shell-less Turtle-Man climbs through the clouds and collapses onto the platform beside Luke. His back, where the shell had been ripped off, is still bloody.

"Hey Mitchell," Larry says. "I'm afraid this is humans only."

"No," I say. "He's one of the good guys. Like Crystal. And you. Plus, look at what Cole did to him."

"I started out on the wrong side," Mitchell says. "Sorry, girls."

"You were on the right side when it mattered," I tell him. "I'm sorry about what happened to you."

"Coleus is coming," Mitchell warns. "For both of you."

"Isn't he down for the count?" Jon is perplexed.

"You'd think. We need to go. Now," I say. "Otherwise, Cole will come up here and do who-knows-what to these people."

Ebby gives Beth a hug. I realize that with all that was happening I didn't have a chance to properly introduce her to Ebby and Jon. They promise to get to know her better when we're home.

Eager to end this conflict, Beth strolls to the top stair and without looking back, disappears through the cloud. I follow.

Rain pours down on us as we descend. My chest begins clogging up again and the coughing starts. All the body aches rush back. "Don't worry. I'll get through this," I assure my concerned sister.

When we reach the bottom, sure enough, there is Cole limping through the farm to the grassy field. Croc-Man is shielding him with poor Mitchell's shell. A crowd of Creepers trail behind them, ready for battle. I struggle through a coughing fit and don't have much energy left for a fight.

"We should hightail it back to the house," Beth says. "Find Mom, go home."

"I can't outrun them. I'm not feeling so good."

"I have a gun. Bet I can shoot right through that shell."

"Only as a last resort," I remind her.

"Fine."

We face off with Cole and his Creepers at the border of the muddy farm. There are blood stains on his torso, arms, and legs. He looks like he was hit by a truck. The expression on his face is of pure rage. He's mad as hell, with an army at his beck and call.

"Where's our Mom?" Beth asks.

"She fled," Cole sneers, "You're on your own."

"I don't believe you."

"Believe what you want. I'm done playing games." Cole gestures to his gang. "Kill them both. Make sure they suffer."

Croc-Man continues to hold the turtle shell in front of Cole. The Creepers charge. I try to shoot darts into as many as possible, but only hit Bee-Man and Rat-Girl. Snake-Man is about to tackle. Beth shoots a dart into his chest and with her other hand, pulls out the handgun. She shoots two bullets into the shell, with no results. Resourceful as always, Beth shoots a bullet into Croc-Man's knee. He roars and collapses, dropping the shell on Cole's foot.

"Ahh!" Cole screams, diving to the ground. "Kill them! Kill them!"

I'm surrounded. Creepers have closed in on us. I'm coughing, trying to find more darts.

Beth aims the gun at Cole's chest and fires.

CLICK.

I don't have time to reload. Butterfly-Man flaps his wings excitedly, takes flight and hovers in front of me. He watches me coughing, an evil grin spreading across his face. "Allow me to put you out of your misery," he cackles and kicks my chin, knocking me backwards. He twists Beth's arm, forcing her to her knees and making her drop the gun.

Cole slaps the ground, laughing maniacally. "You're both done! Fellow Creepers? Whoever makes them suffer the most can have the house. Along with everything in it."

Their excitement is obvious; however, I'm feeling sicker with each passing minute.

"We can't possibly outrun them all!"

Beth offers me a hand up as the Creepers close in, but with one gigantic leap Grasshopper-Man knocks her backwards. Greeta's tentacles whip outward from her face and one suctions to my cheek.

As it's sinking in that this might very well be the end for me and the sister who I tried so hard to save, there is a flash in the sky. Dark and cloudy seconds ago, it's brilliantly lit up like a giant lightway. The rain stops and the light dissipates. No one moves.

Darkness wraps around us, not night-sky darkness but black like the abyss we jumped into in Doom World. The one Mom calls Oblivion. An image forms above us—Mom! A giant hologram of her face is looking down on us as if we're connected on Skype.

"No way!" Beth takes my hand.

"Before any of you even think about harming either of my girls, let me tell you a little about myself." Her voice echoes from all around like surround sound speakers. "My name is Debra Wade. My husband Ian and I brought you all to life. We created this world and I have the power to obliterate it, like it never existed."

"Don't listen to her, she's lying!" The Creepers nervously congregate around Cole.

"About lying." Mom is so calm it's unnerving. "Since your fanatical leader has brought that up, let's discuss it. Coleus earned your trust by telling you that he freed you from the lethal siren that confined you to the sewers."

"That is what happened!" Cole tries to stand, but the pain is too much. "I…freed every one…of you."

"Did you? Wasn't it your disfigured girlfriend who turned on the siren? Aren't you the one who convinced her to do it? After your parents were killed…by a Creeper?"

The Creepers mutter amongst themselves, glaring at Cole, some moving away.

"That's a lie!" Cole shouts, looking worried for the first time. "I told you they would say this. The humans killed my parents! You know this."

"The funny thing about lies—they are fragile. They are easily disproven."

Where is Mom going with this?

"There are many things about the world you live in that you don't know," Mom goes on to explain. "Let me share one of those things with you now. The Garden world my husband and I built wasn't only a community. It was first and foremost a testing facility. And like most testing facilities, everything is recorded."

No friggin way.

Mom's face fades and a grainy black and white video replaces it.

"She's in the house. We can stop her!" Cole screams to his army.

He tries to stand again. Croc-Man holds him firmly in place. "First, let's see how this plays out."

The video offers a bird's-eye view of a cabin in the Garden.

Mom's voice booms around us again. "This is the home of Adam and Root, and your fearless leader back when he was a boy."

The video zooms in like it's Google Earth. Someone exits the cabin. A boy. A boy with not one face, but two. Young Cole is holding a baseball bat. He checks to make sure nobody else is around, and then tosses it through the door. He lights a match and throws it into the cabin. The cabin erupts in flames. He watches the fire briefly and then runs around the

Garden, frantically banging on cabin doors for help.

The projection in the sky fades. All eyes move to confront Cole, but he isn't there.

I scowl at Beth. "The coward must have limped away."

"There he is, almost at the orchard!" Beth casts an inviting look at the stunned crowd of Creepers. They finally see the truth.

"He lied to us!"

"He played us for fools!"

"Let's get him!"

A lightway shoots from the ground in front of Cole. Mom steps out of it, holding a shotgun. She shoots him in his good knee. He collapses, screaming.

Mom shoots a round into the sky and the charging crowd of Creepers stop in their tracks. She drags Cole back, two Creeper dogs prowling along with her, one on each side.

"This murderous coward kept me and my husband trapped for years!" she shouts to her audience. "He has murdered my husband in cold blood." She shoves Cole down and presses the shotgun against his forehead. "Now, he's mine."

"Mom, don't kill him!"

"Seriously?" Croc-Man snaps.

"You promised," I remind her.

"Yes, I did promise not to kill him," Mom says, lowering the shotgun.

"What are you doing, Mom?"

"I won't break my promise, Synthia. However, I did make a different promise to someone else."

And with that, a long strand of web shoots down and latches onto Cole's back. He is thrust up into the air, swinging back and forth like a metronome. At first, we only see Maya's shadow. As she moves into the light, we see her in the flesh, half of her face and body extensively burned.

"You murdered my mate, Coleus. And all but one of my children."

Jeremy slides down on a strand of web next to his mother. Their eyes are glued to Cole, scornful and menacing.

"P-please. I-I beg you."

"Pathetic," Maya sneers.

"Maya," I shout. "Please, don't do this."

"Please," Cole is gazing down at me, the face of a psychopath now looking more like a homeless man begging. "Listen to her. I'll do anything."

"There is only one thing you can do that will satisfy my hunger. Synthia, my dear, you and your sister should close your eyes. We're not the most well-mannered dinner guests."

I don't have time to scream before blood starts to spray from Cole's neck. I close my eyes to the horrendous scene, but it's impossible to block the horrifying sounds of flesh being ripped apart, and blood being slurped like the remnants of a milkshake through a straw.

Chapter 46

The Sun Will Come Out

I HOLD MY SISTER TIGHTLY. Correction, my sister holds *me* tightly. Beth's eyes are surely wide open. She must be satisfied that justice has been served. I don't share that sentiment. Even though Cole's death lifts a weight off my shoulders, it provides no satisfaction. When I finally open my eyes, the two flying Creepers devour what I assume are the scraps of Cole's remains that have fallen from Maya's feast. I vomit on the grass.

* * *

It's been hours since Cole met his end. Beth and I are sitting on the platform above the spiral staircase with Ebby, Jon, Luke, Lily, Crystal, Mitchell, and a few others.

Not only is there daylight up here, the sky is clear and the sun is shining. With Lundy's assistance, Mom has restored the Garden's warm weather. Apparently, changing the weather is "easy-peasy." Who knew?

My parents came face to face with Maya when their parachutes landed near the tree where she and Jeremy were recuperating after the horrible destruction of their family. Maya, of course, wanted vengeance against Cole, but spending time with her remaining child after the brutal murders had to come first. She recognized my parents and filled them in on the latest events, and where their two daughters were likely hiding.

When Mom and Dad left the sewers, Mom sought out Maya and made a deal. Mom would capture Cole and Maya could have him to herself to do with as she pleases. Mom also wanted to return order and peace to the Garden. Not because she cared about anyone there, but because she was planning to restore the Garden's healing factor and wanted me to have a peaceful place to live a healthy life.

After Cole's death, my mom informed the Garden's residents—humans and Creepers—that everyone would live together above ground. To help keep the peace, Maya agreed to be in charge. Mom, who can't return to our world because of Masie Winter's programming, would advocate for any humans who had grievances and would take them up with Maya. But Mom's time would be spent mostly on fixing what I had broken.

Luke is fully healed and knows that if he leaves the platform his wounds will resurface. Mom says that if he stays on the platform long enough, his wound could permanently heal. She has promised to look after him along with Rose and Lily, Dawn and Nell.

Lundy has decided to stay since he's wanted for theft and murder. He's made friends in the Garden and believes that he can be happy here. He's agreed to help Mom try and fix what I broke.

Mom hopes I will return to the Garden if she can restore the healing factor. I tell her I'll think about it. After what happened to Dad, I don't want to leave her on bad terms. You never know when the end will come. So while I might visit, I won't live here. Ever. What the people here have dealt with these past few months may not be all my fault, but too much death and suffering has occurred because of me. I don't deserve the Garden and the residents sure as hell don't deserve me.

As I'm daydreaming about what it will be like to have Beth at home with me, Lundy peeks through the cloud. "Hey guys, your mom asked me to tell you that your dad's burial will begin whenever you're ready."

Beth lowers her head. Ebby and Jon, Lily, Rose and Flint, and a few other friends are invited to join us. After the burial, Beth and I will return home and the other victims of Cole's carnage will be buried later.

Luke is lying on his back, enjoying the sunshine. It's time to say goodbye. "I can't thank you enough, Luke. Beth and I wouldn't be here now if you hadn't stepped up for us. I'm just so sorry that...."

"No regrets, Syn. Have Beth bring me the things I asked for so boredom doesn't kill me and I'll be fine."

"You got it."

Ebby and Luke share a heartfelt moment and then Luke says he wants to come clean with her about something. He winks at me.

"What is it?" Ebby asks.

"Syn and I have secretly been dating for the last couple months."

What? We're doing this now?

Ebby bends over, bursting into laughter.

"What's so funny?" I ask.

"You guys, I know my brother's gay."

"What?" Luke says. "How....since when?"

"Um, since always, dummy."

"But you're always trying to get me and Syn together."

"Yeah, because it's fun to watch you squirm. Serves you right for keeping things from your little sis."

"I told you she'd be cool with it," I tell Luke.

"You thought I wouldn't be? I'm happy if you're happy." Ebby gives Luke a big hug. "Even if you aren't dating my bestie."

We share one last laugh and descend the stairs into the sunny Garden, chuckling amongst ourselves. At the halfway point, pain from my bruises returns and my lungs begin to fill up with mucus. I cover my mouth and start coughing. My cough is dryer than usual. There are splatters of blood on my hand.

"Syn," Ebby says soberly. "You have to go home. Now."

"I don't want to miss Dad's burial. I'll be fine."

"I don't think so," says Beth.

I frown.

"I'll go find your mom!" Lily takes off.

Jon, Ebby, and Beth escort me to the chicken coop where we will find the lightway home. It's a long way and I'm having a hard time. When we arrive at the pond, a familiar voice calls to us.

"Hey," Greeta shouts. She and Croc-Man are approaching. "You're not looking so good." Her tentacles are waving around her face.

"Let me give you a lift," Croc-Man says. "It's the least I can do."

When we reach the coop, Croc-Man lowers me.

"Mom isn't here yet," says Beth.

"I'm feeling terrible. I need to go now. Ebby, Jon, you guys stay with Beth until our mom gets here. Join me after."

"Not a chance," says Ebby. "We are all staying with you, right guys?"

Of course they all agree.

"You go get better," says Greeta. "When you return to the Garden things will be different."

I try to form a smile, but am hacking non-stop. I crouch down to enter the coop and step into the lightway. As time slows, I look at my friends who will follow me home. Behind them is Mom, frozen in mid-run.

The light brightens. When it dissipates, I'm in the shed at home. Ebby and Jon arrive first. Beth twenty seconds later. She probably said a quick goodbye to Mom. I kneel and stare at the blood I'm coughing onto the brick tiles.

"It's not far to the house," Jon says.

"No way!" Ebby shouts. "We'll stay here with Syn. You go get her aunt! *Now!*"

Chapter 47

The Cat Came Back

IT HAS BEEN EIGHT MONTHS since my return home from the Garden. My life since then has been a mixed bag

I spent another four months not sleeping in my own bed. That time was spent at Redfern Memorial with a serious lung infection. The infection left my lungs scarred and breathing is more difficult than before. I need to be connected to oxygen 24/7 and usually roll it behind me, though it can be strapped to my back too. The plastic tube that connects my nostrils to the tank isn't exactly sexy.

My immune system has been weakened from the infection. With my condition, even an ailment as simple as a cold can have serious repercussions, so this is especially concerning. The Dr. Freeman who administered Mom and Dad's treatment in Bugtopia warned me about this. The effects could be devastating for me some time down the road. But, if the treatment had not been given, I wouldn't have survived my journey back to the Garden. If I could turn back time and do it again, I would.

So, my health sucks. That being said, I'm happy to be alive, and happy to have Beth with me. Since Janna, I haven't bonded with anyone like this. Janna was like a sister to me—Beth *is* my sister.

During a few occasions in the Garden, I saw darkness in Beth, especially her shooting Cole with the intention to kill. But who knows the horrors she has faced over the years? Considering she was five when she started to live on her own, hopping from one world to another, I'm amazed and thankful she turned out to be as wonderful as she is. Since coming home with me, she hasn't shown a shred of what she demonstrated in the Garden or in Doom World. For the first time in five years, Beth has people who care for her, a family, and a place to call home.

Aunt Ruth welcomed her into the family with open arms, and treats her the same as she treats me, like we're her own kids. While at first Beth was apprehensive about trusting someone new, she soon warmed up to Aunt Ruth.

Speaking of Aunt Ruth, as my note instructed, she didn't call the police while I was gone. When I told her my far-fetched story about a world full of hybrid creatures, an evil two-faced villain, a deformed version of myself, and alternate earths, she believed me! However, she had difficulty believing that her own sister, my mom, was alive after more than a decade of believing otherwise.

A few weeks into my four-month hospital stay, Luke, looking good as new, surprised me with flowers. Luckily, the police don't have enough evidence to charge him with anything related to that nurse's murder. I had the pleasure of sharing his and Ebby's reunion from my hospital bed and hearing more good news from Luke.

Luke told me that Lundy took Nell to a hospital in another world and the doctor confirmed that she has vertigo. No brain tumor or anything life-threatening. Not that it doesn't affect her life, but at least it's treatable. He says that Nell is happy. It's great to have loose ends taken care of and know that my friends are doing well.

I had a lot of time to think during my four months in the hospital and am plagued with unanswered questions. About Oblivion and the visions I had while falling through it; the monster in the voltway; where the cameras are that document everything in the Garden; who has been killing my family in alternate worlds; why the murderer spray-painted that message telling me he'll see me soon.

Who is the murderer who caused Cole to revolt against the Creepers in the first place? I had assumed it was Cole because he murdered his parents. Yes, he would have been a boy back then and could swing a baseball bat, but he certainly wasn't strong enough to carry victims up the spiral staircase or throw them over the railing. But if not Cole, then who?

Beth goes to the Garden often to visit Mom and it's tempting to ask her to get answers. What would that solve though? I much prefer the pleasant stories Beth tells me.

I haven't returned to the Garden and Aunt Ruth won't go without me. As much as I want to see Mom and my friends, I'm in no hurry to leave home again.

My friends here have accepted Beth. Even though my sister is younger, she is as much a part of the gang as anyone. She is more mature than most kids her age. Smarter too. Years of sneaking into classrooms in alternate worlds and reading everything she could get her hands on paid off. Beth is the top student in her class. Not bad for a kid who has never been enrolled in school before now.

The thing about Beth is that there is, of course, no record of her. No one, including me, knew she existed. Aunt Ruth came up with a far-fetched story about her living on the streets abroad before discovering she had family in America, and that she stowed away on a commercial airplane to find us. Aunt Ruth fought to get custody rather than let Beth live in foster care—like I'd ever let that happen.

* * *

As usual, today I am walking home with Beth after school, rolling the oxygen tank behind me like luggage. I insist on walking unless the weather is bad. When we enter the kitchen we are surprised to see a man sitting at the table, typing on a laptop. He is middle-aged, has uneven stubble, and is balding in the back. Aunt Ruth is standing next to him.

"Hey, girls, I'd like you to meet Douglas, an old friend of mine. We go way back. Beth's life will be a lot easier because of him."

"How?"

"Well, Syn," Douglas says, "Beth is now officially a person on record. In fact, she always has been."

"Huh?"

"I'm in the system!" Beth is a step ahead of me.

"Exactly. You have a digital history. A birth certificate and all your other records." Douglas closes the laptop. "The federal and state agencies won't have a clue how they missed you." He motions to Aunt Ruth. "I should head out."

"Of course." Aunt Ruth escorts him to the entry hall. "Douglas, it's so good to see you after all these years. And thank you. I knew I could count on you."

"Of course. Anything for a friend. Girls, it was nice to meet you."

Once the door is closed, Aunt Ruth glances at Beth. "How about that?"

"Why couldn't he have done this eight months ago?" Beth says, smirking.

"I've been trying to track down Douglas for years."

"Why so long?"

Aunt Ruth grins. "Well, he did the opposite for himself that he just did for you. He erased his own records."

"He's a ghost?" I ask.

"Yup. He must have hacked into some government databases he should have stayed out of. I'd prefer not to know the details. He's an old friend and he helped us. That is good enough."

"I'm glad you found him again." Beth darts to the stairs and pauses. "You coming, Sis?"

"To feed your latest TV obsession?" *Buffy the Vampire Slayer.* "Right behind you."

"Syn, wait," Aunt Ruth says earnestly. "Can you stay for a minute? I want to speak with you."

"Hurry, Buffy waits for no one!" Beth charges up the stairs.

I set my things on the floor and sit down at the kitchen table, expecting bad news.

"I have some excellent news." Aunt Ruth defies my expectations.

"What is it?"

"Your name has been added to the waiting list for a lung transplant."

Aside from a cure, the only thing that could give me a chance at living a long and normal life is having a lung transplant. I think about this for a minute.

"Finding a donor who's a match is a long shot," I finally say.

"There is still hope." Aunt Ruth kisses me on the cheek. "Let's go out to dinner tonight and celebrate."

"Wait. If I get a second chance at life, it's only because someone else lost theirs. That's not something to celebrate."

"Syn, we can't control fate. But we can have hope. Hope that while one life sadly ends, another will carry on for many years to come. That's all I hope for."

I can't argue with that.

"You said you don't want to return to the Garden to live. This is the next best thing."

She's right.

"I didn't make anything for dinner, so we're going out. Beth and I will celebrate. You can just fill your stomach if it makes you feel better."

"Where are we going?"

"We have a reservation at Alberto's in an hour. I'm going upstairs to see what this vampire slayer looks like, and then take a shower." Aunt Ruth tousles my hair playfully and struts out of the kitchen.

I need a snack and decide to grab some cheese from the fridge. I'm checking texts and nibbling on the cheese when a shadow passes by the window. The doorbell rings. When I open the door, a woman is standing there, about to ring the doorbell again.

"Mom!"

"Hello, Syn."

Beth comes thundering down the stairs and flings herself into Mom's arms. I should be happy too. Right?

As I'm shutting the door, Fluffy skirts through the crack. The bald, but lovable feline rubs against Mom's leg, startling her.

"What is that?"

Beth laughs. "This is Fluffy."

"That thing doesn't have any fur." Mom cringes.

"She's a hairless Sphynx." I click the door shut. "Hypoallergenic, so Aunt Ruth doesn't break out in hives."

"That's odd. I don't remember Ruth having allergies."

Interlude

Knock Knock

IT HAPPENED TWO MONTHS TO the day that Ruth received the call about her sister Debra and her husband's disappearance. She was frantically dusting bookshelves and tidying her apartment. A social worker was flying in from Washington State to interview her. Though Ruth didn't understand why they couldn't simply place Synthia in her care, she accepted that this was part of the process of applying for guardianship.

While she had only met her niece twice, before she was two, the girl's well-being had become important to Ruth and she wanted to leave the best impression possible. Ruth had just laid down the feather duster and entered the hall closet to fetch the vacuum cleaner when there was a knock on the door. She looked at the clock. The social worker wasn't supposed to arrive for another hour.

When Ruth opened the door, she was greeted by a woman about her age, with a clipboard tucked under one arm. "Sadie Garner," she announced, briskly shaking Ruth's hand.

"I was under the impression you were coming at two o'clock."

Sadie checked her watch. "Gee, I'm an hour ahead of myself. My apologies."

"Oh, well. Not to worry. Please come in."

The apartment was reasonably neat but Ruth was nervous that Sadie might notice that the rug hadn't been vacuumed or that the duster was lying on the bookshelf. Sadie barely gave the place a glance. She strolled into the living room and sat on the couch across from the purple leather chair where Ruth sat. She declined coffee or tea.

Sadie asked basic questions about Ruth's interests, job, and her routine. Then the line of questioning began to catch Ruth off guard. Questions about the house where Deb and her family had lived. The house that Ruth was raised in. When Ruth could move in.

"Excuse me," Ruth said. "I think there has been some miscommunication. I wasn't planning on relocating to Redfern. I expected that Synthia would live with me here in Chicago."

"Oh, I see," Sadie replied despondently, and scribbled a note on her pad.

Worried, Ruth added, "I realize this apartment is small and has no elevator, but if I have Synthia in my care, I'd be prepared to move someplace more ideal. Perhaps even a house in the suburbs."

Moving to a house with nice property was something Ruth had always wanted to do. She dreamed of reading on her front porch as birds chirped and the wind whistled through the trees. Adopting Synthia might encourage her to finally do it. For the first time, she warmed to the possibility of a change in lifestyle and everything involved in caring for her niece. In fact, she was surprised to admit that the idea excited her. She couldn't recall the last time something excited her this much.

"That would be fine, Ms. Lowery. I imagine it would take some coordinating since her doctors are in Washington. But having a warm home and a loving guardian is obviously more important for Synthia than staying in her family's house." She jotted something down on her pad and asked to use the washroom.

Ruth relaxed in her chair. She pictured herself swinging in a porch chair, facing a quiet, suburban tree-lined road, reading to Synthia. The young girl in her imagination was mesmerized by the story, which delighted Ruth. It was a wonderful daydream.

Her daydream savagely ended when a plastic bag was slipped over her head. Ruth instinctively tried to pull it away, but the bag was wrapped tightly around her neck. She fought to breathe, fought to push her attacker away. Her breaths became shorter, feeble.

Dreams of a future with her niece were replaced by terror and frantic thoughts of confusion. Who would do this? Why? These questions were followed by the realization that this was the end. How tragic it was that her life was ending just as she was about to have a new beginning.

The last thing Ruth Lowery pictured before losing consciousness was the niece she had last seen in a photo Deb sent the previous year. A young girl whose fate was terribly uncertain.

The woman who had introduced herself as Sadie Garner loosened her grip and felt her victim's pulse. She checked Ruth's pockets. Empty. She removed Ruth's glasses and slid them into her own pocket. The woman then dragged the dead body off the chair and rolled it into the ornamental rug beneath it. The woman put a hockey puck-shaped metal object on the floor, stepped on it, and leaped back as a stream of light beamed from one wall of the living room to the other. The woman rolled the body into the light. The light then vanished, as did the body and the rug.

The woman picked up the metal object and slipped into in her pocket just as there was a knock at the door. She glanced at her watch. "Right on time."

Still, she checked the peephole before opening the door. The man was wearing his baseball cap low to hide his face. He quickly ducked inside, took off his hat, and slid it across the dining room table. The woman watched calmly as he set up a laptop.

"Time?" he asked.

"Thirty minutes, tops."

"Wallet?"

The woman spotted Ruth's purse on a chair, took out a bulky wallet, and tossed it onto the dining room table. The man connected his laptop to Ruth's. He opened the wallet, took out Ruth's driver's license, and balanced it on the keyboard.

In the washroom, the woman pulled her hair into a ponytail, then wiped off her makeup with a tissue and flushed it down the toilet. She slipped on Ruth's glasses and couldn't see a thing. She removed them and replaced them with an almost identical pair she had brought with her.

In the bedroom, the woman scanned the closet and replaced her own navy-blue slacks and red blouse with plain brown pants and a beige top. She was studying herself in the mirror with satisfaction when the man called from the other room.

"Done!"

"That was fast," the woman said, as she hurried into the dining room.

"What can I say?" He tugged his hat on confidently, shielding his eyes, and then slid his laptop into its case. "We're done here."

The woman followed him to the door, looked through the peephole again. "I knew I could count on you, Douglas."

He slipped outside quickly.

It was done. She leaned against the door, scanning the apartment to make sure everything looked okay.

Satisfied, she relaxed on the couch. Barely five minutes later, there was a knock at the door.

The woman stood up, patted down her outfit, and went to greet her guest with the warmest smile she could muster. The door swung open to reveal a short, older woman with red hair that had obviously been dyed.

"Sadie Garner from Social Services," the red-haired women said as they shook hands. "And you're Ms. Lowery, I presume?"

"Of course. Please come in. I've been expecting you."

Chapter 48

Bombshell

"MOM, HOW DID you get back?" Beth asks.

"Lundy gets all the credit. The programming Masie used to keep me from returning was only accessible here. So, Lundy traveled to a world very similar, found Masie's notes, and figured out how to reverse things from over there. Technology has come a long way. That kid now processes all the functions of the Garden from tablets and mobile phones." She pauses to watch Fluffy insistently stroke herself on her legs. "Where's my sister?"

"Taking a shower," Beth replies. "We're going out to dinner to celebrate."

"Celebrate what?"

"Syn's on the lung transplant list!" Beth blurts excitedly. "She has a real shot at living a long, normal life!"

"That is terrific. But you know, the Garden's healing factor has been restored. There is an understanding between the humans and Creepers now. You have friends there."

I sigh and roll my oxygen tank into the family room.

"I'd be living there with you. Beth too," Mom says.

I plunk myself on the couch. Mom sits on a chair opposite me.

"It's not that."

"Then what, Syn?"

I don't want to get into a heated argument. She just got back, but thoughts of the terrible things I said to my dad before Cole killed him…. Well, it makes me think hard before saying anything too rash.

"Mom, my life is in this world. The real world. End of story."

"The Garden may have been a testing ground to find you a cure," Mom says. "Now, that is something I can't do without your father. But the backup plan was for us to live there permanently. That's why we brought people over. So you'd have a community. Friends."

Brought people over? Kidnapped them, more like it! Must keep calm.

"Those people. The Creepers too. All the terrible things they have gone through all lead to me."

"No, Syn."

"Yes, Mom. It's true. When I smashed the blue dome—the deaths, the carnage—that is all on me.

Them even being there in the first place instead of in their own worlds. Cole being there. Cole existing! It all comes back to me and what you and Dad did to protect me. I can't take a chance and allow anything else to happen to them because of me. Honestly, they don't deserve having to see me there all the time, living alongside them."

"Listen, Syn…." Mom trails off, interrupted by Aunt Ruth walking into the family room.

Her hair is still wet and she's wearing a bathrobe. "Did I hear the doorbell?" Aunt Ruth stops abruptly, her face losing all color.

Mom leaps from her chair. "What are *you* doing here?"

"D-Debra. Let me explain."

"What's going on?"

Mom lunges at Aunt Ruth with clenched fists, backs her into the kitchen and against the table, and wraps both hands around her throat. Aunt Ruth is looking right at me. I can't read the expression in her eyes. She doesn't resist Mom's attack.

My world suddenly feels surreal, like the chaos from the Garden has followed me home. "Stop!"

Mom persists. She seems to have a death wish for her own sister!

"I said stop!"

Mom loosens her grip.

"Mom?" Beth is confused. Scared.

Exactly how I feel. "What are you doing? Your sister has taken care of me for years."

"My sister? This is not my sister!"

"Of course she is!"

Beth's voice trembles. "If she's not your sister, then who is she?"

Aunt Ruth is staring at the floor. Mom grabs her chin and forces her to look directly at us. "Go ahead, tell them who you are!"

Fluffy tears from the room, her claws scratching the floor as she skids around the corner. I feel sick to my stomach.

Aunt Ruth's eyes bore through me.

"Tell me!" I plead. "If you're not my aunt, then who are you?"

"Tell them your name!" Mom demands.

The woman I have always known as Aunt Ruth finally opens her mouth. I watch her lips speak the name that will haunt me forever.

"Masie Winters."

SAVAGE WINTERS IN THE
GARDEN
OF
SYN

MICHAEL SEIDELMAN

Book Three In THE GARDEN OF SYN Trilogy

Coming Soon

Join Michael Seidelman's mailing list at
www.michaelseidelman.com
to be notified when it is released.

Acknowledgments

It's amazing to have my second book in your hands! I would like to thank the many people who helped me get here.

Once again, my parents, Shelley and Perry Seidelman, are my biggest supporters. They read (and reread) the book and provided me with invaluable feedback before I was brave enough to share the manuscript with anyone else. I thank my sister, Sara Solomon, for also being instrumental to the quality of the book you are holding. Thanks to Tracey Lutz, Lorne Greene and Lillea Brionn for their honest and constructive feedback. Many thanks to Dr. Mark Gelfer for allowing me to consult him on the medical aspects of the novel. Any mistakes are my own. Thanks very much to my wonderful editor, Davina Haisell, and to my talented cover artist, Carl at ExtendedImagery.com.

I want to give a shout-out to the Cystic Fibrosis community for supporting and embracing the first book. The last thing I ever want to do when writing a story of fiction about a protagonist with a real disease is to offend anyone who struggles with it in real life. But going further, I hoped readers with CF would be inspired by the story and enjoy being able to root for a hero with challenges they can relate to. It brings me joy when this is confirmed by someone who suffers with CF, or is close to someone who does. I hope that the second book in the trilogy will further inspire and entertain the real heroes fighting this devastating disease.

Finally, a big thank you to everyone who reads this book, reviews it, shares it or recommends it to a friend. Writing fiction is my dream job and having this book enjoyed by as many people as possible helps bring my dream to fruition.

About the Author

When Michael Seidelman was growing up, his passions were reading, watching movies, enjoying nature and creative writing. Not much has changed since then.

Working in Online Marketing for over ten years, Michael felt it was time to pursue his passion as a career and began writing *The Garden of Syn* trilogy.

He is currently working on the third book in the Garden of Syn series and, beyond the trilogy, has many ideas plotted out that he looks forward to sharing with the world!

Michael was born in Vancouver, BC Canada where he continues to reside.

You can learn more about Michael Seidelman at MichaelSeidelman.com. You can also follow him on Facebook, Twitter, Instagram and GoodReads.

This story is fiction but cystic fibrosis is very real.

70,000 children, teenagers and adults in the world suffer from the disease. While treatment is far above what it once was, there is still no cure. Let's help find one.

Please check out these sites for more information on cystic fibrosis and how to donate to help find a cure.

Cystic Fibrosis Foundation (US) https://www.cff.org

Cystic Fibrosis (Canada) http://www.cysticfibrosis.ca

Cystic Fibrosis Trust (UK) http://www.cysticfibrosis.org.uk